Demon Tales

Bruce W. Johnson

Legal Disclaimer

The scenarios outlined in this publication are fictitious and have been included for entertainment purposes. Names, characters, businesses places, and events are used in a fictitious manner. Any resemblance to actual persons, whether living or recently deceased is purely coincidental.

Edition 2.0

Dedicated to my great friend Richie Turnbull,
my companion through many dark night adventures.
We have slain a few demons together.

17th March 2019

Contents

Getting his own back 1

Beyond the circle 14

Business unfinished 33

Third time lucky 48

The Exorcist 59

Their Satanic Majesties 65

Digging for gold 81

Old men 93

Adventurers 136

The true story of Doris Bither 145

Underworld 147

Asylum 169

Primitive religion 185

A messy divorce 189

A cautionary tale 196

Author's Note 198

About the Author 201

Getting his own back

Miles had always been a gambler. Not that he won much, but then that wasn't really what it was about. He knew that. If he lost a hundred quid this week it didn't matter. Brush it aside! He could take it! It was all just part of the game. But if he won a hundred next week then he could bask in the glory, buy a few drinks for the guys down the social club and let them all know that he had picked a real winner. In reality, he might have a good weekend just once in every three months but that was what he lived for, the thrill of that one big win. All the other weeks were simply pushed out of his mind and forgotten. The losses were forgotten and even the debts were forgotten, until the day that the letters came.

The building society lawyers knew what they were doing. There were three copies of the letter delivered to the house, one addressed to Miles, one to his partner Eileen and one simply addressed to "The Occupier." By the time he got home, there was no point in pretending, she already knew the whole story. The court-case was due in thirty days and it was a dead cert that they would be evicted from their home. The house had always belonged to Eileen, left to her by her parents when they died. There hadn't been a mortgage back then but Miles had persuaded her to borrow a bit for the cost of a holiday, and then extend it a bit for a new car, and then he had added on a bit more to clear some of his longstanding gambling debts. One thing had led to another and now here they were, in a sticky spot.

He was honest with her that night. He always took pride in that. He told her the whole story. The mortgage payments were almost a year in arrears. There had been letters warning him what would happen but he had torn them up and put them in the bin. He had convinced himself that he just needed one decent win on the horses and he could pay it all back. And he had tried, indeed he had tried. Every bank account he had was overdrawn to the limit, and the credit cards as well, an indelible record of his ongoing attempts to achieve that one big win.

The hardest part was the jewellery. That was when she started to cry, when she knew all that had gone. Stupid really, to be so attached to a bit of jewellery. She was going to be homeless in a month or two, so why make such a fuss about the jewellery. By the weekend she was a bit better and she even gave him a few quid to go down to the social club for a beer but even that was too good to be true. When he got back home she was gone, and so was the girl.

There was a note. There was always a note. Any time that Eileen had got sick of him and gone off on her won she had always left a note, but usually it said she was going to stay at her friends. This was the first time she had ever mentioned a new man in her life. To hell with her then. It was too late to do anything after a bellyful of beer so Miles just went to bed and left it till the morning.

On Saturday it all got worse. Miles was taking a short cut through the alleyway that ran down the back of the Grand Hotel when came face to face with Johnny Diamond. Not the great Johnny Diamond, of course. Not Johnny Diamond the nineteenth-century tap-dancing artist who toured with Barnum, of course not. In fact, this particular Johnny Diamond wasn't really called Diamond at all. He was a loan shark, some might say a gangster, and well known to be a very hard man. So that was why they called him Diamond, because he was rock-hard. Right now Miles owed Johnny a lot of money and he was in absolutely no position to pay it back.

There were only two ways that this particular meeting could end. One way would involve Miles spending the rest of the weekend in the casualty department at the general hospital, and so quite naturally he chose the other way.

"I've 'ad a bad week Johnny, a dreadful bad week mate, I can tell you. The Missus has run off and left me and I've been off me head worrying with it all. But listen, I can sort this out for you. I'm seeing the bank manager next Thursday to arrange a bank-loan for a new car. My record's good, I've got me house for security and it's not even mortgaged, so I know he'll give me whatever I ask. So, there you go, I can square you up right there and then, sound as a pound. In fact, if you could just be so kind as to tip me a couple of hundred, just to get me through the rest of the week, we can have it all sorted by next weekend. I promise you."

The lies came easily, and Miles was a regular customer, so Johnny relented and more money changed hands. By three o'clock Miles had picked a winner at 7 to 1. By five o'clock he was buying rounds in the social club. At nine he decided to chance his luck with Suzy-Sue, a gothic looking girl who would give a punter a good time for thirty quid. Just before midnight, he was walking home drunk when two young guys knocked him down and robbed him of everything he had.

It was another week before he found out where Eileen was. He had his contacts and he knew they would come through for him. Nothing stayed secret for long in a small town. This particular mate was the caretaker at the special school. He was a good old boy and he knew who his friends were.

Eileen had a daughter, just the one, called Cathy. She had got the child when she was still very young, before her and Miles had even met, and she never talked about who the father was. Cathy was a pretty little thing in her early teens, very pretty indeed, but she had lots of problems. Severely autistic was what they had been told. Miles couldn't care less what that was all about as long as Eileen took care of her and stopped her having screaming fits. Eileen loved that girl. She was devoted to her, and she wouldn't be parted from her for any reason. Now the caretaker had given him the girl's new address from the school computer, so that gave Miles a chance to go and find her.

Elm Avenue was considered to be a most desirable location as it ran along one side of the golf-links. In fact, there were only houses along one side of the avenue so the wealthy residents could simply look out of their front doors and windows to see ladies and gentlemen taking their shots on the second fairway. Unsurprisingly these homes were expensive, as was appropriate to the means of the accountants and the doctors, the businessmen and the lawyers who enjoyed that majestic view of the grassy banks and bushes of the golf course.

On this particular Friday evening, however, the view in Elm Avenue was far from majestic, the dark silhouettes of the trees being illuminated by the blue flashing lights of two police cars and a van. There was no crowd gathered in the street of course, they were all much too respectable and middle class for that, but from behind their twitching net curtains the locals were watching with interest.

Miles had arrived to confront Eileen. He had it all planned. He would promise to give up the gambling and the drinking. He would tell he had booked a holiday. He would remind her of how much he had done for her and how happy they had been during all their years together. He would talk her round. He had done it before and he was confident that he could do it again.

But this time, it just didn't work like that. Eileen wouldn't come to the door. The house belonged to an Asian doctor from the hospital where Eileen worked. He had tried to be reasonable, but Miles was up for an argument. Accusations led to racial abuse and then to death threats, by which time the police had arrived.

In the end, it was an old police sergeant who persuaded him to leave.

"Miles, you should have better things to worry about son. We heard a bit of local gossip about you and Johnny Diamond. We heard you messed him about regarding a debt, something about the bank manager. He's after you Miles and you need to lay low somewhere in case he finds you. Coming round here and making this fuss is just going to get you the wrong sort of attention. You want to get out of here now son. Go on. Go now and I can look the other way."

And so Miles went, but he had nowhere to go once the pubs closed and at last he found himself sitting on the wall of the church-yard sharing a cigarette with Suzy-Sue and telling her how he would do anything in the world, absolutely anything, if he could find a way to get out of all the trouble he was in.

"I would sell me soul to the devil, so I would, if I thought it would help."

"Nah you wouldn't." Suzy blew a smoke-ring towards him. "You probably don't believe in God anyway."

"Yeah, well just because I don't believe in God, that don't matter. All the more reason to sell me soul. It ain't no use to me, is it? What about you? I bet you don't believe in God neither."

"I've met a few devils in me time." Suzy took one last draw and passed him the cigarette.

"Well, you would in your job." Miles attempted a smile then went off to urinate behind a tree.

When he came back Suzy-Sue had gone but Miles wasn't ready to call it a day. The main door of the church was open and he took himself in there, out of the cold. For a moment he thought about praying, but to hell with that. He took a book from the bookcase inside the door. It

4

was a prayer book so he put it back and tried the other shelves till he found a bible. Then he went round to the back of the church and found a dark spot where he couldn't be seen. Burning the bible seemed like a pretty dramatic gesture and he stood there with the flames flickering beside his feet as he raised up his hands to increase his feeling of importance.

"Listen to me!" He called out across the graveyard. "If you are listening this is what I want. I want my woman back and I want all my money problems sorted, and I want Johnny Diamond off me back. I want all this and I promise you I will do whatever you want. I'll give you whatever you want, anything. This I promise on my immortal soul."

He stood for a moment, half expecting some demonic beast to appear in a flash of thunder and lightning with the smell of sulphur, but nothing happened. He could still hear the traffic on the High Road and he could still smell the food from the kebab shop, and the light rain still drizzled on his face like mist. So Miles just stamped out the last dying sparks of the burning bible, then he lit a cigarette and walked home.

By the time he reached his garden gate he had pretty much given up and was feeling emotionally numb to all of his problems, but the sight of the house did awaken a certain sadness. He had been there a good few years now and he would be sad to see it go. Still, it was her house, so no loss to him in financial terms. Just a pity that he would need to find somewhere else to stay.

He must have been preoccupied with such thoughts because he failed to realise that someone was approaching him from behind as he struggled to fit the key into the lock. At the last moment, he sensed the presence of another and he spun round expecting the worst.

"Good evening Mr. Walker" piped the stranger "Let me introduce myself. I am Simon Terode. Awfully pleased to make your acquaintance"

Mr. Terode was at least fifty years old, possibly more. He was a short, fat man with a broad face and a wide mouth, with thin lips and a tongue which flickered in and out as he talked. He wore a classic style trench-coat and a trilby hat, like the stereotype of an old-style journalist working for the News of the World on a sex-scandal story.

Expecting some trouble from Johnny Diamond, Miles glanced around to see whether Mr. Terode had any heavies with him, but he didn't, and on his own he didn't seem particularly threatening, just a bit distasteful for some reason.

5

"What can I do for you Mr. Terode?"

"Ahh, Mr. Walker, it's more a matter of what I can do for you!" Mr. Terode replied. His manner was slimy and obsequious.

"Here! Here's a small sum of money. Just a trifle I know, but enough to see you through. Take it! Yes. Just take it Mr. Walker. Tomorrow is Saturday and I know you enjoy a flutter. Follow your gut instincts and don't hold back. Have a good day and I will be seeing you later. Don't hold back Mr. Walker. Mark my words. Don't hold back"

With that, Terode turned away and left Miles standing on the doorstep, open-jawed with astonishment and with a roll of money in his hand. He counted it before he went to bed and there was four hundred pounds. The next morning he checked it again and to his amazement it was real.

Saturday was a blast for Miles. It seemed he could do no wrong. He doubled his money in the first hour and doubled it again on the next race. When he wanted to put a thousand on an outsider at thirteen to one they phoned head office to get clearance. Sure enough, the horse came galloping home five lengths ahead of the field. He had won again. By three o'clock he had twelve grand in his pockets and they wouldn't take any more bets, so he went round the corner to another bookie's and put a thousand on a multiplier for the last three races. All three came romping home in royal style and he set off for the social club riding on a wave of euphoria, stopping off at the newsagent's to put on his lottery tickets and buy a packet of cigarettes. As he reached the corner of Bar Street he all but bumped into an old fellow, whom he recognised at once as Mr. Simon Terode.

"Ahh, Mr. Walker, so lovely to see you, Sir. How was your day?" Terode didn't wait for an answer. "Let me put it to you now Sir. Your luck may have changed. Indeed it may have changed, but you have to ask yourself why? And for how long?"

Miles offered a handshake to his benefactor and raised his head to speak but Terode was oblivious and simply licked his lips and then continued.

"I deal in legal matters Mr. Walker, contracts and that sort of thing. Yes, very much that sort of thing. Yesterday evening, Mr. Walker you were overheard in the churchyard, asking for help with certain issues and offering certain things in return. I'm sure you know what I am talking about, burning that bible and all.

"Now, you Mr. Walker, you have been a bit down on your luck if you don't mind me saying, and as you can see I am here to help, but it's up to you. It has to be your choice. If you want you can give me back all that money and just walk away, or if you still want our help we can go ahead. What's it going to be Mr. Walker? Do you really mean it? Do you want to keep on winning?"

"Well, yes! Of course!" gulped Miles, his mind in a spin.

"Jolly good," said Terode, his tongue flickering in and out as he spoke. "Jolly good indeed. I shall see you when I see you. Goodbye for now, and make the most of it, Mr. Walker. Make the most of it while you can." Then he turned on his heel and swung back into Bar Street and was gone, leaving Miles quite bewildered.

Ten minutes later he was buying a round for his friends in the social club and he raised his glass in a toast, "To my new-found friend Mr. Slimy Toad"

Sunday morning came with a loud knock at the front door. It was the police. Miles had no idea what they wanted, maybe Eileen had pressed charges for something although he couldn't think what. Anyway, he had the feeling that Mr. Toad would be able to sort him out with a decent lawyer so to hell with her. He pulled on some trousers and a jumper and opened the door. When the coppers started talking he had to ask them in and offer them a seat. This was too much of a shock to take standing up.

Johnny Diamond had been murdered, stabbed on Saturday evening in the toilets of a pub near the railway station. The police needed to eliminate any possible suspects, and Miles was just one of many on their list. He gave them his movements for the relevant time frame, two betting shops, and the social club. It was never going to be a problem. He had plenty of witnesses, and there would be the surveillance cameras and the betting slips, though for some reason he didn't mention Mr. Terode. What a turn up! When the police were gone he made himself a cup of tea and put the telly on. Then came another shock. His lottery numbers had come up. He was rich.

A lot can happen in three months for a gambler on a winning streak. Miles was determined that this time, just this once, he would be sensible with his money and so he took some legal advice. Not from Terode, that guy had disappeared and was no-where to be seen. Instead, he went to a local law firm that did a bit of everything. He paid off all the debts on his own accounts but not the ones that he had run up in Eileen's name. He used part of his lottery money to buy the old petrol station which had gone out of business a year or two back, as well as the derelict patch of land just behind it that was used as a scrapyard. He had always fancied a business selling cars and that seemed like a good way to start. Most of all he made sure that everything, absolutely everything, was sewn up in his name only. They had never officially got married so Eileen couldn't touch him for a penny. He still thought about her though, sometimes in a sexy way, sometimes in an angry way, but he did still think about her.

Life was good now. It was very, very good. With plenty of cash in his pocket, he was quite a popular man about the town. He even got nominated for the management committee down at the social club, but he didn't want it. He had no time for boring committee meetings, there were better things to do in life. He let the mortgage company take the old house. It wasn't his anyway so he saw it as a good way to get his own back on Eileen. He bought a nice big place on the outskirts of town and arranged for Suzy Sue to drop in twice a week. Now that he could afford to pay her a bit more, she would do some of the kinky stuff that he liked.

Then his Christmas came early. A story broke in the local newspaper that someone had made allegations against Eileen's new boyfriend. Nasty allegations these were, the kind that can end a career, especially for a doctor. The house in Elm Avenue was raided by the police. Bedrooms were searched. Computers were taken away. An angry crowd turned up in the dark and broke the front windows. Eileen and Cathy had to be taken away by the police for their own protection and the social workers tried to get a statement from the girl, but of course, she could tell them nothing due to the severity of her condition. In the end, they left Eileen with a simple set of choices. She needed to move out and put some distance between her and the boyfriend, to take the daughter away to somewhere safe. Otherwise, the girl would have to be taken into care for her own safety, but Eileen had no-where to go, so she came home to Miles and begged him for another chance.

There would come a time when Miles would look back on that night with regret, but at the time he thought only of triumph. He wasn't a forgiving man and he wanted to make her pay. He locked Cathy in her room to keep her out of the way. Then he took his revenge on Eileen with a thick leather belt and a garden cane. The more he beat her, the more she begged, and the more she begged, the harder he beat her, whilst all the time her autistic daughter screamed and howled in the back bedroom. When at last he was done and Eileen lay sobbing, naked at his feet, he felt pleased with himself and he promised her more of that to come "hard and often."

Now he was the winner and it felt so good. He came and went when he wanted. Nothing was off limits. Late night drinking, all night-parties, he could do whatever he wanted then come home to Eileen when it suited him. The only problem was Cathy. The girl just seemed to get worse and worse. He could never really enjoy his life with Eileen when that girl was around.

One muggy evening in February, Mr. Simon Terode appeared on the doorstep, unexpectedly as always. Miles welcomed him in with a warm handshake and opened a nice bottle of twelve year old single-malt whisky. He had never really understood this man, where he came from or what he wanted, but somehow, in some strange way, he knew that Terode was connected to his own good luck and that was really all that mattered.

"So how can I help you Simon?" Miles asked after a bit of small talk.

"Ahh, Mr. Walker. It's how I can help you." Terode's tongue ran along his top lip. "Yes, yes, that's always the main thing, Sir. I am simply here to help you."

"No Simon." Miles shook his head. "There's nothing I need. Everything is fine and dandy now. I haven't a care in the world. You were a total gent standing by me when things were a bit tricky, but it's all worked out and I thank you for your good advice, honestly, there's nothing else I need now."

"It's about that girl, Mr. Walker," Terode leaned forward and his eyes narrowed till they were almost shut, "That girl Catherine, your step daughter. We have a place arranged for her. We know she isn't normal and you can't really get on with your life as long as she is around, what with her needing care all the time. We can set her up with a special place and that will give you back your private life. You can go out for meals, go on foreign holidays, even just enjoy your home life more. We have everything ready, and it won't cost you a penny." Terode winked and sat back in the chair.

"Where will she be?" Miles was suddenly attentive.

"Oh, there are places which train these people for certain types of work." Terode made a sweeping gesture with his hand, as if he was simply pushing a problem to one side. "Special places that get them out

9

of your hair. There are private hospitals. There are foreign schools. There are many, many places, some quite nice, some not so nice. It's not your problem. You really don't want to know the details or that wife of yours will be dragging you up there every weekend. Just leave it to us. We know what we are doing."

It was all very quick and easy. Eileen didn't like it but she had to do as she was told and within a fortnight Cathy was gone. Miles had her room ripped out and turned into a private office for himself, mainly so that he could surf the internet without Eileen disturbing him.

Eileen for her part could never forget about Cathy. She asked about her all the time but his answer was always the same. These special homes wanted the patients to settle in. Visits upset them. It was best for the girl just to leave her alone. That was what Terode had told him and that was what he wanted to believe. In no time at all the girl just disappeared from his horizon. Life was so much easier now. In the summer they went to Thailand for two weeks. It was the first foreign holiday he had ever had. It was perfect.

In the last week of August a letter arrived unexpectedly. Some building firm that Miles had never heard of wanted to buy the garage and the scrapyard, to use the land for residential developments. They were offering to pay a fortune, even more than the lottery win. His lawyers advised him to accept the deal but with one additional condition, a proportion of the rent from the apartments to be allocated to Miles as a regular income. He would never need to work again. His luck was still holding good, it seemed, and he phoned for a cab into town to celebrate. It dropped him off round the side of the King's Arms. Suzy-Sue was smoking by the side door and he gave her a smile but she didn't seem pleased to see him.

"It's wrong what you done to that girl." Suzy snapped at him. "You gotta be a bastard giving her to those people."

"What the hell are you talking about?" Miles was taken by surprise "What do you know?"

"I know plenty! I know what they do! Trafficking they calls it. I've seen it in some of them films, young girls what they make them do stuff. Half of them is off their tits on drugs so they don't know what's happening, but that little girl you had, she didn't even choose it for herself. You should be bloody ashamed."

Miles just ignored her and went off to drink at the Royal Oak instead. Cathy was nuts. It wasn't his fault and he wasn't going to worry about it. Any problems he ever had could be sorted by Mr. Toad. That was how it was and that was how it was going to be. His life was easy and uncomplicated and he was quite happy to keep it that way, right up to the time when he had the health scare.

When Miles fainted and fell over in the betting shop he thought it must be a bit of a hangover, but when he fell down the stairs the following week they took him to the hospital. They stuck him in some big machine to take pictures of his brain, like sticking your head in a tumble-dryer, he thought. But the results when they came back were nothing to joke about. He had an inoperable brain tumour of a highly aggressive nature. They gave him three months, but it might even be less. They set up some appointments and allocated him a visiting nurse. They even arranged for a hospital bed to be set up in the front-room of his home. He would get the best of care, but he would still die.

That night he lay awake calling out for Terode, but it did no good. No one came. After two days he started to have headaches. After two weeks he needed to be put onto powerful painkillers. It was time to put his affairs in order while he could still think straight.

He decided to make out a will leaving everything to Eileen. It was the least he could do considering how he had treated her. He knew that. In the end the solicitor persuaded him that it was better to marry her in order to avoid death duties and inheritance tax. That suited Miles fine, he never liked paying taxes anyway, so they got a special licence and the registrar came to the house and they got married in the room with the hospital bed.

He thought she would be pleased but when all the people had gone and she stood there with the papers in her hands there was only one thing she wanted to talk about and that was Cathy. There was nothing he could tell her. He really didn't know where the girl was, only Terode knew that, and if he told her the rest it would only upset her, so he said nothing despite her begging and her tears, till in the end she told him that she hated him and that he was absolutely the worst thing that had ever happened in her life and she cursed him with really harsh words the likes of which he had only ever heard used in horror movies.

That night Miles lay alone in the darkness and like so many nights before he called out for his one remaining friend. "Terode, Terode, where are you? I need you."

Then to his absolute astonishment, Terode appeared, right there in the room. He just appeared as if he had been there all the time.

"Mr. Walker, Mr. Walker, what can I do for you?" Terode seemed bigger somehow, perhaps he had put on weight.

Miles had no reserves of courage, no smart comments left to make. He simply blurted out the one all-consuming thought on his mind. "I don't want to die!"

Terode sat down by the bedside and took Miles gently by the hand. He was smiling and nodding as if to show he understood.

"You can't live forever, Miles, really you can't, and even if you could, what kind of life would it be, lying in this bed, sick and in pain?" Terode squeezed his hand gently. "No my friend, you do have to die, but there may still be something I can help you with."

"Please help me" Miles twisted awkwardly in the bed, the wires and tubes holding him back.

"Well, here's the deal." Terode leaned even closer. "You can end it yourself anytime. Take the whole pack of those painkillers and you will be dead in an hour. That's beyond my control, but I can promise you that you will be born again, reincarnation they call it. You can be good-looking, you can have a wealthy family, everything you need and best of all you can keep all of your memories. Just think how much fun you can have being young and healthy again but knowing all that you know now."

"Will that work? Can you really do that?" It sounded like nonsense to Miles, too good to be true, but he had nothing to lose, he was dying anyway.

"You have my absolute word." Terode took off his trench coat and hung it on the hook on the back of the door. "Remember all the other things which have happened. Have I ever let you down?"

"Pass them over here." Miles struggled to sit up in the bed.

"And that glass of water". He had a little difficulty in swallowing but he managed in the end. All the pills went down. Now it was done and he slouched back against the pillows.

"It won't take long." Terode turned towards the door and hung up his trilby hat. It was the first time Miles had ever seen him without the hat, and it came as something of a surprise to see that Terode had horns. Not big, long horns like an antelope or a bull, but stumpy little horns, about as big as his thumbs, curling back through the hair on the top of his head.

"So now Mr. Walker, you are taking your own life, which is a mortal sin, putting your soul outside of the protection of the church, but let

12

me reassure you that we always keep our promises." Terode licked his lips. "You are going to be born again as a pretty young girl. You will be born as Cathy, Eileen's daughter. You will have all of your memories. You will know exactly what is happening, but because of your autism, you will be unable to communicate with anyone. You will be locked inside your own little world. Now, for the first fifteen years of your life, you will have a loving mother, that's true, but you will live in constant fear, already knowing the full horror what's to come. You will rail and scream and even try to kill yourself, but because of your condition no-one will ever know what your problem is.

Miles could smell something, like a chemical, like a struck match, but getting stronger and stronger like the smoke from a big firework display.

"After that," Terode continued, "Well I think you know what happens after that. You will be trafficked to people we know, sold to men with certain bizarre appetites. You will spend the rest of your life in a secret world of underground clubs and brothels being tortured and abused, day after day, night after night, year after year."

Terode's features seemed to melt a little. Perhaps, thought Miles, it was the drugs beginning to have an effect. His face really did start to look like some giant bloated toad, the wide mouth flopping open as he spoke, the long tongue curling and uncurling as it flickered in and out of his mouth.

"Modern theologians don't believe in hell anymore, Mr. Walker." Terode's breath had the stink of rotting meat. "But I can assure you that hell does exist in many forms, and for you, it will begin with a whole lifetime spent in an absolute living hell and suffering sadistic abuse beyond anything you can imagine. Then, when you do finally die, well then we will be waiting for you and that is when the real suffering will truly begin. Think of it Mr. Walker, think of being tortured for the amusement of my kind, for all eternity.

"But it was your choice, Mr. Walker, it was always your choice. Up till now, you have given so much misery to other people, but now you shall be getting it all back. It was your choice all along, and nothing can possibly save you."

Beyond the circle

Janice didn't really have a Saturday job, but sometimes she would help Uncle Rufus by watching the antiques shop if he had to go off somewhere to give an estimate for a house clearance. Antiques they called it, but it was mostly just junk as far as Janice was concerned. Some poor old soul would die and a few weeks later their best china and their dining-room chairs would appear in the antiques shop. There were other things, of course, a few nice swords, a porcelain wash-stand, a metal fireplace from a house long since demolished, a Victorian family bible, an old china chamber pot and some gardening tools, and, of course, there were books, lots and lots of dusty old books.

It was truly amazing, thought Janice, that anyone had ever written most of the books on the shelves of her uncle's antiques shop, and even more amazing that anyone had ever bought them. She had once come across a first edition of the Hobbit in a hardback cover of blue and white and green, but apart from that almost all of those dusty old books seemed to be both boring and obscure. A 1922 copy of "Ulysses" by James Joyce and some old green book about "Leaves of Grass" were piled up with some blue copies of Tiffany's mail-order catalogues, and various 1960's DIY books full of rooms with atrocious orange wallpaper. Janice grimaced at the very thought of trying to read any of that. But one volume did catch her eye, while she was out at the back, putting water in the kettle. She thought it might even give her some ideas for her Art project.

The book itself seemed very old, the covers being made from some sort of leathery skin, a bit like a chamois wash-leather, she decided. It had a design like Japanese writing on the cover but the pictures inside were more like fantasy art. One was Stonehenge, except it wasn't really

Stonehenge, but perhaps an artist's impression of how Stonehenge might have looked a thousand years ago with all the stones still in the right places and a huge coppery sun hanging low on the horizon behind it. There was even a big stone slab with a circular inscription on it. She felt fairly certain that the slab wasn't there anymore and it didn't feature in any other pictures of Stonehenge that Janice could recall.

The other images were all fantasy settings, other-worldly landscapes suggesting an artist with a rich imagination. One portrayed a castle of sandy rock perched beside a lake of silvery water under a golden sunset sky. She tried to imagine herself standing on the battlements of the castle while a knight in shining armour sang love songs to her from the grass below. The next page featured a different kind of world, with a dark moon hanging suspended in a deep purple night sky over a black ocean shrouded in pale purple mist. It couldn't have been earth, not even at night, because the moon was much too large. In fact, it was rather difficult to believe that such a big moon could ever stay up in the sky at all, but then, she thought, that would be why it was called fantasy art.

Another page revealed luscious meadows of wet grass, lining the banks of deep-flowing ultramarine streams running through the bottom of a deep rocky valley. The sides of the valley were studded with trees of what looked like deep pink cherry blossom, while from far above pastel shades of light filtered in from a sky that could only just be seen above the tops of the mountains.

Unfortunately, there were no unicorns, which was a pity because Janice really did love unicorns and if she was producing a book of fantasy art she would definitely have had some unicorns in there, somewhere. But even without unicorns, there was so much she loved about these images. Some part of her inner-child wished that they were real, places she could run to, to hide out, to be a mysterious princess, to live out her fantasies and dreams. She loved the quality of the artwork and she reflected that she would give absolutely anything even just to be able to paint such pictures as these, but strangely there was no title on the book, no artists name, no author, not a single word of text. Just one sort of large geometric design on the front cover but it meant nothing. She looked again at the pictures, searching for an artist's signature but there was none, not that she could see. Then she realised that somewhere in every image there was a kind of magic circle. It wasn't a real magic circle, not the pentagram, not the five-pointed star set inside a circle, which of course she had seen in so many paperbacks and horror movies. This was a different design, a circle with arcane lettering, but it was clearly a magic circle of some sort. In each picture, it was found on a piece of flat rock, or at the focal point of a garden, or on a podium, or in the centre of a ruin. Even on the very last page, which had been left completely blank, there was a copy of that circle very clearly portrayed in the middle of the blank sheet.

One picture showed a foreboding dark ocean, purple perhaps but almost black, under a deep violet sky with only the merest hint of sunlight beyond a dark and dusky horizon. Out of that ocean rose a single rocky outcrop, a natural tower of blood-red stone cut by darker streaks where shadows lurked between the natural ribs in the rock. Massively it rose, towering up towards the violet sky, until at perhaps one half of its height there appeared to be a natural ledge and a small, steep, stairway of sorts spiraling up some distance further to a point where a small cave appeared to provide an entrance. Sure enough, the inscribed circle had been cut into the ledge where the stairway began. Perhaps this circle was the artist's trademark. She tore a page from the back of her notebook and carefully copied the design, then she locked up the shop and went home for the day.

An evening of searching the web brought her nothing. There was no slab or altar anywhere at Stonehenge and no reference to any such book, nor any such circle. If everything in the book was so unknown, then it might be rare, and if it was rare then it might even be valuable, or was she just wasting her time?

On Monday morning she skipped college and went into the shop instead, "Just to check that everything was OK..." she told Uncle Rufus.

"Yes of course," he assured her, as he tried to work out whether "Audubon's Birds of America" should go under 'Natural History' or just under 'America',

"And thanks for standing in on Saturday." He nodded. "Here's a J. K. Rowling book you might like, "Beedle the Bard," Do you want it?"

It was leather bound with no cover pictures, which made it seem rather old-fashioned but Janice accepted it with a polite smile and popped it into her rucksack with her packed lunch. Then she went out to the back to put the kettle on for a coffee and to use the toilet. That gave her a moment to go back to her mystery book and snap a few pictures with her phone. Stonehenge, the red tower, a temple in a jungle and a desert with some sort of pyramids, but not the real pyramids, lots of levels and terraces, like an Aztec ziggurat. She even snapped the circle on the blank page at the back, just in case that was important for some reason. They all had that same magic circle design. She also took a picture of the design on the front cover of the book, though her mother had always told her not to judge a book by its covers.

That night Janice uploaded the pictures to image search, but there were no results, not a single one of those shots was anywhere on the web. That pretty much told her the book had never been commercially published. She unfolded the paper from the shop with her sketch of the circular design and scanned it into her laptop, but still got no result from image search.

Looking again at the picture with the red pillar of rock, reaching up into the purple sky, she realised that her drawing of the circle should have had an image at its centre, a kind of rune. So she drew it in and peeled herself a tangerine. Then she tapped the desk, thoughtfully, and to her everlasting amazement, her finger went straight through the paper and into the wood beneath!

It took her a moment or two to digest what had happened and to pluck up the courage to try again, but this time nothing happened. Her finger simply touched the paper and stopped. But somehow, for some reason, the symbol at the centre of the circle had disappeared, so she drew it again, but this time in ink. Gently touching the centre of the circle she beheld the awesome sight of her finger disappearing into nowhere. She pulled it back and wiggled it about, and everything seemed normal, except that the symbol she had drawn on the paper had disappeared again, ink or no ink.

Janice reached for the half-empty bottle of vodka that was hidden behind the psychology revision textbooks in her bedside cabinet and took a gulp, though she didn't really know why, except that this was the most exciting, most crazy, most utterly unbelievable event that had ever happened in her entire short life and so taking a good stiff drink might somehow be the right thing to do.

She unrolled a large poster-sized A1 sheet of white paper, and picked up her phone, a bag of artist's charcoal and a couple of sticks of chalk and ran off to the garage, getting down on her hands and knees on the concrete floor to draw the circular design as large as possible on the big sheet of paper.

"Would it be dangerous to go through the circle?" She asked herself.

"Maybe." She answered her own question. Then she decided to reach through with her phone in her hand, to take a snapshot on the other side before she decided whether to go through in person.

It took her ten minutes to draw the design, from the paper that she had copied, from the mysterious book in the shop. After ten minutes, nothing happened. The sheet of paper lay there on the concrete floor. She could not push her finger through it, nor her phone. Whatever it was, it hadn't worked.

Janice stepped back for a moment and stuffed all her bits into her pockets, then thought about it for a moment or two. What if the circle wasn't complete? Microscopic breaks in the charcoal, maybe, caused by bumps and cracks in the concrete beneath. She got down on her knees and went over it all again, stepping out as carefully as she could to avoid smudging any of the marks.

A moment of apprehension. She reached out one foot, as if putting her toe into a hot bath, then changed her mind. She stepped back and paused for a moment to take a deep breath, then jumped in with both feet together, and she was gone.

Janice stood looking out upon a restless dark ocean, with deep rolling waves but no white foam. As far as she could see there was no land in sight and no ship upon the swell, but it was hard for her to be sure as the light was dim and dusky. The sky was purple and there was no sun, just a deep purple moon. She was standing on a flat rocky platform the size of her mum's back garden. The lines of the circle that she had just drawn with such care were unmistakeably etched into the rock around her feet. She turned slowly and looked behind her, to behold a massive rocky pillar the size of a large city tower block, maybe bigger, stretching up above her head to a dizzying height and seeming to grow wider so that it overhung her slightly, shutting out the violet sky. The rock was some kind of red, the colour of raw liver, granite, maybe, or obsidian perhaps.

Janice recognised this place, from the picture in the book. She had copied her inscription from exactly that image and here she was. The wind off the sea was cold and damp and the sea didn't quite smell like a normal sea, but she was here, somewhere perhaps that no living person had ever been before, but then she decided that someone must have been here in order to paint the picture. A question sprang to her mind and she followed the platform to the right, till she found, as expected, a small twisting staircase cut into the rock and rising upwards into the gloom above.

She couldn't climb that. Her knees were trembling with fear and she felt as if she wanted to be sick. That was hardly surprising. She was taking Psychology at A Level so she knew how to recognise the symptoms of stress. The only important thing right now was how to get back home from this amazing place.

Janice looked at the centre of that mystical circle which was carved into the rocky platform and at once she realised that the rune in the middle was missing. That was wonderful. She was sure, now, that she knew what to do. Taking her phone from her pocket she clicked on the image of Stonehenge and zoomed in on the central design. Then she knelt down on the red rock and sketched a copy of the glyph into the centre of the circle with a stick of chalk. That was the symbol for earth. She was sure of it. Then she stepped out of the circle, and jumped back in, like a child in a playground game.

In the moment that she jumped she was suddenly afraid. Modern Stonehenge didn't have that design, it didn't have that stone at all. What if she couldn't get there? What if she rematerialized three thousand years ago, or ten feet below the ground? What if ...

But she didn't arrive at Stonehenge. Nothing so dramatic. She was back on top of that big sheet of paper, spread out on the concrete floor of the garage. Nothing had changed. The time on her phone was the same as the time on the central heating boiler and she could smell the stew that her mother was cooking in the kitchen. She was home.

Tuesday passed pretty much just like any ordinary day. Janice went to college and tried to pretend she was listening. She knew she wasn't ready to go through that circle again, though she never for a moment stopped thinking about it. Should she tell someone? Was there anyone at all in the entire world who she really could tell? Was there anyone who might actually believe her? The answer to that one had to be no. If she even breathed a single word about this to her friends they would put her down as a liar just seeking for attention.

As for teachers and parents, if she mentioned it to any of them they would probably refer her to social services for counseling. Arcane books and interdimensional travel were not generally considered to be part of normal teenage development.

She did it on Friday, quite early in the morning, as soon as her parents had left for work. She wore her Converse All Star sneakers and a pair of black army trousers with plenty of pocket space. She was going to wear her leather jacket to protect against the wind, but in the end, she took a thick fleecy black shirt and a black body warmer, as well as a black beanie hat that she could tuck her hair into. She partly filled her rucksack with a rope, some bars of chocolate and some bottles of water. She looked good in the mirror, completely in black, like some girl out of a SWAT team, and she took a selfie to mark the start of her big adventure.

Right to the last minute she didn't really believe that it could work again, but it did, and she jumped through the circle and onto that red, rocky platform, on the side of the massive granite mesa, looking out onto that wide seething ocean. It was not so dark this time although there was still no sign of a sun, just a baleful purple light filtering down through muggy lilac clouds. There were even some tiny shapes, like black seabirds, wheeling and circling over the waves far out in the distance.

She thought about a guy called Harry whom she had chatted with online a few times. He was into base-jumping, going up high buildings and jumping off with a parachute. At least, he said he was into it, but she wasn't sure if he had ever actually done one. What would he make of this huge tower of red rock standing on its own in an ocean of purple water? Wouldn't this be an amazing place for a parachute jump? Or maybe not. What if you landed in the sea? And how could you get back up from the bottom?

Janice took a deep breath and began to climb the narrow steps. It was longer and harder than she expected, perhaps because she chose to crawl up the stairs rather than walk. She wasn't exactly afraid of heights, but this was pretty scary and she didn't want to take any risks. She told herself not to look down, which was always the advice people gave in the movies and at last she reached a small niche in the rock where the stairway ended. It was the entrance, it seemed, to a cave.

And indeed it was a cave, but not just a natural cave, for someone had already been here. At the entrance there was a metal gate, some bars of wrought iron twisted into shape, like the security grids they had on the local pub to stop people breaking in at night. The gate was open and was wedged back against the wall with a heavy wooden carving, like an African tribal god, lying down on its side.

"From tribal god to door-stop" Janice murmured. "What a come-down"

In fact, there were several caves linked together by smaller caves and passages. This in itself was hardly remarkable, but the caves were not empty. On the contrary, they were untidily strewn with all manner of items. In that first cave alone there was a pair of leather boots, the kind of long leather boots that pirates and cavaliers wore in old movies. There were boxes and there were bottles. There was a really large trunk, big enough to hide in, filled with silky fabrics that looked very expensive. There were tools and there were trinkets. There were bags and there were bundles. There was even what appeared to be a kind of brass trumpet.

Janice crept carefully to the adjoining cave, through a short passageway which sloped steeply upwards towards a very low archway where she had to duck. In the second room there was a large chair, more like a throne, and a couple of smaller chairs upholstered in leather with studs of brass. There was a table, but no food, and a large box full of maps written in languages she had never seen. There was something which looked like a kind of crossbow and 3 copper pots of different sizes. She picked up some clothing from one of the chairs, a sort of cape, or was it a cloak? It was soft, velvety and almost black, not quite black but very dark grey and it had a huge hood which could fall down right over her face. That seemed like fun so she put it on.

Opposite the doorway was a mirror, a strange mirror with an iron frame. It had a big rune at the top, and smaller ones round the outside which made it look like a sundial, or maybe a clock, but the designs and letters meant nothing to her. Looking into the mirror she realised that in the shady darkness of the chamber she was unable to see herself in that great big cloak, she just seemed to disappear.

She threw back the hood and suddenly her face appeared in the reflection. This was all too much now, way too much. What if it was a magic cloak? What if it was a cloak of invisibility? That would be well beyond the wildest stories. She opened her rucksack and ate a half a bar of Swiss chocolate then drank a little water. Her knees were getting wobbly again and she needed to calm down. She took off the cloak and left it draped over a bookcase. She realised that the bookcase didn't disappear, and neither did the cloak, so perhaps it wasn't really a magic cloak of invisibility, maybe it just didn't show up in the darkness, but it would still be really good for hiding in dark corners.

She would have loved to have gone further, but the rooms became darker as she moved away from that doorway at the top of the stairs and there were no candles or lanterns, and she was still very nervous. So she didn't go any further but instead she picked her way back through the various bits and pieces and gathered up a few souvenirs. There was a nice set of spoons, maybe silver. She wasn't really sure but Uncle Rufus might know. There was a small ornament that looked like a woman with a bow and arrow. There was a little wooden cube which looked like some kind of Chinese puzzle, some coins, a string of beads and a kind of dagger. There was a small leather pouch on a string with several bits of junk in it, like a lock of hair, a piece of bone with carvings on and other assorted tokens. None of them seemed strange at all, nothing magical or weird. She rolled up the marvelous cloak and put it in her rucksack on top of everything else. As an after-thought, she also took the mirror. No point in taking too much, she still had to get back down those awkward steps, and for a moment she thought about just leaving the mirror, but she really liked it, so that was that.

She felt confident now that she understood the way the circles worked. Whatever rune was drawn in the middle would determine the traveler's destination. Then the rune would disappear so that no-one else could follow. When she was ready to jump she felt so confident that she clicked her heels three times and said: "There's no place like home". Then she jumped. When she got back to the garage she rolled up the large sheet of paper and tied it around with a piece of string.

On Saturday she went back to the shop and told Uncle Rufus she had some stuff to sell. She said it came from one of the neighbours who was having a clear-out. Uncle Rufus seemed happy with the items she showed him, not that he recognised them all, but he did manage a few. The little knife caught his attention first.

"That's from Kurdistan." he seemed confident of that. "Not really used in battle but the old men in the villages wear them as a decoration. Supposed to be for killing demons but just a tradition really, more of a status symbol."

"How do you kill a demon with a little knife like this?" asked Janice, with more than a hint of ridicule.

"Ah well, it could be a small demon," said Uncle Rufus. Then he laughed at his own joke. "But it has nothing to do with the size really. These people say that demons cannot tolerate contact with iron because iron is a base metal and demons are ethereal creatures. It hurts them and weakens them and can potentially kill them.

"Ah ha!" Janice suddenly got it. "So iron to a demon is like kryptonite is to Superman?"

"Err, yes, something like that." replied Rufus as he poured the milk into his first cup of breakfast tea. "Speaking of Kryptonite, I have this book here published by Taschen. It's signed by the author, a fellow called H.R. Giger. He does spacemen and all that stuff you like. You can have it if you want it."

But Janice shook her head. She was much too preoccupied with her loot to read a book on spacemen and aliens.

The small bag of bits, Rufus said, was a "fetish" made up by witch-doctors and worn for good luck. Janice didn't quite know how to respond to that one. She had heard some of the art students talking about fetishes and that seemed to be something completely different to what was in the small bag.

She gave him a small pair of candlesticks to put in the shop window and sell for her, and the string of beads and the Chinese puzzle thing, whatever it was. She asked him about the mysterious book out at the back of the shop but he really couldn't tell her much. It had probably been part of a job lot from a house clearance, he assumed, no special reason to remember it. She told him it would help her with her art project and he agreed that she could borrow it. Then she set off home, taking the Doctor Who annual and a really old magazine called "War of the Worlds" to read on the bus.

That night she lay in bed gazing up at the new mirror on the wall, it had a big rune at the top, exactly the same as the one on the last page of the book, so she assumed they came from the same culture, whatever that was. She was still unable to believe that anything so fantastic could really happen in her own normal, everyday life. She was too excited to sleep, although at times she began to drowse and had dreams, not proper dreams, just fragments of dreams, half-hearing snatches of conversations which made no sense, seeing shadows moving in the mirror when there was nothing there. Eventually, she decided that she was absolutely never going to be able to get to sleep at all. Then suddenly she became fully awake and she realised that she had slept, just a little. Now it was the new day, Sunday, and she had nothing important to do, so she could go questing once again to her wonderful secret place.

She was determined to look more carefully this time and she prepared for the expedition like a true professional. She took a packet of fruit pies and a packet of vegetarian sausage rolls, and the left-over chocolate and water from her last trip. She packed a sketchbook and a camera and a flashlight. She wore the big old cloak that she had found last time because it was warm and she liked the smell of it somehow. She also wore the little bag of charms around her neck, figuring she could use all the luck she could get, fetish or no fetish.

When everything was ready, all it took was a little jump and Janice dropped through the circle and out into sunlight, not the white sunlight of our world on a summer's day, but a cold blue sunlight which reminded her of the lighting effects in Santa's Grotto when she was little and her parents had taken her to Winter Wonderland. At last the sun was up in this strange world. It was almost like the moon she would see from earth, but she could feel a slight degree of heat in its rays and she was sure that it really was a sun. Its pale blue light shimmered on the heaving ocean, making the waves seem higher and faster moving.

The first thing Janice did was to mark the rune for earth in the centre of the circle, so she wouldn't forget what she needed to get home, just in case she lost her notebook and phone. She snapped a few pictures then headed for the spiral stairway. Once she got inside the tower the flashlight made all the difference. She moved up through the two rooms she had already seen and on into the next which was very small, just a link between two larger caves.

She carried on moving inwards and upwards through dusty spaces filled with old weapons and bookshelves and even, in one room, a kind of altar with wooden decoration carved around its edges. There were seven rooms altogether, each one a little higher so that the overall effect was like a corkscrew gradually moving upwards inside the rock. The top room even had a window, like those narrow windows castles have, or churches. As with the door below this window had wrought iron shutters, but they were open and there was no glass, so she stuck her head out. She could just see the platform down below where she had arrived through the circle, and she looked around at the stonework on the outside in case there were any more steps or openings further up, but there was nothing. "Worth a try though," she mumbled.

The wrought iron shutters made her think. If her uncle was right then maybe these doors and windows were meant to keep demons out, or even to keep them in, so she closed the shutters on that window at the top and fastened them with the metal catch.

There was clearly no-one here right now so she decided to work her way back down, searching all the bags and boxes as she went. That didn't last long, though. There were too many things to look at and as soon as she started on one she got distracted by another. It would take her weeks and she would need to keep lists of where things were.

This was a dream come true. She wondered if she could ever bring anyone else here. Would they think she was mad? What if she was ever on the run and needed somewhere to hide. No one would ever find her here, never ever.

One room, half-way down, had a table. It was a very ornate table carved from some dark wood like mahogany. It must have been difficult to get that up the stairs she thought and that made her wonder who had brought this stuff here and why. Perhaps it had been here for hundreds of years, she thought, thousands maybe. She looked underneath the table and there was another pair of boots. These ones seemed to be made of felt, or suede even, anyway they were very soft and she tried them on. They fitted perfectly so she kept them on, rolled down to her ankles, and put her All-Stars into her rucksack. She looked back under the table to see what else was there and she realised that there was a gap at the back, a dark space. At first, she thought she had discovered another passageway but it was just a small alcove full of extra stuff. A box with brass hinges caught her eye so she crawled underneath the table and gave it a tug.

"The jackpot!" Janice gasped with delight.

The casket was full of jewellery. If even half of this was gold she would be rich, although she would need to be careful. It might not be easy to sell all of this in her part of London. The police might want to know where it came from. Maybe the shop? Perhaps Uncle Rufus could sell it for her. He must know people. She hung a couple of nice golden amulets round her neck, popped a ring on her finger, then stuffed the rest of the jewellery into the leg pockets of her army trousers. This was brilliant. It was the very best thing that had ever happened to Janice in the whole of her life. She opened her rucksack and took out a mini fruit pie, apple.

Then, all at once, came a noise. It was a slap-slap-slap noise, like the shutters on a security grid coming down. What it really was, Janice just couldn't tell, but her every instinct told her it must be bad. She switched off the flashlight and crawled backwards under the table. She pulled the big cloak around her so that no part of her was showing, not even her

25

hands, and from beneath the hood, she peered out anxiously into the gloom.

For a little while, there was nothing, but she could hear a kind of scratching sound, in one of the other rooms, maybe. She waited as quietly as she could. She could hear her own heart beating, like a drum thumping in her head. Then the scratching noise got closer. Something bestial moved in the darkness. Its body was tall enough to fill the doorway blocking out almost all of the dim light which had filtered through from below, but still, Janice could see enough to know that this creature was in no way human.

Crouched beneath the table her best view was of the monster's feet. The toes were longer than human fingers with large lumpy nodules where the knuckles should have been and vicious long claws like a bird of prey. The legs, in so far as she could see them, were short, thick and muscular. As the creature went by Janice lay paralysed with fright not daring to move, even though the sound of her own heartbeat rang inside her head like a heavy motor racing out of control and she had to stop breathing because she was certain that the beast would hear her at any moment. As it disappeared through the opposite door she had the merest glimpse, if only for a moment, of long, thick, leathery wings folded back behind its shoulders.

Janice waited for a few long seconds and then she crept out on all fours from beneath the table and crawled out through the doorway and into the room beyond. As she rose to her feet and slipped her rucksack onto one shoulder, the two heavy golden amulets swung and knocked together making a clonking sound like a coin being tossed into a pot. It wasn't really loud but it nearly scared her to death. She felt for the chains around her neck and lifted them off, up and over her head, and the little leather bag of charms came off at the same time.

Somewhere in the chambers above, the demon gave a terrifying howl. In that moment she knew that she had been detected. Perhaps it had noticed something missing. Possibly one of the necklaces had been protecting her and she had removed it. Maybe there was something else that she simply did not understand. It made no difference anyway. All that mattered was that she had been discovered. Lurching forward she flicked the three chains back around her neck again and threw herself through the next door and down into the room beyond.

She could hear the thing moving behind her as she spun into the bottom room. In front of her, the open doorway looked out on empty space and she blanched with fear as she realised how vulnerable she would be, struggling down the steep narrow stairway on the outside of the tower. For a moment she stood undecided on the edge of the top step as the creature and the shuffling and scraping sounds grew louder. Then she made her decision, wrapping the cloak right around her, climbing into the largest wooden chest and pulling a bundle of silky material over the top of her. There she lay, trembling in fear, as the demonic creature, whatever it might be, came into the room to search for her. Lying beneath the fabrics and wrapped in her cloak she could see nothing, but she sensed that the room grew darker as the monster walked towards the open doorway and stood there blocking out the pallid light. She could hear a noise which seemed to be part hissing and part moaning, which reminded her of the way dragons breathe in movies, just before they spit fire. The blood was thumping so hard in her head and in her heart that she was afraid even that would be loud enough to give her away. Then she heard the creature move again and she was terrified that it was about to tear away the coverings from her hiding place, but instead it began to shout out loud, so that its voice echoed up through all the caves. To her amazement Janice found that she could understand its words.

"I know that you are here, little thief, come to steal my treasure. I know that you are here and I shall find you."

How could a monster speak English? She wondered, and even if it could speak English, how could it know that Janice spoke English? Perhaps this was telepathy, she thought, but then remembering Bilbo Baggins, she deliberately slipped off the ring, and the monster's words suddenly became just a porridge of snorts and snarls. She slipped the ring on again and its words made sense once more;

"... I can wait here forever and when I find you I will eat you ..."

Janice fought back a desire to be sick and just lay as still as she could until the scratches and hissing began to sound further away and then faded away altogether. Hopefully it was no longer in the room.

In the darkness of her hideaway she waited and waited, desperately hoping that her cloak really was making her invisible and the amulets, or at least one of them, really was protecting her from whatever senses the demon might have which could otherwise betray her presence.

At last she managed to gather sufficient courage to pull her cloak back, just a little, and to push aside the fabric just enough, so that she could peep out with one eye to confirm that the monster had gone and the room was clear.

"Magic!" said Janice, and with that she climbed out of the wooden chest and sneaked out of the door and began to descend the narrow stone stairway which curled its way down the side of the tower of red rock, with her rucksack slung over her left shoulder.

Suddenly she heard a roar. It was a triumphant roar, like a lion's roar, and she turned her head to look upwards, the hood of her long black cloak falling back onto her shoulders. The demon had been waiting for her, sitting high above the doorway, perched on the very top of the tall red rocky pinnacle, and now, as she had emerged, it had seen her.

As she tried to gather her wits she looked up again to see the winged monster soaring into the sky above her, growing in size as it wheeled and turned and began its diving attack. Its claws were extended, its jaws were open wide and its eyes seemed to burn with rage. Struggling to cope on the narrow stairway, Janice knew in her guts that the vengeful creature would easily reach her before she could get back down to the circle on the rocky ledge.

As the sound of the wings battered her ears she swung the rucksack up into the air above her head, hoping perhaps for some tiny chance of protection. The demon seized upon it, grasping it in those vicious talons and soaring back out above the ocean. Then it realised that it had only manged to capture the bag, not the intended victim and it let it fall, tumbling down and down, until at last it disappeared into the seething purple waves of the ocean below.

That small portion of luck gave Janice the time she needed to scramble back up the stairway but on the top step she missed her footing and found herself lurching into empty space, just managing to catch at the iron gate, which slammed shut as she pulled it towards her, leaving her canted out over the edge of a horrific drop with one hand gripping the metal bars and one foot just on the corner of the top step, only just saving herself from a deadly fall.

She heaved herself forwards and crashed in through the doorway slamming the gate shut behind her just as the demon came soaring back towards her for another attack. She grabbed at the effigy of the tribal god and wedged it between the gate and the wall of the cave.

As Janice stood breathless in the doorway, the demon which had stalked her landed deftly on the top step and glowered into the room through the wrought iron bars of the gate. Its body was muscular, its skin soft like black leather but moist and slick with a sheen of viscous slime and pungent secretions. As it stood framed in the narrow portal its wings snapped out and filled the space around it, a black leathery membrane stretched tight across a framework of sharp bony ribs.

It flailed its arms towards her. The claws on its hands and feet were curved and vicious, the yellowed colour of old ivory. Janice kept her hands away from the bars in case the creature should seize them, and instead piled more chests and boxes against the gate to help to hold it shut.

The demon snarled at her from just inches away, its long tongue almost reaching out to her and its lips peeling back to reveal the full menace of its jaws. Those jaws were long, too long to seem natural, like a ferocious guard-dog with an extra-long snout sticking out much too far. The long jaws were bristling with nasty teeth, long wicked hungry teeth, sharp teeth which could cut through any natural tissue, teeth which could tear and rend human flesh with just a single bite. Above those terrifying jaws were a pair of evil, burning, red eyes which seemed to pulse hatred into the gloom, and those eyes were set in deep, dark sockets which were heavily protected by thick surrounding ridges of bone.

The enraged creature snarled again, with droplets of yellow spittle spraying out through the bars, but it didn't touch the metal gate and in that long moment they confronted one another, the angry demon and the terrified teenage girl, held apart by nothing more than a single barrier of wrought iron.

"I can wait forever." Hissed the monster, and it stepped off the stairway and soared away into empty space, effortlessly wheeling its way down to the platform below, where it perched with its wings folded right beside the circle.

And so they found themselves at an impasse. Janice, sitting up in the tower, knew that she was safe for the moment behind that wrought iron gate but the demon, waiting outside, knew that she was mortal and that she could not survive for long without food and water, especially since all of her fruit pies, chocolate and bottled water had been in the rucksack which was now lost somewhere in the purple sea.

The irony of her situation was not lost on her. She had a whole world to call her own, a fantastic castle reaching up into the sky and rooms filled with countless treasures, magic items even, and yet, before long, she might be wishing that she could exchange it all for a large portion of chips and a can of fizzy drink. Such were the rules of supply and demand. What a wonderful study that would make for an economics textbook.

But economics was not what Janice did best, and as she stood in that doorway she searched back through her own treasure troves of rich and colourful ideas. What would Sun-Tzu do at a time like this? What policies would Machiavelli recommend? or even Robert Greene for that matter? What about the Book of Five Rings by Miyamoto Musashi? She had always been fascinated by philosophy and psychology, by sociology and by strategy. There had to be something in all that reading which could help, but nothing useful sprang to mind. The pale light began to drain from the purple sky and still they stood vigil, the girl and the demon, locked into a situation with no resolution. She stood looking down from the metal gate towards the circle and the demon stared back with eyes of fire.

With the passing of time her thoughts began to wander off track. She thought of her old History teacher, who liked to talk about Alexander the Great, cutting through the Gordian Knot, sweeping away the problem rather than answering it. She knew that Captain Kirk was all for that approach, reprogramming the Kobayashi Maru, winning the unwinnable scenario by thinking outside of the box. If only she had a starship maybe that could get her out of here, but that wasn't going to happen, not unless she decided to draw one for herself, but a drawing of a starship was not the same as a real starship.

Then something clicked.

"Forget the books." said Janice out loud. "Start thinking like an artist."

Retreating back to the second room, she cleared a space on the floor, using her hat to wipe away any scraps of dust. She pulled out a felt marker pen and paged through some of the pictures on her phone. Then, slowly, carefully, patiently, she began to sketch out a copy of the circle just like the one she had drawn on the big sheet of paper at home. When she was finished she drew the symbol for earth in the middle and to test her handiwork she prodded the surface with one finger. To her delight and her relief, the finger disappeared into the rock.

"Bingo!" said Janice, aloud. "Time to go home."

She gathered together as much loot as she thought she could manage to carry without the rucksack. Then she stood beside the circle and took one last look at the fantastic caves which for a short time had been her own little private world. She put both of her feet together and clicked her heels three times for luck. But then, in a most brilliant moment of inspiration, she changed her mind and rubbed out the rune from the centre of the circle.

It had grown dark outside and the roiling ocean waves had turned black with the fall of night. Janice looked down towards the platform where the vicious red eyes of the demon burned all the brighter in the gloom. She swung the iron gate open with a loud clang and stepped backwards, disappearing in to the shadows of the doorway as the monster leapt into the air and soared up towards the entrance. It burst in through the open gate with a roar of fury and stooped low to get under the smaller archway which led into the second chamber.

Through the niche came the angry demon, its leathery wings folding in behind its back, its face drawn into a mask of hatred, its teeth bared and its claws spread, rushing straight at the human child who had dared to trespass upon its magical domain. As it came on towards Janice the monster stepped into the circle which she had drawn on the floor and in that moment it immediately disappeared from the world with the purple ocean.

"A drawing of a trap can still be a trap!" said Janice with a grim smile.

She was pleased with herself. She was pleased at getting rid of the demon and sending it off to wherever it was now. She had a feeling that it might not be able to get back, but she wasn't so sure that she wanted to wait around, so she quickly drew another rune in the circle. This time it was the right rune, the one for earth, not the other rune that she had used to get rid of the monster.

By now there had been plenty of adventures for one day so she just drew the rune for earth and made her jump. In an instant, she was no longer on some other planet fighting demons in some other dimension, but back in her Dad's garage, on top of that big sheet of paper with the drawing of the magic circle. She fell over sideways, rolled across the floor, and looked up with an expression of sheer terror, but to her everlasting relief, there was nothing else there. The rune on the other side must have disappeared and nothing could follow her through the portal. Without hesitation, she ripped the whole big sheet of paper in half to destroy the circle, and mercifully nothing else happened. No demon came crashing through the garage roof, nothing. Just to be on the safe side she went down the back garden to the old barbecue and burnt every scrap of the paper and still nothing happened, except that

31

she felt very sick and had to go round to the back of the garden shed where she threw up a couple of times. But that was nothing, it was just fright, and she was pleased she hadn't wet herself like she did when she was a little girl and she had got bitten by the vicar's dog.

It took her a while to settle down and she started to shiver a bit so she wrapped herself in a warm tartan blanket and had a few cups of tea, but in the end she was fine. It had been a great adventure. She thought about the mysterious book. How many other places were in there and could she visit any more of them? Would she dare?

In the days and nights which followed Janice didn't always find it easy to sleep. Sometimes it was two o'clock in the morning, or perhaps even three, before she finally drifted off into a restless slumber. Even when she did sleep she had sometimes had troublesome dreams. And on the wall of her room there hung a mirror, a very old mirror, a strange mirror with an iron frame which looked like the outline of a sundial, or maybe a clock, bearing a large rune which was the same as the one at the back of the book, and sometimes in the mirror there are glints of red light, like burning red eyes, watching her while she sleeps, and waiting.

Business unfinished

I was always the brightest one in the family, and when I started university, in 1973, it was like stepping into another world. I was a working-class kiddie from a northern industrial town and I suppose I was a bit out of my depth among the public school types who had sports cars and were members of the sailing club. My first term went well, as far as my studies were concerned, but I was a bit of a loner, and I knew it. Strange how you can be surrounded by hundreds of other young people and still feel lonely. I was naive, inexperienced and young for my age. Just the sort of person they liked to find. Early in the Spring Term one of the other guys in my group invited me along to the University Christian Union, where a couple of nice girls made a fuss of me and gave me free coffee and chocolate biscuits. I went along again the next week and all of a sudden I had friends who cared about me and I had a place to go on wet Wednesday evenings. I was hooked. I got religion and became one of the "God Squad".

When I went home for the Easter holidays I wasn't really keen to discuss it with my parents and my old school mates, it wasn't what they wanted to hear, but I needed to find somewhere that I could still enjoy the sort of fellowship I had been getting used to, so I popped into a couple of the local churches and looked for people who had their own floppy leather bibles with notes hand-written in the margin, always a good way to spot a true believer. It didn't take long for me to find the perfect place, an evangelical Christian fellowship that catered to a group of keen souls who attended various different churches around the town but also came together for additional prayer meetings and bible study groups.

Felicity Hargreaves was the leader of the group. She was a very attractive blonde woman, and for a church leader she was very young, maybe 21 or 22. She stood out as far as I was concerned because she was both intelligent and pretty, but it was more than that. She had charisma. She had that extra special quality that made people want to get close to her, a little bit of magic that made you want to listen whenever she spoke. The first time I went she took a real interest in me and made me feel welcome. I remember she had a guitar, an acoustic one, with bright coloured stickers on it which said things like "Jesus is the Way". At one point in the evening she led us all in a song called "Bind us together," where everyone had to have their hands on the shoulders of the next person in the circle. For some boy like me who was naturally very shy that was maybe the only time in the week I was going to have my arm round a girl so of course, it felt pretty special. Then towards the end of the night, they went round the circle and everyone in the group had to say what they had enjoyed most about the evening. Looking back now I would say that was a bit of psychological manipulation, getting people to comply with the group mentality, but I didn't think like that at the time. I mumbled something about fellowship, then we said one final prayer before we left.

The second time I went along a guy sat beside me. He was older than me. He looked poor and a bit undernourished in a pair of scuffed shoes and an old tweed jacket. Old men dress like that but he was only in his early thirties. He was new to the congregation so we talked a bit. He told me his name was Melvin and he was married with kids, five kids in fact, but he had decided to come along to the group because he was suffering from back pain and that had stopped him working and now he was unemployed and that was making him feel depressed. A friend had suggested that coming along to the prayer meetings might help to cure him, although I wasn't sure whether it was meant to cure his back or just cure his depression. Anyway, he seemed like a decent sort of guy but at the next meeting, I deliberately avoided sitting next to him because I preferred to try to sit next to some of the girls.

I went back to university after the holiday, but I kept in touch with Felicity Hargreaves, the group leader. I sent her one or two picture postcards that I bought from the Christian bookshop. To be honest, I really fancied Felicity, but she was two or three years older than me and realistically I knew that nothing was going to happen. So those picture post-cards were the only contact I had with her in the next ten weeks.

34

When the summer holiday came around I went back up north and got myself down to the fellowship in the very first week. They were all pleased to see me but it had changed a little bit. This new guy, Melvin, had really stepped up to play a part in the ministry. He was doing a lot of the public bible readings and joining in the discussion groups. He was also helping out as a prayer leader when we broke up into small groups for private prayers. He had become very friendly with Felicity. His wife was coming along as well, but not to all of the meetings as she had to stay at home and look after their five kids.

One night there was a woman who said how she desperately needed to give up smoking but no matter how hard she tried she just couldn't do it. I remember that I wasn't impressed. As a lifelong non-smoker, I have always been very intolerant of people who say they can't give up. All you need is willpower. Seriously, I thought she was just weak and inadequate but to my amazement, after they had all prayed about it, they decided that she needed an exorcism. Well, that certainly got my attention.

Now you have to bear in mind that the Hollywood movie "The Exorcist" had only been released a year earlier, and it was considered to be pretty shocking for the time. When they all talked about doing an exorcism of this woman I had visions of her crawling along the ceiling with her head spinning round back to front, vomiting black bile on the whole congregation, but in the end the kind of exorcism which they carried out was very innocent and harmless, just a few people laying hands on the woman and praying for her.

I don't know if she stopped smoking but what I did notice was that along with Felicity, Melvin was the main one speaking in tongues. This was one of the really trendy things which was going on in evangelical Christianity at the time, and it could seem very strange to a non-believer. Sensible adults go off into a kind of trance, shouting and babbling in some strange unknown language that no-one can understand. They can't even understand each other. They all have their own different sort of babble. They say that it's the Holy Spirit speaking through them, although cynics and psychologists might describe it as attention seeking behaviour.

I know it seems a bit odd, but to a certain degree I envied them the attention they got from all this. I still found Felicity very attractive, and I did consider confessing that I had a problem with alcohol and maybe letting her pray over me to exorcise me from that, but at the next meeting one of the members confessed to the sin of self-abuse and we all crowded round him and laid hands on him and said prayers.

Afterwards I thought it was so bloody awful, so totally embarrassing for someone to own up to that in public. I cringed and I laughed and I promised myself that I would never, never, be so utterly stupid as to make an announcement like that in public. That might have been the first time that I started to have misgivings about the whole religious thing. It certainly wasn't the last.

During the next few weeks I heard about Felicity and Melvin arranging all-night prayer vigils, sometimes with other group members and sometimes all alone, just the two of them. It seemed obvious to me that he fancied her, and maybe she fancied him. I felt a little bit jealous at first, I must admit, but after a while, I started to feel concerned. It was obvious that if I had noticed it when I was only back for a holiday, then other people must also have worked it out as well.

Then at a meeting one Saturday evening, all hell broke loose. We were at a point in the worship where people get to stand up and share their feelings. Sometimes it's a verse from the bible which has inspired them, sometimes it's a problem they want their friends to pray for. This time it was Melvin's wife, Elizabeth. Right out of the blue she said how she was suffering great inner anguish because she felt that her husband was being unfaithful to her and committing adultery with another woman.

Of course, the whole congregation knew exactly what she was talking about. There was so much tension in the air and yet no-one actually said anything. Every single person just looked at someone else and waited for whatever was going to happen. I just didn't know where to look. Really! I remember twisting my fingers together and ruffling through the pages of my bible as if I was looking for a special page, anything just to try to conceal my embarrassment. I was mortified, but things just kept on getting worse.

Melvin stood up from his seat and raised both arms in the air shouting at the top of his voice about how he was under attack by demons, and how an evil influence had cast its shadow over him. This was just too much. I still remember how I couldn't stop myself from turning round in my seat and trying to see the expressions on other people's faces.

Then to my everlasting amazement, Melvin turned away from his wife and started pointing and shouting at Felicity Hargreaves.

"You! You have led me from the path of righteousness! You have come between me and my family! You! You are evil and I denounce you!"

His face had completely changed. His eyebrows were drawn up into points, like a vampire in the movies, and his lips were drawn back so that his teeth were bared. Suddenly he launched himself at her, crashing through all the people and stumbling over chairs with his hands spreading out like claws trying to reach her.

I was quite a fit young guy in those days, rowing for the university team. I held onto him as best I could and, with help from two or three others, I was able to hold him back. He was screaming at her now, speaking in tongues most of it, so I really couldn't make out what he was trying to say, but the overall effect was that it sounded like a wild animal screaming. Felicity was screaming back at him, and she was speaking in tongues as well, shouting just as loudly and just as aggressively, and I couldn't understand her any more than I could understand him, but now the whole congregation was crowded around and things weren't getting any better.

After a little while, it seemed to me that Felicity had lost contact with the Holy Spirit because she stopped speaking in tongues and was just calling out "Jesus, Jesus, Jesus". Then Melvin's wife Elizabeth joined in and she was calling on Jesus as well, but Melvin just kept on howling and roaring like a wild animal. This went on for a while and then people led them all away and got them out of the church, like teachers breaking up a fight in the playground and eventually the rest of us good Christian folk went home.

The next day was Sunday and I have to say that the worshippers were all rather surprised to see Melvin arrive at the church, but I think some sort of apologising had gone on behind the scenes. He claimed that he had no actual memory of what had happened but he wanted people to pray for him, and Felicity got up and gave a little lesson about the importance of forgiveness and its role in Christian love, and then they gave him public forgiveness and full absolution in church in front of the whole congregation. This all seemed a bit strange to me. I was very suspicious. If I had to guess I would say that they were all really embarrassed and had made up some kind of peace agreement to save face in front of the other members, and then passed it off as all part of the religion. I didn't know how much it was all due to divine mercy and how much it was just down to basic human nature but it all made me feel very uneasy.

During that summer I became a lot closer to Felicity. She was 22 now and I was 19 and the gap didn't seem quite as big as it had a year earlier. Looking back I think she liked to be seen spending time with me because it was a way to try to prove that she wasn't really involved with Melvin. She totally denied any suggestions of adultery, but just denying it was never going to be enough. Being seen with me made her seem a bit more normal. For my part, I just enjoyed the time we spent together. She really was very attractive, not just physically, but in her whole manner. I don't know what it was, but she had it.

Towards the end of the summer, it was becoming obvious to everyone that Melvin's condition was getting worse. He often said things to people that were stupid and abrupt. He accused members of not liking him. He reported hearing voices. We also heard that there were arguments at home. Some of the elders in the congregation began to suggest that a proper church exorcism might be the only way to restore Melvin to his sanity. I was against it myself. In my opinion, Melvin's behaviour was symptomatic of people with mental health issues, but those evangelical types like to have a religious explanation for everything and they were convinced he needed an exorcism. I was starting to wonder if these people were losing track of the division between real life and Hollywood. I said it many times but people didn't want to hear that, they felt that it challenged their faith. I had to go back to university in September so I wasn't party to any further arguments. There was a local vicar, the Reverend Rushmore, and in the end, he decided to approach the church hierarchy for permission to carry out an exorcism on Melvin.

During my whole life, since that time, I have often wondered why people argue about religion. You can argue and argue but in the end, some people will always believe one thing and other people will always believe something else. It splits right down the middle into two groups, and they might all be nice people but they can argue forever without ever changing their beliefs. There was once a civil war in Russia over which way people should point their fingers when they did the sign of the cross. That's the sort of stupidity you get when religious dogma takes the place of common sense.

It might surprise you to know that there is nothing in English law to provide protection for people who are involved in exorcisms. There is no system of health and safety checks, no code of ethics, and no supervisory body. Most amazing of all it's assumed that the person on the receiving end is demon-possessed so they are given no choice in the matter, no right to withdraw, no lawyer present, no medical checks. If a doctor or a policeman acted like this they could be sent to jail, but none of this seemed to matter to the good people of the congregation. At the start of October, Felicity told me on the phone that a date had been set for a service. I bought a train ticket and went home for a long weekend. I was worried about her, really worried. I don't know why, but I just felt I should be there for her sake.

The exorcism started at midnight on Saturday the 25th of October, and I must confess that starting at midnight seemed a bit over-dramatic to me. There were two ministers, one Anglican, and one Methodist which surprised me a bit because I thought it was only the Roman Catholic Church which went in for demon possession. There was a sizeable audience if I can call it that. It wasn't the whole of the congregation but a significant part had decided to attend.

It all started off fairly sensibly, I thought, with Melvin sitting in a chair and the two ministers praying for him, but he soon began to twitch and swear and shout, all of which was seen as a good sign that the demons could be conquered. The first stage is getting a name, so they command the demon to identify itself and it usually does. Maybe the priests have the power to force it, or maybe those demons just want to get a reputation. I would not know, but as they identified each one they kept demanding the names of more, like a witch trial in the seventeenth century, till at last, they had a list of about forty demons, representing such sins as lewdness, heresy, incest, bestiality, blasphemy, masochism, and carnal knowledge. It seems that all of these demons had managed to take possession of Melvin, but somehow none of the rest of us had been affected in any way whatsoever. It was all very hard to believe.

The ceremonies dragged on long into the night. The general idea was just to keep on praying till the demons came out, but if Melvin started to struggle they would have to hold him down and so it quickly became a very physical affair with men of the congregation taking turns at restraint while Melvin kicked and screamed and wriggled on the floor beneath their weight. At one time I went to the toilets in the back of the church and when I came back Melvin was on the floor with three men sitting on him as if they were riding a horse, while he tried to force himself up like a man doing press-ups, though of course, his body couldn't move, only his arms which just kept on going slap, slap, slap, against the flagstones of the church floor.

After a while his violence began to tire them out, so they tied him up and carried on, but that didn't stop him from scratching and spitting and screaming. They poured holy water on him, they shoved a crucifix down his throat and then they burnt it to destroy the demon which they claimed had gone into it. For my part, I was getting more and more uneasy. When I went to the church door, for a breath of fresh air, I saw odd couples, husbands and wives from the congregation, standing out in the church yard taking a break. Some were even having a smoke.

When I went back in Melvin was still tied up on the floor getting wrestled and slapped and prayed over. It was almost as if it had turned into a kind of spectator sport. Perhaps it was my experiences at university, or perhaps a degree of natural cynicism, but I was very ill at ease with what I saw.

And yet, we so often comply with the will of the masses, going along with the mob and saying nothing against them for fear of disapproval. There may have been others who shared my concerns, but none of us spoke up and it wasn't till eight o'clock in the morning that they finally called a halt. The priests believed that almost all of the demons had been driven out. Only three remained, bearing the names of insanity, anger, and murder, so it was decided that we would take a break, and everyone, including Melvin, could go home to sleep, then we could meet again to complete the exorcism the following day. Looking back, it was sheer stupidity. If you really do believe in demons why set someone loose who is known to be possessed by insanity, anger, and murder?

I walked Felicity back to her house, but our conversation as we went showed quite a gulf between our thoughts and beliefs. I was of the opinion that the whole thing had been overdone. I was beginning to think that I didn't really believe in demons and this was just creating some sort of pantomime which had everyone mesmerised. Even if there were such things as demons I could not see any reason why they would all be crowded inside poor inadequate Melvin.

Felicity took the opposite view; that this whole show proved beyond doubt that demons were real and that he should never have been allowed to go free and that those three demons inside him could now be much more dangerous than ever because they knew they were under threat. By the time I said goodbye to her at her parents' house I was really starting to think that she was almost as crazy as Melvin.

Walking home, I could easily have gone down the street where Melvin lived, but I deliberately chose to avoid it and went down the next road instead. It was shortly after nine o'clock on a dry autumn Sunday morning and no-one was really out and about. Despite being tired and a little uneasy I found the walk relaxing. Well, it was relaxing until I heard the roar. I call it a roar because I don't have a better word to describe that dreadful sound. It was as menacing as a growl but much, much louder. It was more threatening than any shout. It was unreasoning, wild and chaotic. It made me afraid.

I turned into someone's gateway and walked down the side of their house and out into their back garden. Again I heard that terrible roar. I jumped the back fence and over into the garden of the house behind. From there I was able to peer through into the next street and I could see that the front door of Melvin's house was wide open, but no-one was there. I sneaked up towards the front street, keeping close into the bushes that lined the side fence so that I could survey the road without being seen.

In the street beyond, I beheld a creature of sheer horror. It was what appeared to be a naked human male, and I assumed it was Melvin, although he was totally unrecognisable as his head, his face and his matted hair were heavily smeared with fresh blood. I have heard it said that even a small amount of blood looks like a lot in an accident, but this really was a lot. No part of his naked body was free from the sticky red mess and as he staggered about the street he left gory footprints clotting in his wake. Even his male member, which stood fully erect, was heavily caked in dark sticky blood as if it had been smeared on with a purpose.

As I watched from my place of concealment he raised up his hands, like the winner of a boxing match, and once more let out that fiendish roar, then something disgusting sprayed from his mouth, blood perhaps or even red vomit. I have never seen anything like it in my life, and God help me, I pray that I never will. Melvin turned away and walked half-crouched down the road, shouting incoherently, with the fresh blood still dripping from his hair and his fingers as he went.

I stayed hidden until he had disappeared from sight and then I crept out of my hiding place and crossed the road to the family home. As I stood on the porch I could hear the regular ticking of a large carriage

41

clock in the hallway but aside from that, there was total silence, which worried me as I had thought to hear his wife crying maybe, or phoning for help. I went through the hall and into the living room, backtracking the trail of bloody prints and smudges on the carpets, until I reached the lounge where I came upon a scene of horror which I shall never forget.

The room had been completely wrecked, with broken furniture and smashed ornaments just strewn everywhere. Everything was covered in blood, but not only blood, for torn flesh and even brain matter had been scattered all around. In the middle of the floor lay Melvin's wife, Elizabeth, and I later learned that he had strangled her with his own bare hands, although that would not have been the sole cause of death, because in his deranged and maniacal fury he had also gouged out her eyes and bitten out her tongue then bitten and ripped at her face till she was completely unrecognisable, just strands of tattered flesh clinging to a bloody skull. They say she died of shock and asphyxiation, either through being strangled or through choking on her own blood. I can only hope that it was quick because it cannot have been painless.

Poor Elizabeth had not been the only victim. Beside her lay their pet dog, a King Charles spaniel well known to the neighbours as Bessie. The poor beast had literally been torn limb from limb. One hind-leg lay against the window-ledge, another on the sofa, the rest I could not see. The poor dog's body had been thrown onto the armchair, its head twisted round to an impossible angle and its eyes gouged out. He had even ripped out its teeth, what kind of person could possibly do that to an animal? I thought, was Melvin truly demon-possessed?

I felt certain that I was going to vomit, although in fact, I didn't. I think my mind was concentrated so much on survival that I just focussed on getting out of there. I left the building and followed Melvin's bloody trail, walking towards where I had last seen him. As I turned the corner I was aware that a police car was arriving at the house I had just left behind. They had been summoned by the neighbours I supposed.

Ahead of me, in the next road, Melvin was still roaring and speaking in tongues, almost dancing in the middle of the street. As I got closer I began to make out one phrase amongst all the nonsense, "The blood of Satan!" He kept saying. "It is the blood of Satan!"

A small crowd was gathering around him, obviously horrified at having a naked man covered in blood standing there gibbering away to himself on a Sunday morning. Then another police car arrived and Melvin fell to the ground and curled up in a foetal position, still ranting about the blood of Satan. They tried to calm him down while they called an ambulance but nothing was really having any effect. How do you calm a man who has just torn apart the mother of his children?

Later, in the cells, it seems that he was able to talk rationally about what had happened to him, the ordeal of his long night of exorcism in that church. Newspaper accounts said he told them that he loved his wife and that he didn't remember anything about the murder, but when they asked him how he felt about her being dead he replied;

"Praise the Lord. I once was lost but now am found. I have been released. God's work has been done and I have been released. The demon that was in her has been destroyed."

It was sixth months before the trial took place and I was nearly at the end of my second year at the university. The prosecutor opened with a resounding statement;

"The evidence that will be put before you" he thundered, "will sound, at times, like something from a medieval witch trial, not a modern court of law" and that much at least was fair comment.

I had given a statement to the police, but they didn't call me as a witness because I hadn't actually seen him do it, and there were plenty of others who had seen what I had seen. In any case, the defence didn't try to deny that he had done it. They accepted all of the facts but tried to put up a defence of insanity. They argued that Melvin had already been mentally disturbed when he went along to the Christian Fellowship Group and that the congregation were a bunch of cranks and fanatics who had indoctrinated him and manipulated him. Melvin's lawyer made no bones about it. He blamed religion in general and he blamed the fellowship in particular, labelling them as a bunch of lunatics who enjoyed being lunatics and were breeding other lunatics.

I could certainly follow that line of argument, but I also had to ask myself what would the congregation have to gain from this, it went against everything they wanted, everything they stood for. They were decent, peaceful people and they had never wanted any of this. I refer to them as "they" not "we" because I was no longer attending any of their meetings and I'm sure that was true of many others. This whole business had made people think. Anyway, that line of defence seemed to work for Melvin and he was sent off to the special hospital for the criminally insane at Broadmoor, not to a prison. A couple of hundred years ago they would have just hanged him, I suppose, or maybe even burnt him alive.

Now here's a thing I noticed; You might expect that after such a desperate affair all the people would be of one mind in condemning what had happened, but it wasn't ever as simple as that. Within the fellowship about a third of the members stopped going straight after the murder, and then there were others, like myself, I suppose, who gradually drifted away but still kept in contact socially. I certainly still tried to keep in touch with Felicity. Then there were the rest, about a third of the original number, who kept on going. They would even be heard to say that this terrible incident was proof that they needed to be better Christians, to have more faith and to pray harder.

Around the town, as well, opinions were split in many different ways. The local priests who had carried out the exorcism still, apparently, believed in demons. They still claimed that Melvin had been demon-possessed and many of their parishoners agreed with them. True, one of the vicars said he felt sorry that they had bungled the exorcism, but the other one even went so far as to say it was a good thing as it was all part of God's plan. However, there were also plenty of other people who you could hear talking in the supermarket or the working men's clubs, complaining about religious mumbo-jumbo and blaming the "God Squad" for driving Melvin mad.

As for me, I had given up all my religious delusions by the time I graduated. My Social Science degree led on to a Masters in Psychology and then a Ph.D. in Criminal Psychiatry. I was fortunate enough to get a good job with the Home Office in London and I enjoyed a successful career far away from my home town. I really had no reason to be involved with any of those people again, but I have lots of family and friends in the area so I always kept myself aware of the local news, and from time to time Melvin would surface again. After four or five years he was let out of the asylum. That caused a bit of a stir. Later there was at least one suicide attempt when he jumped off the motorway bridge, which you might say was not surprising considering all that he had been through. I often wondered how his children reacted, young adults now, living in the same town as the father who slaughtered their mother.

Then maybe ten years after the suicide attempt came another big shock. Melvin was arrested for some sort of sexual interference with an underage girl. That pushed him over the edge again and he seemed to relapse into the various types of mental illness which he had been suffering from at the time of the murder, but instead of getting a prison sentence he was put into psychiatric care as an outpatient. This led to complaints from various people in the local community, which was hardly surprising. In the mind of the general public, it's bad enough having a murderer for a neighbour, even worse if he's a paedophile as well. I was over forty by now and well respected within my profession, so the consultant psychiatrist dealing with the case rang me up for a chat and asked me to share my background knowledge.

That was the trigger, I think. I had often thought about Felicity during the intervening years but I had not kept in touch. Now with the increasing use of computers, I was able to trace her address and I went back up north to pay her a visit. Perhaps I shouldn't have done it. You might say it had no real value to the case and I was just taking a walk down memory lane. I could never really argue against that, I could only say that sometimes we do what we do and we can't properly explain it. In any case, she was not living locally and after sending her a letter to make her aware of my intentions I drove up to the address I had been given in a run-down area of Stoke on Trent.

The terraced house was cold and bare, clearly the dwelling of someone who did not have the money to buy new carpets, or furniture or even ornaments. Those furnishings which did exist could easily have been bought from a second-hand shop or donated by a charity. But plenty of money had been spent on security. Every window in the building was protected by anti-burglar grilles, the stylish modern ones which have strips of white-lacquered metal crisscrossing in a diamond pattern, and to every metal grille was fixed a cross, or a crucifix, sometimes several of each. In every room and hallway which I entered there was a low voltage lamp switched on to burn incessantly both day and night, and candles with matches placed ready in case some power cut or technical fault should threaten to plunge the dingy place into darkness.

At the centre of this iconic web sat Felicity on a studio couch, which appeared to serve as her seat by day and her bed by night, huddling herself into an old eiderdown blanket which reminded me of one my grandmother used to have when I was young. But Felicity was not as I remembered her. She was only two or three years my senior, but here, in this dim lodging, she could easily have passed for seventy compared to my forty. Her once blonde hair hung dry, wispy and white. Her furrowed brows betrayed too many years of stress, and where once she had been confident and enchanting she now fidgeted nervously with the pages of an old worn and tattered bible whose leather cover had long since fallen away.

I could gain no useful information from her, let alone any form of social conversation. Her concentration was woeful, her emotions fragile, and she reminded me of many of my patients, not the spirited young woman I once admired. Only one notion, one idea, seemed to return over and again in her conversation. She claimed that someone was always watching her, trying to get to her, wanting her. When she said these things she cast tense looks towards the stairwell, not the windows, to such an extent that I feared there might be some intruder or abusive partner hiding upstairs, so I excused myself and ascended towards the upstairs bathroom with a certain amount of caution. However there was no one in any of the rooms and I stood looking around at the squalor, thinking how sad it was that my beautiful friend had grown old in a place like this.

Then suddenly through the bedroom window, I realised that a grotesque creature was staring at me from the branches of the dead elm tree in the garden behind the house. A grim feral face with great teeth set in hanging jaws, it leered at me with hate filled eyes, glowing red like burning coals. In its size and its shape it was, at a first glance, like a jaguar, that particular species of giant cat which hunts from the limbs of trees in the jungles of South America. But this was no cat of any sort, its body being too heavy and muscular, its hands too human, and its movements too purposeful. Then, I noticed it had horns, short, straight upright horns, like a European Alpine Goat, and exactly at that moment it began to move towards me, walking out upon the limb of the tree, or rather it seemed to be effortlessly gliding through the air just as easily as a shark moves through water lightly touching the branches as it passed between them.

I was instantly overwhelmed by a sense of fearful helplessness and a perception of limitless evil. I ran to the ground floor, calling the police, and thanking God that we now lived in the age of the mobile phone. When they arrived they searched the garden and its surroundings but found nothing. I think if it hadn't been for my title, and the nature of my work at the home office, they might have labelled me as some sort of crank, but I won them over and before I left I had I made them promise to check in on Felicity from time to time.

46

I drove home through the darkness with a remarkable feeling of stress and foreboding and slept little that night despite the consumption of several glasses of good quality Scotch. At work, the next day, I found it hard to concentrate and I was hardly surprised when the police contacted me during the afternoon to tell me that Felicity had been found dead. Natural causes it seemed, her heart had simply given way.

My life has changed forever since I saw that vile creature lurking like a predator on the edge of Felicity's property. I left the United Kingdom three months later, and I don't think I shall ever return. I have a job as a teacher of English at a small international school in Rome. The money isn't great but the children are from wealthy families and all very polite. All that matters to me is that I am in a cathedral city surrounded by priests on every side. Hopefully, here, I can live out what is left of my natural life and die with my soul safe. I had abandoned my religious faith as a young man, but now it is all I have left.

Third time lucky

Egy kitűnő barátnak dedikált

Vikki's life was shit. There was no other word for it.

It wasn't her fault. Andrew had caused all their problems. He had run up debts to pay for drugs and gambling and all sorts of other stuff that she didn't even know about but now they were in deep shit and she was in just as deep as he was. Two nights previously they had lain in the darkness pretending not to be at home while strange men banged on the door and shouted threats from the stairwell. They had said that they would be back, and she believed them. Now she was terrified at what they might do.

The next day, when Andrew got back from the pub, he was in a positive mood.

"I've managed to find a guy who can give us some money." He grinned at her with a stupid, drunken smile that made her want to slap his face.

It should have seemed like good news, except of course that no-one ever really gives anyone money. There is always something that they want in exchange, and in this case, that something was always going to be Vikki.

Andrew made it sound good, a part in a film, maybe even a big break, but Vikki knew it was going to be porn. She was expecting it. She had worked as a stripper in the past, and as a topless waitress in a cocktail bar, so when Andrew suddenly said they had money coming in she knew she was going to have to be the one who had skin in the game. She didn't really mind taking her clothes off, not if it was somewhere respectable like on the beach in Spain or in the theatre when she was doing the drama course. What had her worried was the filming, the idea that her pictures could be spread all over the world, and how far they would want her to go, but Andrew didn't want to talk about any of that, he just needed the cash.

The studio was a warehouse place, on an industrial estate somewhere near Tottenham. There was a security guard on the door but she didn't know if that was a good thing or bad. He took her in to meet someone called Gregory, an ugly little man with lots of gold rings who clearly had no dress-sense. His shirt was bright blue, the sort of thing you might buy for a Caribbean holiday, only partly buttoned up and showing off his hairy chest and a big tasteless medallion. He had green canvass shoes and baggy chino jeans in a shade of brick red or dark orange, it was hard to describe exactly.

Vikki knew his sort. The entertainment industry was full of them, self-important little men trying to show how big they could be. Even the way he spoke to her was totally imperative, "You need to do this." and "You have to do that." She really didn't like him and she really didn't want to be there. But life isn't always what we choose and she had come with a job to do. The filming wasn't pleasant. She was prepared for sex but this was worse than she was expecting, the things men want from pornography that they can't ever get from their wives. She just had to switch off and let the time pass, and then, at last, it was over.

"Here you go, girl!" Gregory stopped her just as she was going out of the door. "Go on! You're the one that earned it. I'm giving it to you, not to him."

It was a rolled-up wad of money. In her whole life, Vikki had never held so much cash in her hand at one time. She took it home and gave it to Andrew. Then she went to the bathroom and locked herself in. She took a long bath and cleaned herself up as much as she could and didn't come out until she had had a good cry.

The money gave them a break but it didn't last long. Andrew was soon in trouble again. It was one thing paying off a few weeks' worth of debt, but the figure in the background still kept going up. That was how those people worked. They trapped the punters into debts that just kept getting bigger. Once a body was on their hook it was well near impossible to get off again. A couple of months went by but in the end, there was no choice, she had to go back to Gregory and arrange some more work.

She spotted the little man from the other side of the car-park. He was sitting outside of the building on top of an empty beer keg, having a smoke and drinking coffee from a disposable plastic cup. He looked for all the world like a little garden gnome, thought Vikki, although even the most tasteless garden gnome would have steered well clear of that colour scheme. Today he was wearing pink satin trousers, a sort of glittery-silvery shirt and those funny plastic sandals with big holes in that had been really trendy for a little while. And of course, there was the medallion.

This time the film set was very different. Almost the whole of the building was one large room inside, and that had been lined with black drapes. At one end was an altar with huge candlesticks, the size you would normally find in churches, except that in churches the candles were white and these candles were all absolutely black. Vikki wasn't happy with the candles being lit so close to the black drapes but Gregory assured her that it had all been fireproofed according to the regulations.

In the centre of the black painted floor there was a huge silver circle with a five-pointed star inside it. She had seen all that before in horror films.

"That's the magic circle, isn't it?" asked Vikki. Not that she really cared but if you have to work with people then you have to find something to talk about.

"We would prefer to use the term thaumaturgical circle" Gregory replied. "Thaumaturgy is the science of what you would call magic."

"Suit yourself." She just didn't like his attitude. "How do you want me?"

This time the filming had taken longer, much longer. The ritual part alone must have taken an hour to enact, with Vikki spread out naked on the altar and no chance of a break for a cigarette or the toilet. Then, at last, they were finished and they moved on to what they called the bacchanalia, which was what most respectable people would call an orgy, although Vikki just thought of it as a bit of party and wished some of the men had been a bit younger. Never mind at least there was plenty of chance to drink and smoke during that part and the money was going to be very welcome. They even offered to let her have a copy of the DVD, although, to be honest, she found it all a bit boring. Sex was meant to be more fun than that, and besides, that big empty place had been a bit too cold.

Life went back to normal for a while, but just for a few weeks, then like a clap of thunder from the heavens she realised that she was pregnant.

"That really wasn't supposed to happen," she told Andrew. "There must be sumfin wrong with them pills"

"The only things what's wrong with them is you keep forgetting to take them, you silly cow." Andrew was far from sympathetic.

"Your trouble is you're so pissed when you go to bed and so hung over when you get up that you never really know if you has took 'em or not."

"Fuck off and gimme a break, Andrew." Vikki could give as good as she got. "If you wasn't so fuckin randy all the time it wouldn't have happened."

But she was worried all the same. Andrew was cute looking, but he was totally irresponsible and no way suited to bringing up a child. The weeks which followed were far from easy. Vikki suffered all the usual problems of pregnancy, morning sickness, cramps, and incontinence, heartburn and indigestion, back-ache, constipation, and swollen ankles. If this was what being a mum was like she really didn't need it. She tried to cut down on the drinking, but nicotine was a lost cause, she needed her cigarettes to get through the day and nothing was going to change that.

Then, late one night, the police came, a man and a woman together and she knew it was bad news. Andrew was dead, stabbed outside a pub in Canning Town. They asked her what she knew but she knew nothing, not until the day after the funeral when she had the phone call she was dreading. Andrew still owed money, lots of money, and now the debt was down to her.

She phoned Gregory and she begged him to help, and to be fair he was sympathetic, but it was a lot of money, a lot to ask. This would take quite a few jobs he told her, and some of them might not be nice.

Then she broke down on the phone and it all poured out. She couldn't do any parts in a film because she was pregnant and she was terrified, that they were going to come for her and she was going to lose the baby and she didn't have anyone in the world she could turn to for the money and she wasn't pretending but she would do anything, she would do absolutely anything, if he would just help her out of this mess.

There was a long silence, then a short reply. "All right girl, let me come round and see you."

He hadn't changed much in six months, still the same self-important little man. He was perhaps a little more tanned as a result of some cheap winter holiday in Grand Canary. That made his chest hairs seem a lighter shade of white by comparison. He was wearing bright blue stay-pressed trousers and a loud Hawaiian shirt with white patent leather shoes. He had the same tasteless medallion but more gold rings on his fingers than she remembered.

"Are you Jewish?" she asked him, thinking about the gold.

"Never fancied the operation" he grinned, cracking his knuckles. "Now let's talk about you, not me."

But they didn't have the opportunity to talk because at that very moment someone started kicking the front door, and shouting, and Vikki screamed and fell to her knees behind the coffee table clutching her hands to her face.

"Don't go! Don't go!" She begged him.

But Gregory ignored her and went to the door. She heard raised voices, then some sort of argument, and then it all got a bit quieter and eventually Gregory returned.

"Vikki darling, I can deal with this if you want me to, but nothing comes free in this life. If you want these lot off your back then I'll be coming back to you after you've had the kid and I will want you to do what I ask. Whatever I ask."

Still crouched behind the coffee table, Vikki didn't answer but just nodded and sobbed into her hands. Gregory returned to the door and spoke to someone for a little while and somehow, for some reason, they went away. He came back in and double-locked the door and brought toilet paper from the bathroom for her to wipe her face and blow her nose. Then he lifted her to her feet and helped her to the window where they looked down on the car-park, seven floors below. Five men were getting into two cars, one red and one silver. There might have been drivers in the cars as well, that was impossible to tell from above.

"There they go, girl." He whispered gently. "They're going away and you won't have to worry about them no more."

Instead of answering she leaned towards him and kissed him on the top of his head.

"What's that for?" he chirped.

"It's for what you did, Gregory. I've never seen anyone so brave in me whole life."

"I can deal with the money, girl, I can sort that for you. But don't forget that you're gonna owe me. You are gonna have to pay me back one day."

"What about my Andrew?" she asked as an afterthought. "Who's gonna pay me back for losing him?"

The little man shrugged and left without another word.

A week later there was big news in both of the local papers and even on the national TV. Two cars had been set on fire and all the men in them had been murdered. Some were shot, some were burnt, but they were all dead. One car was red, one was silver. The police put it down as gang-related. Vikki tried hard not to think about it. One thing she had learned growing up on mean streets, the less you knew about these people the less chance that they were going to hurt you.

A year went by. Vikki had the baby, a little girl called Cindy who had blue eyes and curly hair and smiled a lot. She had a new boyfriend as well. Barry was a computer technician, not her usual type maybe, but he was clever and she respected him for that. He read books about almost everything from Archaeology to Zoology and especially Science Fiction. She didn't understand his jokes and he listened to some pretty odd music, but he was nice and tall with long dark hair and he even wrote poetry about her. Most of all he was a lot less trouble than Andrew.

When Cindy was one year old they got a new place together on a modern estate in Romford. She was glad to be away from those flats with all their bad memories, and she felt that her life was starting anew.

It was September when Gregory appeared on the doorstep, wearing banana yellow flared pants and a burgundy shirt. She really didn't know how he had found her, but she guessed that someone had given him the address. He was making a film about Halloween, he said, but she told him she didn't need any work right now.

"I don't want you, darling. I need the baby. Just for a couple of days. I'll be coming back on Tuesday to collect her and I don't want no arguments. You owe me, remember"

When he had gone she began to cry. Barry was sympathetic but he just couldn't see the problem. She told her story as best she could although it didn't make much sense to him. He told her she could just refuse. He told her she could just go to the police, but nothing he said made any difference. Vikki was beside herself with grief. She had made a promise that she would do absolutely anything to get out of debt and get that gang off her back, but now Gregory was asking her for the only thing in her life that she wasn't willing to give.

Barry did suggest that they could run away together, run away somewhere and never be found, but she didn't think that would work. These kind of people always knew where to find you. He suggested hiring a few heavies, but she wasn't sold on that idea either. Gregory, she was sure, could easily find more people and nastier people than anyone Barry could come up with. So they just waited for the next three days. Barry retreated to the spare room with his books and his internet and he re-laid the carpet in the living room. Vikki tried to hug Cindy as much as she could, to love her as much as she could while there was still time.

On Thursday morning Barry went out early to collect some DIY stuff. Vikki stayed at home and sat miserably in the furthest corner of the bedroom dreading that Gregory would come but by the time Barry got back he had still not been.

Barry though, was like she had never seen him before. "Still waters run deep." her grandmother used to say, and in his own strange and quiet way, Barry seemed to be waiting intensely for the little man to return.

At last, there came the knock at the door. It was Gregory, just as they knew it would be. He was wearing yellow leopard-skin trousers, a green silk shirt, and open-toed sandals with white socks. He had a gold ring on one little finger and his medallion round his neck.

Barry sat him down in an armchair and offered him a glass. Gregory said no, so Barry just poured one for himself, a big one, and sat beside Vikki on the sofa. They talked for a little while, Vikki begged and pleaded, Gregory insisted. Barry asked a few questions of his own but none of them made much sense to Vikki.

In the small bedroom Cindy began to cry, but when Vikki started to get up Barry gently pushed her back down onto the sofa.

"I'll get her. You stay here."

Barry brought the child from the bedroom and laid her down on the settee beside her Mum, then he started to give Gregory some of the things he was going to need; a baby buggy, a plastic potty and a bag with food in. The little man looked bit awkward with his hands so full but Barry just added a few more bits until Gregory really was overloaded. Then he turned, smoothly and quickly, and before anyone else knew what he was doing, his hand was round at the back of

Gregory's neck and he had grabbed hold of the medallion chain, pulling it up and whipping it off, over the visitor's head. Then he stepped back quickly towards the sofa.

The response from Gregory was instantaneous. The little man flew from his seat, wide-eyed in rage and his fingers spreading like claws. But he never reached the settee. Instead, he recoiled with a yelp of animal pain.

"What have you done?" His face was suddenly a great deal more ugly as he paced about the room, struggling with himself, it seemed, but for some reason, unable to get to the sofa where Vikki sat desperately hugging little Cindy.

"You know exactly what I have done." Barry always spoke quietly, as if he just couldn't be bothered to get excited. "Or at least you can easily work it out. I took up the carpets last night and painted the magic circle and all the protective charms on the underlay. I believe you would use the term thaumaturgical circle, wouldn't you? Anyway, you know what it means. The circle is protecting us and you can't get in here."

"How did you know?" Gregory's nostrils flared with anger, making him look somehow more bestial than normal.

"Ah well, I have a webcam set up to cover the front door. I watched the film of your first visit. That gave me a good start." Barry rolled a cigarette but didn't light it.

"When you are with a person they can't see you properly because of your enchantment, but the digital images stored on the hard-drive are just images. They show you as you really are. It surprised me a bit when I watched it but, hell, better than being kept in the dark, eh? Oh, and, nice tail by the way."

"And it's not just the camera," Barry was smiling now. "You know the internet has changed the way people do things. As much has changed in the last ten years as in the last five thousand. You should try surfing the web some time. You might learn a lot. As for me, I like to research things, Archaeology, Religion, Languages, Folklore, Demonology and the Occult, loads of stuff." Barry twirled the little man's medallion in his hand like a hypnotist spinning a pocket watch.

"That sigil on your medallion tells me that your name is not really Gregory, is it? It's Grigori, your demon name. Am I right?"

The little man seemed to wince at the name and his eyes flicked from side to side as if seeking some sort of advantage or even a means of escape.

"This is nonsense." His voice was now quite soft and his manner reasonable. "Don't mess with me son. Give me back the medallion and I will leave you alone. That's fair"

"That seems very fair" nodded Barry, amazingly calm considering the situation, "But what if I don't give you back the medallion?"

"Then you won't ever leave this room alive." Grigori snarled, and his body began to morph before their eyes. Within moments the small man had ceased to be, and in his place stood a creature with a squat muscular body, its brown skin oozing yellow bile from multiple pustules, its hands and feet ending in claws. Its head looked like no natural visage but could best be described as resembling a bat with oversized ears. Its eyes were tiny slits from which some sort of green metallic light seemed to shine out. Its tail was thick like a crocodile and it had small stumpy wings which seemed much too small for flight. Of all it's bizarre features however, nothing was more compelling than the smell which emanated from it, a cloying, repulsive smell like a mixture of human excrement and fish-guts on a hot day.

"I can stay here forever, literally forever." The demon hissed. "You need to know that because you can't get past me and you will starve to death in a few days, all of you. So give me back the medallion and I will go."

"Ah, the medallion, Grigori." Barry dangled the jewel in front of him and gazed at it quizzically.

"Is that what it is, Grigori, a medallion? Or could it really be what people call a demon amulet? Is it true, Grigori, that for a demon to exist, here in the human plane, it must keep its own life safe in an amulet? Is that what we have here, Grigori?"

The monster's claw snatched out towards the jewel that Barry was swinging so provocatively in front of him, but the protective barrier held and once again the creature recoiled in pain and confusion."

"Give it to me," Grigori demanded. "It's no use to you. I can do you a service, maybe grant you a wish. Yes, I will, you can make a wish."

Barry shook his head and gazed at the monster with a sad stare of disapproval.

"The Russians have an ancient proverb Grigori: 'He that would sup with the devil should use a long spoon.' It means that the devil is so cunning, that it's dangerous to try to deal with him. I think we have learned that any help which comes from you will come at a high price. I am pretty sure that we will all be a lot safer if I just destroy the amulet."

"You cannot destroy it," cackled the monster. "That metal will resist any force that you can muster, puny human"

"Puny human?" Barry snorted. "Puny Human! What sort of language is that?"

"That's what we call a cliché Grigori. It's already been featured in too many films and comics. It's considered bad form to use such an overworked expression. If you spent a decent amount of time on the internet you would know about all of these things. You would also know that the best way to get what you want in life is not to make deals with demons, but to order stuff on line for click and collect."

Vikki sat open mouthed in amazement. Here they were confronting a foul-smelling demon with a tail like a crocodile, in their own front-room, and Barry actually seemed to be enjoying himself.

"You see this tumbler here?" He dangled the medallion over the glass. "You saw me pour myself a drink from that vodka bottle but you didn't see me drink it. That's because this isn't vodka. It's a little concoction that I bought from an online dealer called DIY Warehouse Direct. If you had a degree in inorganic chemistry you could call it nitric acid hydrochloride, although you old-fashioned types might know it better as Aqua Regia. That's what it was called by medieval alchemists, Aqua Regia, the Water of Kings, the universal solvent. Anyway, nowadays it's guaranteed to clear any blocked drain in seconds but they have to sell it in glass bottles, or plastic, because it dissolves metals almost instantly, including both gold and platinum"

Barry slowly lowered the demon amulet towards his glass. The monster screamed in despair and threw itself forwards with all the force and willpower it could muster, writhing like a fly caught in a spiders web as the protective magic of the circle caused its flesh to spark and burn. Then Barry released his hold on the thin golden chain and the medallion fell with a tiny plop into the liquid and began to effervesce, twisting and turning in the stream of bubbles until it came apart and crumbled into small pieces of debris which sunk to the bottom of the glass.

At that point, quite suddenly, the demon seemed to collapse inwards upon itself, shrinking in size like a deflating balloon, till there was nothing left but a small pile of slime, rather like a large dollop of dog-poo, which Barry took out and burnt on the barbeque. That was the last they ever saw of the horrible little creature, although the smell remained for quite a while and eventually they had to order a new carpet.

Vikki, of course, was completely taken with Barry from that moment on. He became her superhero, her genius, her dark-knight in shining armour and she loved to tell people how clever he was, although she generally kept quiet about the demon because no one would have believed her and they might even have reported her to social services for being a nut-job.

On his birthday she arranged a babysitter and took him out to an Indian restaurant in Romford, where they overdid it on the poppadums and the onion bhajis and could hardly finish the main course.

He was wearing a black shirt with baggy sleeves and black drainpipe jeans, and his long hair was tied back with a little loop made from black leather. As they were eating she thought about how calm and good tempered he always was with her, even in the most difficult of moments, and she asked him a question which had often played on her mind.

"Right at the end there though. When it was promising you all sorts of things and when it said it would grant you wishes and all that if you would just give it back the amulet. Did you never think you might want to do a deal?"

Barry gazed at her for a moment then shrugged. "It was never going to happen" he smiled gently "Anyone who dresses like that deserves to die."

The Exorcist

In 1973, when I had only just begun my university studies, I took on a part-time job as the projectionist at the university theatre. This served two useful functions, I got paid for being the projectionist and I got to see the films for free.

Things were different then. There was no video, no cable TV and terrestrial television didn't get the rights to screen top movies until years after they had been released. So the only place to see the latest Hollywood sensations was on the big screen at the movie theatre. There were three scary movies that I remember being infamous at that time; Deliverance, The Wicker Man, and The Exorcist.

Now whether you choose to call them "Horror" or just "Thriller" they were all certainly scary, but in a way they were also very different. The Wicker Man and Deliverance were (as far as I know) entirely fictional, and yet their stories were perfectly possible. They only involved normal human activity, if indeed you believe that murder can actually be considered a normal activity.

It was only in "The Exorcist" that there was any suggestion of supernatural or paranormal activity, and yet, surprisingly, this was the only one, out of all three films, that was actually based on real-life events.

In the aftermath of the film there were several reports of individuals attempting suicide and of clergymen trying to exorcise demons from people who had watched it, even though most people in Britain at that time regarded demons as nothing but fiction. I myself can remember very distinctly, in the student union bar, having a conversation with one student, a big strong lad from the rugby team. He had been seriously upset by watching the Exorcist and was trying to bring peace to his mortal soul by drinking large quantities of beer, whilst at the same time asking how to get counselling from the college chaplain.

It puzzled me how impossible events could be based on a true story. Perhaps for that reason, I have often reflected on that film over the years and from time to time did some research into its origins. Here, to the best of my knowledge, is the true story, of the real child, whose life was the basis of what some would regard as the most frightening horror film ever made.

***

In 1949 a story appeared in the Washington Post and was later discussed and publicised in many other sections of the media. The child was referred to as "Roland Doe" and also as "Robbie Manheim" in order to protect his confidentiality. The generally held account was that Roland, or Robbie, was born in 1935 in an American protestant family. It was said that the family lived in Cottage City, Maryland. As an only child Roland often amused himself by spending time with his Aunt Harriet, who was herself a spiritualist and when he was about 13 years of age she taught him to use an Ouija board for fun, but following her death strange events were reported, such as items of furniture moving of their own accord in the house where the family lived. It is said that the family then began to fear that Roland had become possessed by the ghost of his dead aunt, and so they took advice from their church pastor, Luther Miles Schulze, who just happened to have an interest in such issues.

Pastor Schultze arranged for the boy to spend a night at his house. The next day he reported that objects such as household furniture had moved by themselves when the boy was near, and he advised the boy's parents to "see a Catholic priest." The boy then underwent a number of exorcisms. The first was conducted by a Roman Catholic Priest named Edward Hughes, at Georgetown University Hospital, which was funded and managed by the Roman Catholic Jesuit Order. It was claimed that during that first exorcism Roland was tied down on the hospital bed but he managed to get his hand free from the restraints and broke a bedspring from his mattress, which he used it to slash the priest's arm. At that point, the first exorcism was halted.

The family then sought help from Professor Raymond J. Bishop at St. Louis University and his friend and associate William Bowdern, both of whom were Catholic Priests. When they met the boy they reported the bed shaking, Roland speaking in a harsh, husky voice, and also speaking fluent Latin. They even reported that words such as 'evil' and 'hell' appeared on his body in blood. It was also said that he reacted with revulsion to any religious words or objects.

Bowden carried out another exorcism, this time at The Alexian Brothers Hospital in South St. Louis, Missouri, which was has since been demolished. Additional Jesuit priests were called in to help, including Walter Halloran, and William Van Roo. Halloran claimed to have seen the words "Hell" and "Evil" appearing in blood on the boy's skin. During the exorcism it was reported that the boy's bed began to shake and that at one point he punched Halloran in the face and broke his nose.

In 1949 the story appeared in the Washington Post and was later discussed and publicised in many other sections of the media. This was the story which inspired the 1971 novel, *The Exorcist* by William Peter Blatty, which was then made into the 1973 horror movie. But as I stated earlier, this was supposed to be a true story, and yet it involves events which many people simply could not believe to be true, so what could be the explanation?

***

The film was made for entertainment purposes and certainly added many shocking details which went far beyond the original reports, for example, the child in the film was a little girl, not a boy, in order to enable the scene where she is pictured masturbating with a crucifix. This simply could not have happened in the case of Roland. Other additions included the child's head turning all the way round, vomiting black bile, and the famous "Spider Walk" scene where the child defies gravity by crawling across the ceiling. These were some of the most sensational moments which made the film so visually shocking, but they all appear to have been invented entirely for the movie.

In fact, they had actually been "borrowed" from another historical account. In 1906 a sixteen year old girl, called Clara Germana Cele, had been playing with an Ouija board and had allegedly prayed to Satan, entering into a pact with the devil. A few days later, her body was taken over by strange impulses. Her family had taken her to a local convent where the nuns tried to look after her. They reported that she made terrible, animal-like sounds, and spoke in a range of different human languages such as Latin. In this case the nuns actually did report that the child had been levitating into the air and that she was horrified by the sight of a crucifix. In this particular story two priests actually carried out a successful exorcism and the girl had no further problems. Some people might suggest that this was attention seeking behaviour by the girl and religious hysteria by the adults, but the fact remains that features reported as part of Clara's story, whether true or false, seem to have been used to "top-up" the script of the Exorcist.

Even so, the rest of the story still seems both frightening and convincing, particularly considering how many serious men of religion were witnesses. This evaluation changes, however, when we begin to check out the specifics.

Author Mark Opsasnik actually went to the local neighbourhood and spoke to people who had known Roland, including his boyhood friends. Overwhelmingly they gave the impression that Roland had been a very manipulative child, a clever prankster who liked to invent tricks which would frighten his mother and the neighbours' children.

J. B. Rhine, a parapsychologist who studied the case, raised doubts about the integrity of Pastor Miles Schultze, who had first brought the story to public prominence. Schulze took the boy to spend a night at his house, then claimed that he witnessed household objects and furniture seemingly moving by themselves, but Rhine wondered if Schulze had unconsciously exaggerated some of the facts. It is entirely possible that Schultze and Roland were each meeting the other's needs; Roland wanting a chance to show off and Schultze wanting a story to tell. They might even have conspired together.

The media coverage of the story points to Father Albert Hughes as the first to clergyman to attempt an exorcism, but Hughes apparently suffered a nervous breakdown at around that time and disappeared from the area, so there was never any possibility of checking his involvement. There is no independent evidence that he ever visited the boy, or attempted an exorcism, or that he was cut with a bedspring.

In fact every rational investigation of the case has found that there was no actual evidence at all, except for a few minor incidents, such as a bed shaking, which could easily be faked by a naughty child. For example, the boy was said to have had words appearing in blood on his body, but at least one of the priests noted that they had seen him scratching himself with a fingernail and smearing his own blood on his torso. Experienced police officers, social-workers and psychologists are all fully aware of a simple way to differentiate between self-harming and harming by another. In Roland's case, the words only appeared on areas which could be easily reached, and never on his back. As for the Latin words which the demon-spirit is said to have uttered, they were probably just words he had heard from the priests themselves.

The Washington post had never bothered to report these critical details as they just wanted a convincing and exciting story. After publication of the newspaper account, it seems that the boy, Roland, faded out of the public eye and went on to live a fairly uneventful life with no further instances of demon-possession.

In 1993 author Thomas B. Allen published a book *Possessed: The True Story of an Exorcism*, which claimed there was a consensus among most experts that "Roland was just a deeply disturbed boy, with nothing supernatural about him"

If we try to see the big picture it becomes plain that several parties played a part in sensationalising this story. Roland enjoyed playing a role and tricking his seniors. The various priests were delighted to find a case which appeared to agree with their own beliefs and interests. The newspapers got a story which helped them to sell copy. Then the film company made a huge amount of money from the success of the sensationalised Hollywood movie.

At every level people chose to believe the story rather than question it. Thus, what began with a mischievous teenage boy rattling his bed and tipping over pieces of furniture, eventually ended with a demented teenage girl masturbating with a crucifix and spider-walking across the ceiling of her bedroom, but it was still described and accepted as being "based on a true story."

This should serve as a lesson to us all not to believe everything we read in the papers and see in the movies. But it also teaches us a more serious lesson. When we recall the horrors of the witch-craze in Europe, the genocide of the Native Americans, Stalin's purges and Hitler's holocaust, we must realise that the same forces are at work. A leader cannot unleash such horrors unless he has the support of the masses, who lap up the rumours and the propaganda even though they know it is wrong. All too often people know the truth, but they prefer to spread a good story. In an age of mass media, our real enemy is fake news, not fake demons. Instead of exorcising evil spirits from our children we should be ejecting the dishonest politicians from our governments.

Their Satanic Majesties

Marianne had grown up in the care system. She had been in care from as early as she could remember, passed on through several different children's homes and several different sets of foster parents over the years. She sometimes wished she could have been adopted and had her own family, people who would really care about her and protect her, but it never happened. Apparently, there were some legal issues with her real parents that never quite got sorted out when she was young, and then when she was older, well, no one wanted a fourteen year old girl with a difficult history. So adoption was just a dream. It wasn't ever going to be on offer.

At eighteen the care system suddenly cut her loose. There were rules which had to be followed and budgets which had to be met. The local council, social services, whoever it was, their responsibility only covered children, not adults, no matter how cute-looking they might be, no matter how much they wanted to be loved. So regardless of Marianne's feelings and needs, she suddenly found herself out of care, out of school, out of a job, and out on the street. But it wasn't all bad news. She had met Nick.

She had been waiting at the bar in a pub in Hackney and he was standing next to her ordering his drink, a pint of snakebite with blackcurrant. She didn't even know what a snakebite was and she gave him a funny look. He just smiled, such a lovely smile, and then he started to sing, not quietly humming a little bit, but full-on singing that the whole pub could hear;

"Please allow me to introduce myself, I'm a man of wealth and taste..."

"Do you know that song?" he asked her "It's the Rolling Stones. One of my favourites."

"I've never heard it," she raised her eyebrows in a way that said cheesy, "Must have been way before my time." But that was it, one simple conversation and love at first sight.

Nick had been in care too, at least that was what he told her, but he had run away and survived on his own, homeless on the streets of London. She could believe it. He was sharp, streetwise, a natural survivor. He was always two steps ahead of any argument and never stuck for the right thing to say. She admired him, she adored him and soon she was in love with him. Nick was the first great love of her life.

And suddenly life was worth living. All they had was a tiny room in a house that he shared with three other mates, but that didn't matter. She had a rucksack to keep her things in and there was a mattress on the floor to sleep on and that was all they needed.

Not that they slept much, with Nick she discovered just how good sex could be. Before him there had been a bit of adolescent fumbling with boys from school and the unwelcome attentions of a temporary worker at the care home but it was all pretty meaningless, just trying to keep up an image of being as good as the next kid. With Nick it was different in every possible way. She loved him. She wanted to please him. She hungered for him. She would do anything for him. But even more than that she enjoyed having sex with Nick because he really was very, very, good. Sex with Nick was like nothing she had ever known before. Friday and Saturday evenings were for dance clubs and squat-parties, every other night of the week was for sex.

Marianne got a little bit of benefits but it wasn't enough to survive. Nick got nothing on account of not having any proper paperwork but he was the one that brought in the big money. Usually, it was from drugs. He didn't deal with the little guys. That would be too much time for too little reward. He had the contacts to rise above all that. He would arrive home with a kilo of powder or a big bag of pills and divide it up for the local dealers. Two or three days later it was all gone again, easy money.

Marianne didn't mind. It wasn't harming anyone, as far as she could see, just giving the punters what they wanted. She went along with him and she didn't ask too many questions. He knew what he was doing and people trusted him. That was very important Nick told her. If a drug deal went wrong you couldn't complain to the police so there were only two ways to keep things sweet, either you worked with people you could trust or you might have to get nasty with someone. He always treated people fair and they trusted him. There were other benefits as well. He knew lots of people in the music business and the clubbing scene. There were clubs and there were parties and there were after-parties. Doors were open to Nick, and Marianne was always right there at his side.

One night he brought her home a present. It was a cute little tablet PC, the first one she had ever had. She wasn't sure if he had bought it or swopped it or stole it, but it didn't matter. It was brand new and it was hers and she loved it. One of the guys in the house had Wi-Fi and she could lie in bed in the morning looking for clothes from Hell-Bunny.

Nick liked to use it as well. He wanted to buy her some things, sexy things. Some of them were things that she might have bought for herself anyway and others that she wouldn't really. He loved black, anything in black. Black stockings, black knickers, black corsets, black satin, black rubber, anything black was just up his street. It was fine by Marianne. If it made him happy she was happy. If it turned him on she wouldn't complain. She was young and free and in love. That made everything seem like fun.

Camden was her greatest joy. The shops and markets beside the canal were like a treasure house full of fashions and shoes and junk jewellery. The cafes were cool and the people were funky. Even when she didn't have any money to buy anything she just loved being there, but as long as Nick was with her she usually ended up getting something new. One shop did a line of t-shirts with a caption which said "Good girls go to heaven. Bad girls go to London." She didn't really know what heaven was supposed to be like but she was pretty certain she would rather be in London. She felt herself growing, learning, developing and becoming a better person, and in her own mind, she was sure that it was all down to her relationship with Nick.

One damp night in February they went dancing at a party in a converted railway arch off Crucifix Lane near London Bridge Station, but it all ended early when a police raid closed it down. Outside in the dark, as the crowd began to disperse, a little group of old-style punks struck up a conversation. An Irish guy called Ronnie was asking how many people could get into one Uber. He had his hair done in a green Mohawk and a spiked silver stud through his tongue.

"A pity to stop dancing now eh? We're going to go off to a party we know about. Do you want to come along? It won't cost you. They're nice people. I'm just wondering how many we can squeeze in an Uber."

His friend went by the name of Rattle. His head was shaved and he wore a t-shirt that looked like a skeleton, under a leather jacket with dozens of badges. Rattle was a local guy who reckoned he knew all the shortcuts and thought it would be quicker to walk.

Marianne was scared. She really didn't want to go, but Nick said he was up for it and so they tagged along.

"Sometimes you have to trust folk." He whispered in her ear. "And you have to trust me."

They ended up in an artist's studio somewhere near Brick Lane. It was pretty badly organised but it was fun. They got high and they danced and the hours went by and they chilled-out with new people. Someone did a collection to go out and buy more beer and Nick put some money in. Marianne got talking with an Eastern European girl, called Zofia, sitting on an old leather settee. The springs of the sofa had long since given up the struggle, and the two of them sunk so low that they were almost sitting on the floor but it was warm and comfortable and nobody cared. They talked about London and then they talked about some other cities where Marianne had never been yet but she wanted to go, and they talked about Camden, and artists, and vegetarian coffee bars. Maybe it was the drugs or maybe it was real, but she felt like her and Zofia were really going to be the very best of friends forever. They sat close for a while and kissed a little bit. It was the first time she had really kissed a girl, properly.

After a while Marianne said she was starting to feel a little bit cold so Zofia got a blanket from somewhere and wrapped it round her, and then went off to make her some hot tea. Nick was talking away to one of the DJs. She knew that he liked to play now and then but he hadn't brought any music with him. She just watched him for a little while and thought about how much he meant in her life, how amazingly positive and protective he was, how honest and trusting and totally unflappable. Then she started to have a bad feeling. What if anything bad ever happened to him? What if anyone hurt him or took him away from her? How could she live without him?

Then, somehow, for some reason, the DJ plugged in a set of electronic keyboards, and the music faded. Nick rolled up his sleeves in a big dramatic gesture, put his hands on the keys and started to play.

She never knew he could do that. But he could! He came out with some sort of loud scary classical music stuff, that made her think of a horror film, then after a few minutes he stopped and took a little bow, and everyone clapped and they all had a laugh and he told them that was all for now and they put the dance music back on again.

"What was that?" laughed Marianne as he pulled her up from the old sofa and hugged her. "What you were playing?" She seemed to have forgotten her worries. "What was it?"

"It was Bach's Toccata and Organ Fugue in D Minor," He smiled an innocent smile as if it was the most normal thing in the world to play like that, in the middle of a drug-fuelled bender at a party full of strangers.

Did you like it?" He asked in all innocence.

"Dunno!" She pulled a face. "A bit creepy if you ask me." Then she giggled. "Come and meet Zofia."

It was dark again by the time they went home. They had danced and partied through the whole winter's day. He hailed a black cab from the end of the road and she huddled in his arms as they travelled home in style.

"That was nice in the end." She pushed her head inside the front of his jacket. "They was lovely people. Hope we gonna see them again."

"Told you." He tickled the back of her neck. "Most people are good people. Just accept them for what they are and trust them."

As the weeks went by Nick started browsing websites about fetish clubs and it wasn't long before they gave that a try. She would wear a skin-tight black latex dress with no underwear and patent leather court shoes with five-inch heels. She couldn't walk in the damned things and Nick always had to order a cab to get them home, but it was an amazing buzz to be out there on a dancefloor surrounded by all the most bizarre clubbers in London. One night in the middle of summer they got out on the roof of the building with a little group of liberated people and Marianne made out with a beautiful black girl, the full public performance in front of an audience, as the sun was coming up over Wapping, and the respectable general public were starting to make their way to work through the streets below. In her heart, she knew that she only really did it because she thought it would turn Nick on, and when she asked him he smiled, but she wasn't quite sure.

Life just kept getting better and better. Nick was working his way up the supply ladder and making plenty of money. They moved into their own flat. She had new clothes. She had an iPhone. She had freedom and the chance to be different, really radically different, to do things that would shock the general public and to enjoy doing them all the more for that. But most of all she had Nick and he was the most important, most wonderful thing in her entire life.

The thrills got more intense as well. They were definitely in with the in-crowd, it seemed like every club led on to a party, and every party led on to an after party, and all the time there were more beautiful people, and more drugs and more sex.

But Nick, himself, never did the drugs when they went to the fetish clubs and he didn't drink either. She thought at first he was worried about his sexual performance, but he told her it wasn't that. He was just being careful he told her. There might be strange people in a place like that. Most of them were fine but it only needed one. He wouldn't allow himself to be vulnerable unless he was with people he could trust. She didn't worry. She never worried when she was with Nick. She was pretty sure he could cope with just about anything.

The bigger fetish clubs were really just a fashion show with lots of wannabes showing off ever-more exotic outfits. Top DJ's played and there were glossy websites with official photographs. The smaller ones were more underground and cameras were banned because crazy things happened. She always marvelled at the dominant females, statuesque women with names like Lady Sabien and Goddess Demelza, strutting about in thigh length leather boots while their middle-aged, middle-class husbands crawled along behind them, tethered on a dog-leash or a chain. She asked Nick if he ever imagined her acting like that but he didn't really answer, he just smiled.

One night in October they went off to a party in Shoreditch, something different this time, not just fetish and sex but people with an interest in Satanism and black magic. Marianne didn't fancy it for some reason but Nick was his usual confident self and he told her it would be a new experience.

"Don't get a cab to the door," they had been told, "We don't want the neighbours paying attention. Get dropped off a couple of streets away." So they walked down Hackney Road in the fog. There had been a power-cut and the streets were in darkness, the old alleyways looking much as they must have done in the days of Jack the Ripper; dark, misty and foreboding. Some of the streets still had cobblestones and she was glad she was wearing flat shoes to walk in. They arrived safely at a large

70

four storey Victorian house near Virginia Gardens and were met at the door by their hosts Piers and Victoria. Piers was ex-public school and was working as some sort of city gent. It showed in his demeanour. From the first moment they arrived it seemed he was only really willing to tolerate them, not to welcome them. But they were in, and Nick at least was keen to give it a try.

There was lots of free champagne and lines of cocaine, which was all good news for Marianne although Nick wasn't taking either of them. They mixed with the other guests, "the punters" as Nick would call them, civil-servants, bank managers and IT consultants who wanted to escape their regular vanilla lives, dressing up for the evening to walk on the wild side, enjoying a heady mix of sex, drugs, and Satanism.

Most of the men had already changed into long black kimono-style bathrobes. The women's robes were more flimsy, deliberately showing off a little bit of what was underneath. Nick looked quite macho in his black leather jeans, his motorbike boots and a black cotton shirt. Marianne had a lacey black gothic-style dress. She was worried in case it wasn't right for the occasion but Nick told her not to worry.

"If they don't like it they can fuck off."

In fact, the conversation was amazingly anodyne for what should have been such a sensationally wicked event. A man with ginger hair talked to a man with a moustache about his golf swing. A man with one golden tooth was asking a lad with long hair how much he should pay to have the roof of his garden shed fixed.

Marianne didn't really take to it. She wanted music and she wanted to dance. This was all too subdued, so she just made the most of the free booze, till at last a bearded man led them all down to the basement level, where two or three spaces had been merged into one to create a single long room with a low ceiling running the whole length of the house.

"Behold the Lord Baphomet," said Piers, gesturing towards a statue of a figure with a human body and a goats head, which dominated one end of the underground temple. In front of the statue was an altar decorated with the inverted cross, where a man in long robes was busy setting up some silverware. Piers introduced him as the High Priest.

On the black floor, a large pentagram had been inscribed in silver, a five-pointed star contained within a circle. At first it looked like there were candles round the walls but in reality they were electrical wall lights which only looked like candles. There were also hooks and chains dangling with hand-cuffs and these at least seemed to be real.

In one corner there was a cage, about the size of a toilet cubicle. It was probably meant to hold just one person but there were two blonde girls in there with long white dresses which looked like robes.

"God they are just gorgeous," whispered Marianne, so excited she wanted to shout. "Find out who they are for me."

Nick asked the man with the moustache, who didn't know their names but muttered something about them being a pair of illegals from somewhere foreign. Marianne left the men talking and wriggled her way round to the far end, smiling at a one or two of the middle-aged wives, and picking up another glass of the free champagne as she squeezed past.

"Hiya. How did you end up in there?" she asked the two blondes, not knowing what else one should rightly say to strange women in cages. They didn't reply, so she tried something else.

"Where are you from? Are you from Poland? Are you Polish?"

This didn't look right to Marianne, who was really no fool and could be quick to notice certain things. The girls were pretty, in fact they were more than just pretty, they were beautiful in a truly classical sort of way. They were beautiful enough to be models or professional dancers, and yet they looked dishevelled and their hair hadn't been done. They weren't even wearing any makeup, which seemed like a non-starter for a sex party. As she studied them, she had the feeling that they seemed frightened, glancing at her furtively with questions in their eyes then quickly averting their gaze back to the floor. Their demeanour and body language were simply all wrong and she knew in her guts that these were real prisoners, not someone playing a part.

"Ne Poljski. Serpski." One of them replied in a tremulous whisper. But that was as far as the conversation ever got because suddenly it was midnight and the ceremony was about to begin.

It started with all of the regular members taking off their robes and just standing there naked. That felt kind of funny, thought Marianne, to be the only one dressed when everyone else was in the buff. She found herself thinking that some of the older ones really would have looked better if they had kept their clothes on, but she didn't want to say anything because she didn't want to spoil it for Nick. Then, from the cage behind her, she heard one of the Serbian girls whisper, "Help, please."

Increasingly convinced that something was wrong, Marianne tried to move back towards Nick, but she could see that they were already binding his arms with a length of soft red rope, the kind of stuff that posh people have on their curtains. New members always had to go through an initiation, that was what they had been told. Nick hadn't spoken to those Serbian girls. He had no way to know what was happening. Marianne felt an eruption of fear in her belly and she looked across at him, her big soft eyes appealing for him to say something, but he just nodded his head, acquiescently. Trust was always so important in his scheme of things. He tended to trust everyone and people trusted him. They tied his wrists behind his back and took him to stand at the far side of the altar.

Someone gave a signal and all the worshippers started chanting some sort of prayer, one of those where the leader said something and then all the followers repeated it. Then there were various other things they did, holding hands in a circle, passing round a silver-cup. Marianne didn't actually drink anything because she wasn't happy about what might be in there. Then there were more prayers and chants building up to the main event.

Two men came forward, one with a skinhead haircut and another with tattoos. They nodded to the priest and walked to the back of the long room, releasing the Serbian girls from the cage. The chubby guy seemed to be threatening them with what looked like a Taser and a baldy man with glasses guided them forward with light touches from a thick bamboo cane. Marianne gave Nick a meaningful look, and he kind of nodded but that didn't tell her anything. She found herself wishing all the more that he hadn't let them tie his wrists like that.

The high priest took out a whip, the kind with a short handle and lots of thin leather strips, he passed it to a heavy-set guy who had long ringlets of dark greasy hair which gave him a kind of gypsy look.

"The ceremony requires three." The High Priest was speaking. "It's a symbolic number of course, the unholy trinity..." Then he motioned towards Marianne and two women stepped forward and took her by the shoulders. Getting stripped and whipped was certainly not going to be part of her plan for the evening and she jerked her elbows free and pushed them away. Then the ginger man and the one with the golden tooth closed in to take her by the arms and she struggled to back away towards the altar.

"Nick?"

Nick was smiling, and for a moment she was afraid that he was part of this, part of some shitty game that was meant to scare her for the sake of amusement. But when he saw that she was getting upset his look turned to one of irritation.

"Hey listen. I want you to stop this now." His voice was deep and calm. "This isn't what we want to be doing."

There was a moment of total silence, then a murmur of disapproval.

"This isn't what you want to be doing?" The chubby man cut in with a sarcastic tone. "This isn't what you want to be doing? Well what the fucking hell did you come here for then, if this isn't what you want to be doing?"

Nick pursed his lips, his jaw square set and determined.

"I think we have had enough of this actually. I don't think you are real Satanists at all. To be honest I think you're just a bunch of thrill seekers."

"Well, whatever you think, you've got it all wrong son." The man with a moustache stood dangling a riding crop from one hand. "Because we don't fucking care what you think. Nobody in here cares who you are or what you think. Nobody out there even knows where you are tonight. You probably won't be going home from here and that pretty little girl of yours will do much better in one of them cages."

Marianne jerked forward in horror but strong hands held her from behind and stopped her getting away. It was a trick. They pulled her back and pinned her against the altar. It was a trap. Some of them were laughing. She was terrified. Nick looked straight at her. He looked sullen, he looked angry, but his arms were fastened by the ropes behind his back. She caught the eyes of one of the captive girls, who called out to her in some language that she couldn't understand.

The man with the tattoos opened up a set of metal handcuffs, which were dangling from a chain above the altar. The baldy man pulled one of the girls that way.

"You fucking stop this now, or you will be so fucking sorry!" Marianne had seen enough of this and she started shouting the odds, pulling one arm free and pointing at them. But they only laughed at her. She was a teenage girl with no-where to run to. She was their toy, their trophy, their prisoner, their slave. Now she was going to be part of their sexual entertainment. In that one sickening moment, she began to understand what it was really like to become a victim.

Somehow, Nick had used the distraction to slip his arms free, and there he was tossing away the tangle of red rope. He caught her gaze, for just a moment and it seemed that he was smiling, though it was pretty clear to Marianne that there was nothing to smile about.

Two of the naked men seized hold of Nick and the moustache man tried to grab his wrist, but he just made a kind of a twisting motion with his right arm to jerk it free. It looked like a proper move, the sort of thing she had seen secret agents do in the movies. He dropped into a crouch and punched the gypsy type very hard in the belly which sent him reeling backwards, falling over a chair then crashing onto the floor, curled up in a ball of agony. He turned back to the ginger fellow and punched him straight in the face, a kind of double punch that she had seen in a Jackie Chan film, where his fist sort of hit once, sprung back a little bit, and then hit again in the same spot. It must have been a hard one, thought Marianne because the guy was well knocked back.

There was an uncomfortable pause as the men around the room exchanged glances.

"That's enough," said Nick "Knock it off before things get nasty."

"You really think you can handle yourself don't you?" The chubby man stepped forward and just fired the Taser without warning.

Nick staggered backwards, his body in a spasm, clearly in pain, but then he swung his arm in a circle, looping the wires of the Taser around it, and pulling it all towards him. He grabbed the fat man by the wrist, spinning him round and smashing his face into the wall of the cellar, stepping sideways away from the group to prevent them surrounding him, then grabbing the closest one by the neck and banging his head back against a set of wall lights.

"Yes he really can handle himself you fucking bastard," shouted Marianne. She tried to run towards Nick but the man with the golden tooth grabbed her from behind and locked an arm around her neck. She was proud of Nick for fighting back. She would always proud of him, no matter what happened now, even if they got bloody murdered tonight, she would still be proud of him.

Nick stepped towards her and made a move with his hand, grouping all of his fingers together, not like a fist but all pointing straight like a spear-point. He jabbed it forward, over her shoulder and into the face of the guy who was clinging onto her. He let her go and fell to the floor. She couldn't help looking down, it was a natural reaction. He was writhing in pain with his hands over his face, his eye burst open like an over-ripe plum. Nick spun to catch another one coming in behind him and slapped his face down hard onto the altar. The Serbian girls in their white dresses were standing frozen with fear in the middle of it all, so Marianne stepped forward and pulled them towards her, then she tucked herself in behind Nick and started to scream every rude word she had learned from a lifetime in the care system.

There was only one exit from this basement room. That was via the staircase by which they had come in and right now there was no way they could get to it. Most of the women had backed away down to the far end where the cages were but she could see that the men were arming themselves with champagne bottles and kitchen knives. The High Priest even had the curved silver dagger from the altar. It was too one-sided, there were a dozen or more. A few of them had been hurt, but that had only made them angry. Nick had taken them by surprise the first time. They weren't going to let that happen again.

Strangely, in her own mind, Marianne wasn't worried about herself, she was only scared for what they might do to Nick. So much of her life had been empty of love that she couldn't worry about anything more than she worried about losing him. Maybe he was too trusting, but she couldn't blame him for that. She was desperate that somehow she had to save him. She had to find a way out for him, no matter what the cost was for her.

She got hold of the curtains behind the statue and pulled them down. There was a window there, a basement window, level with the front garden. She could see the houses across the street, and a plane in the sky circling to land at City Airport. She could see the sky, she could see the moon. She could see the free world of London that she loved so much. But there were bars on the window, strong anti-burglar bars and no way to escape.

"Last warning." said Nick, to the naked men.

"You're a fucking game one." The bald man threatened him with the punishment cane.

Then it went dark. Completely black. Every light went off and they were in total darkness.

"Not another fucking power cut." It was a man's voice, but she could hear the wives whispering in the background. Then there was the sound of someone knocking over a drink.

When the darkness did begin to clear she thought it was a bit strange because it didn't go off with a flash of light coming on as one might expect, but gradually the darkness sort of withdrew, like smoke billowing perhaps, except smoke tends to billow outwards and the darkness seemed to billow inwards, concentrating closer and closer, smaller and smaller till it just seemed to disappear into one last central dot, and everything was normal again.

The bald man still stood there with the heavyweight punishment cane in his hand, pointing it at Nick like an old style schoolteacher trying to frighten the boys. Nick waved his hand, pointing at him, like a conductor in front of an orchestra, and he said something, which sounded like it should have come from the bible though she never could remember the words, and to the utter amazement of all those present the stick seemed to turn into a snake, a black and yellow viper which curled round the bald man's wrist and bit him on the arm. He fell down screaming and the snake wriggled off towards a dark corner.

The wind was starting to blow, or something that sounded like wind. Marianne drew in her breath. Nick seemed taller now than he really should have been, almost seven foot maybe? His head was almost touching the ceiling. She couldn't see his proper clothes anymore. He seemed to be dressed in some kind of black flowing robe, a robe of shining darkness if that had been possible. His hair was streaming backwards like long grass in a high wind and it seemed more blue than black.

The priest in the robes lashed out with the decorative silver blade, but Nick caught him by the wrist and then grabbed him by the throat with his free hand, jerking him off his feet and smashing his head straight into the wall. He slid down to the floor and never got up but now the rest were circling around to get an advantage.

Piers, the host ran forward with his hands in the air, perhaps to calm the situation down, but it was all too late for that. Nick simply punched him full in the chest with a sickening force which shattered his sternum and he dropped to the floor with no more than a groan.

Someone at the back screamed and someone by the staircase turned and opened the door. Nick jerked up straight, both hands beckoning towards himself. The door slammed shut, a cupboard slammed shut, a painting fell off the wall and half a dozen glasses fell off a shelf. Then someone screamed again.

The chubby man took a swing with a champagne bottle but it never connected and Nick's hand burst in below his rib cage and ripped out his innards. He turned towards the tattooed man, crushing his windpipe with a punch and then breaking his neck with a violent twist. Marianne momentarily sensed a ripple in the air behind him and for an instant it looked as though Nick had wings, like an angel but black. Then the moment was gone and she all she could see was Nick, dark but somehow shining, tearing into the rest of the men. He ripped the arm clean off from the skinhead and threw his body against the opposite wall. They backed away but now the door to the staircase seemed to be jammed and there was nowhere for any of them to run.

Nick seized on the man with the ginger hair, tossing him as a terrier would toss a rat, sending him bouncing off the wall before he hit the floor. Then he went for the rest, and threw them around like toys, laughing aloud at the panic on their faces,

For Nick was a demon prince who had chosen to dwell in the world of mortals, to take his pleasure in food and drink and music, and in the company of humankind, but these few men, in their folly, had chosen to raise their hands against the woman he loved and the fullness of his fury was now turned against them and they could not stand against his power but fell before him as helpless victims, their flesh torn like paper and their bodies crushed like dry sticks.

The long-haired boy was trapped against the wall. Nick pushed both thumbs into his head through the eye sockets and tore his skull apart. His left hand lashed backwards across the throat of the gypsy type, straight fingers with long, steely claws ripping through the delicate tissues of the windpipe and sending fountains of arterial blood gouting up across the low ceiling. He swung the bald man up into the air and brought him down with a crash on the altar, crushing his skull and then tossing him aside. He ripped open the belly of the moustached man so that his entrails spilled out to the floor and then, without a pause, tore the beating heart from the chest of the guy with the beard.

Total panic reigned amongst the remaining partygoers. The floor was strewn with bodies and the walls were dripping with blood. The naked wives were cowering at the far end of the room screaming hysterically. Those men who had not yet been killed or crippled were trying to hide amongst them, doing anything at all to escape from the fury of this dark avenging angel.

Raising his head, like a lion sniffing the air, Nick made a tiny gesture with his right hand, as if he were flicking droplets of water from his finger. A small black spot appeared on the white plastered wall, and immediately began to enlarge, its centre turning slowly, like a potter's wheel, like a whirlpool, growing bigger and somehow seeming deeper, until it reached the size of a fireplace. Even though it was only blackness it gave an impression of depth. It seemed to create a kind of hypnotic effect and Marianne felt tempted to step into it, to slide down inside it and drift away into a perfect sleep.

Then she found herself snapping back to reality as a strange red, stunted creature scuttled from the blackness of the rift. It was almost formless, hardly more than a blob of red flesh. It seemed to shy away from Nick and staggered instead towards the group of naked wives, cowering at the far end of the temple to avoid the violence. They screamed even more than they had screamed before as it seized upon one of them, dragging her back towards the hole. Marianne watched awestruck as other nightmare figures began to emerge from the vortex. She locked her arms onto the two foreign girls to protect them, and pulled them even closer behind Nick, while the lesser demons made free with the society wives, who had come to the coven for a bit of sensationalist entertainment but would be leaving with a lot more than they had bargained for.

As the grotesque intruders began to drag their screaming captives back down into their hellish passageway Nick coaxed the three girls right into the corner where they would be protected by his own body, then with a rather cute expression of mischief he made a small punching motion towards the barred window and the whole front wall blew apart, showering glass, wood, bricks, and plaster into the front garden and clearing a pathway out into the street beyond. He carefully brought the three women out through the hole beneath the bay window, helping them to pick their way up through the rubble, across the front garden and into the street. Then he turned left and began to lead them off down the road. Almost as an afterthought, he turned to make one last gesture with his fingers and the entire building erupted in flames, a pillar of fire coruscating upwards towards the winter skies like the centrepiece of an expensive firework display.

By the time the fire engines and the police cars arrived, they were already two streets away and he was sitting the girls down in the corner of a small, quiet pub, thankfully looking much like his normal self again. He gave Marianne twenty pounds to go to the bar and told her to get him a pint of snakebite with blackcurrant. Then he walked calmly over to the digital jukebox, singing to himself before the tunes came on...

'Please allow me to introduce myself, I'm a man of wealth and taste ...

Digging for gold

Lisa crossed the plaza by the supermarket and walked towards the train station. She turned and waved to Leonard, with a smile, and then she was gone. The rush-hour service was always busy at this time on a weekday morning, but she managed to find a seat and settled herself down for the ride back across town.

Things had gone well and she was pleased with her performance. She slipped her hand down into her Fendi handbag and checked that the money was still there. Nine hundred pounds. It had been so easy. Maybe she should have asked for more. Still, she would treat herself to some new shoes at the weekend, and maybe a bottle of Lancôme. Why not? After all, it was easy money.

It had all started quite by accident really, not part of a plan, just luck. When she first arrived in London she had lived with friends, in a big old house sharing with other young people just like herself, temporary workers from Ireland, Spain, and Romania. They were all decent sorts and good fun to be with, apart from the overcrowding and the long queues for the bathroom every morning. But that was just for the short term, and Lisa was determined to get her own place.

As soon as she had regular work coming in from a few temping agencies she started to find her way round the websites and magazines where the backpacking fraternity looked for flat-shares, camper vans, and cut-price tickets. It wasn't long till she was looking at the lonely hearts as well, the amazing range of the good the bad and the ugly who were all looking for love, or at least for a partner, somewhere among the sprawling anonymity of the big city.

After a few months she had saved enough money and was ready to rent her own flat but it had all turned rather unpleasant at the estate agents office. How many extra charges could those guys invent for Christ's sake? The first month's rent, the second month's rent in advance, the damage deposit, the agency fee and even a charge for some bastard to come round and read the meters. Lisa didn't like people taking advantage and as they kept on telling her about all those extra fees it began to get very heated.

Roger seems to have misunderstood. He was one of the guys from the big house and he was only there because he had a car and Lisa had asked him to give her a lift to the estate agent's office. When she started to argue about the charges he was quick to chip in with an offer to help out. He said he had plenty of money in his account. He told her he could advance her the extra cash until she got paid. He was a genuine guy who really wanted to help. Lisa didn't actually need more money. It was the principle of the thing which had made her mad, but Roger didn't understand that. He was trying to be the knight in shining armour, riding to the rescue, which was very kind of him, even though that wasn't really what she wanted. But later, when she thought about it, she decided he was a bit naive, just offering to lend her money his money. After all, if she wanted to she could have just taken it and disappeared, and so that was how it all started.

It was all just too easy. In a city the size of London, you could meet people once or twice and then never see them again. She had already dated a few lonely hearts, and she had enjoyed some good nights out but she always let the man pay. There were plenty of trendy restaurants in Covent Garden where she was happy to eat, as long as someone else was footing the bill. Some even turned up with little gifts and that was even better.

There came a time when a couple of weeks went by and there just weren't the right jobs. When she ran short of cash she decided that she would ask one of these fellows for a loan. Roger had been quick to offer money to a damsel in distress, so why not see if that would work with one of her dates. The latest one was Angus, a Scotsman who worked on IT start-ups. She told him she only needed a couple of hundred to get her through to the weekend, but he said no. At first, he seemed puzzled by the very idea that she was asking. Then he said it couldn't be that important, such a small amount of money, for such a short time. He didn't think she really needed it. In fact, he became rather suspicious and they never met up again. At first, she just wrote him off as a tight-fisted Scottish bastard, but later she thought it over and she could see what he meant. It's easy to survive for two or three days, and if you only need £200 it can't be that important. To be a real damsel in distress it needed to be something more significant, something almost life-changing even.

And so Lisa started to develop her act. She would pick a lonely heart who lived right over on the other side of the city and meet him in the centre of town for the first date. Let him treat her to a good meal or a night at a show. She was good. She could talk about her unhappy past and how much she was searching for a good man, how much she needed to find that one special guy, someone she could rely on. And then, somewhere in the middle of all the talk, she would pick up on what exactly the men were looking for. Some wanted to start a family. Some wanted a good looking girl to impress their friends. Some wanted a woman who would enjoy sex the way they wanted it. They were the best ones. They had waited all their lives for a woman who would entertain their secret fantasies, lingerie maybe, or bondage perhaps. It didn't really matter, she was never going to go that far but just being willing to talk about it was like a drug to them. She was good at picking up the clues and then building them up a little bit further each time they shared a phone call. She would also mention that she was moving house soon. Not to exactly where the guy lived, but a lot closer than where she was now.

The second or third date would be at his place, and they might have sex. If she really didn't like the look of him then they wouldn't do the deed, but he would be left thinking that it was pretty close. Then the day before the next date she would phone up all worried and tearful. The ATM machine had swallowed her card so how was she going to pay the deposit on the new flat? Maybe they should cancel the date because she was so upset.

It hadn't worked every time. One guy was suspicious and so she let it pass. She just didn't see him again. The others had all offered to lend her the money. It really was that easy. A meal, two drinks and a night of sex, then the next morning she was away with the money. An argument on the phone the next time he called and she never needed to see him again. She would get a new SIM card for her phone so he couldn't even call her and that was the end. She never brought anyone back to her own place so she knew that they would never be able to trace her. She was good. She knew that she was good. She had a good system and it worked. It was an easy way to make money, and she just kept wondering if she should have asked Leonard for more this time.

Her train reached the station and off she got, crossing the footbridge over the railway. She passed by the park with the cute Victorian wrought iron railings running along the side. Then she was home in her apartment and taking a shower, washing away any doubts and any regrets.

She loved being home. She loved having her own place. She left wet footprints on the polished floorboards as she padded across the kitchen floor in her white towelling dressing gown, the one she had pinched from the Savoy hotel. She took a cup out of the dishwasher and put the kettle on. Then, while she remembered, she took the cash from her bag and hid it in the biscuit tin. Nine hundred pounds, damn, she was getting good at it. Maybe she really should have asked for more.

This time it had been just a little bit different she reflected, as she curled up on the sofa with a mug of camomile tea. The latest guy was called Leonard and he didn't really seem like a lonely heart. He was handsome, no doubt about that, and a very good conversationalist with a wonderfully dark sense of humour.

They had arranged to meet at a pub on Throgmorton Street, the Arbitrager. It was an unusual name for a pub. He told her what it meant, apparently an Arbitrager was someone who settled debts among medieval bankers and money lenders. That made sense because it was right in the heart of the City of London. He had bought her an expensive cocktail in the wine bar down in the basement. It was full of stock-market types on leather sofas and it all just screamed money. This was a man who knew how to impress a girl, and that was the type that Lisa liked best. They ate nearby, at a Sushi restaurant where he had ordered in near perfect Japanese, then they took a black-cab back to Hackney and had a drink at his local, a traditional old-fashioned pub called the Green Man, with dark wooden floors and shutters on the windows. The service was good and the staff all knew him by name. It seemed as if everyone in the place was his friend.

"It's just what comes of being a regular" he explained modestly, as they sat in the beer garden drinking vintage Bordeaux. But Lisa could see there was more to it than that. She guessed that he was the sort of man who became a leader in almost any group.

It was just a two-minute walk from the pub to his home, a classic three storey town-house with antique furniture and a state of the art sound system, where they shared the hot-tub then drank single-malt in bed. The sex was good. Better than she expected from an older man, although he wasn't the sort of guy whose age was easy to judge. Normally she told her partners she would need Seven Hundred and Fifty Pounds for the deposit on her new apartment. This time she had pushed for nine hundred and he had agreed to help her with no questions asked. When she thought about how expensive his house must have been she wondered if she should have asked for more, but it was too late now. The system had worked, she had her nine hundred quid and it was time to move on. She took the next day off work and spent the afternoon sunbathing in the local park with the cute Victorian railings.

It was two days later when Leonard phoned to ask her about their next date, and she had used her usual excuse, she was too busy packing for the house move and she would see him another day, maybe next week when it was all over.

He phoned her back a few minutes later and tried to use both logic and charm. He could help her with the packing. He really wanted to see her again. He felt there was a bond between them. For a moment, and only just for a moment, she did think about seeing him again. For sure, she thought, he was much too good for a lonely heart and she nearly allowed herself to get involved, but she had a system and it worked so why change it?

The third time he called he was more forceful. He warned her not to fool with him. He didn't take well to being messed around. He didn't exactly get angry, but he was very firm, like a teacher spelling out the rules to a naughty child.

Lisa switched the phone off. This was more like the normal response. This was how most men responded when they realised that they had been stood up and their money was gone for ever. Often they would threaten her, they would say they had contacts, their brother in law was a policeman and all that. Leonard hadn't gone that far, but he was no fool, and from his tone she could tell that he knew it was over. By tomorrow she would have changed her SIM card and she would never have to hear from him again. Her only real regret was that she just kept thinking that she really should have asked for more money this time.

It was exactly one week later when Lisa arrived at work to see the puzzled look on the office manager's face. Someone had made a mistake it seemed. The temping agency had called to say she wouldn't be coming in. They had got someone else. She called them up and they quoted an email she had never sent, saying that she was heading off out of the country and wanted to be withdrawn from their books. She called another of her regular agencies and they told her the same, which was very irritating indeed as the monthly rent on the flat was due at the end of the week.

Half-way home she stopped at the bank to check her balance. She knew that she would need to be careful if she couldn't get any work for a while. With a certain irony, perhaps, the ATM machine had swallowed her card. When she spoke to the bank staff at the counter they did a few checks and revealed that her account had recently been closed, which of course she would never have done because all of her standing orders and direct debits came straight out of that account. Something was wrong and she couldn't rule out the possibility that one of her victims had somehow struck back. Was that possible? Probably not. Nobody would know which agencies she was listed with, or her bank details, but then how had it happened?

That evening things just went from bad to worse. Her TV channels were offline and she didn't know why but before she could even start to work it out there was a loud knock at the front door. For a moment she was worried that it might be Leonard, but thank goodness it was just a pizza delivery guy on a moped.

"Sorry," she told him "I didn't order any pizza," but the name was correct and they even had her new phone number so in the end, she paid. It was an extra-large deep-crust pizza with loads of olives and anchovies, both things that she really didn't like and she had to scrape them off into the bin. Then she paused and thought for a minute, and she realised the pizza man had her brand-new phone number, so it couldn't have come from any of her lonely hearts. Before she could work that out there was another loud knock at the door. This time it was a Chinese takeaway and she knew she hadn't ordered that one either.

By seven pm. she had turned away half a dozen unwanted meals and she was getting very angry when she opened the door, but this time it was the police to tell her that her parents were worried about the message they had received that she had been in a road traffic accident. It was obviously a hoax but how had anyone known her parents' contact details? She got rid of the police as best she could but she didn't dare explain her suspicions to them as she didn't want to admit that she had been taking money from lonely-hearts by fraud.

Lisa found it difficult to sleep that night and by six in the morning she had given up and got out of bed. She didn't have any work to go to, so she sat down to renew her registration with the temping agencies, but still her internet connection wasn't working.

"Damn!" This was getting ridiculous, she thought. Somebody must be going to an awful lot of trouble to cause her all these problems. She went off into London for the day and spent a couple of hours getting herself set up again at the agencies, giving them her new phone number and above all begging them not to cancel anything unless she came back and spoke to them in person. She picked up a free paper at the station and crossed at the footbridge over the railway. She passed by the park with the cute Victorian wrought iron railings and stopped at the newsagent's to buy a packet of tissues.

A few minutes later she was home. Every window in the apartment was wide open, every tap was turned on, as was every electrical device, her makeup and cosmetics were spinning round in the washing machine, her shoes were in the dishwasher. All her lightbulbs were gone. Her bed was soaking wet. Her lingerie was festooned around the plants and hedges in the garden outside her bedroom window. This was just too much. It had to stop.

Lisa phoned Leonard and he answered in a calm and even voice.

"Oh, hello Lisa. Good to hear from you. How are you? Have you got a new phone? This isn't your usual number."

"Don't fuck with me, Leonard." She told him. "I know this is all down to you. I know you're behind all this stuff that's been happening to me. How did you do it?"

"How did I do what?" She could sense him smiling with deep satisfaction at the other end of the phone.

"I'll give you back your money Leonard." She was ready to admit defeat. "I was going to give it back anyway. Just tell me how you did it."

"OK then." Leonard purred down the phone. "Tell me your address, your real address, and I'll come over tonight if you like."

"No." She sensed that once he was in the flat it might be difficult to get rid of him. "You already know my address but I don't want you coming here. I will meet you in town at that wine bar we went into, the one below the Arbitrager."

"We can't go there tonight." He told her. "It's bookings only in that place and I haven't booked for tonight. Meet me at my local, the Green Man. You know where it is."

"No." Lisa saw the local pub as his territory, where he would be stronger and more confident. "I don't want to come there."

"Then you will never find out what truly happened and you will certainly never be able to stop it." Leonard sounded so calm and confident. He knew he had the upper hand now.

To hell with him. She just hung up and that was the end of the phone call. An hour later her internet connection was back. She opened her email first to see if any jobs had come in from the temping agencies but her inbox was overwhelmed by hundreds, possibly thousands of messages from unknown contacts. Some were blank, some were rubbish some were clearly spam. It was as if all the spam-filters in the world had been switched off and a massive deluge of digital rubbish had suddenly become concentrated on Lisa's personal email account.

She switched off the laptop, and two minutes later it switched itself back on. She could see the mouse pointer moving around on the screen even though she wasn't touching the mouse. She could see files and folders opening and programmes being started up. Suddenly she realised that the files being moved around were pictures of herself, personal pictures taken long ago, of her posing semi-naked for some previous boyfriend. When she tried to use the keyboard it seemed that the keys were disabled and there was nothing she could do.

Overwhelmed with panic and frustration, she jerked out the cables from the laptop and pushed it straight off the side of her desk, hearing it fall, with a crash, onto the floor behind the wastepaper basket.

In the morning she got almost as far as the footbridge before she saw the pictures in the newsagent's window, the same personal pictures she had seen the night before, but now they had been printed and clipped and cut and pasted, and put up on display amongst the postcards and advertisements offering massage and personal services. This really was the end. She knew she had to give up. She sat down on the nearest park bench, almost in tears, and phoned Leonard back again.

Approaching the pub that evening she felt it was familiar and yet it now seemed more foreboding than it had done on that summer evening, just a few days earlier, when they had laughed and joked with his friends in the beer garden. The lights were dim and the fabric seemed much older and more dreary. Even the Green Man on the pub sign seemed somehow ominous and frightening.

There was no kind word from the barman, only a cursory nod directing her to the back of the room. Passing by the locals she felt their eyes upon her at every step. Did they know what she had tried to do? Had he told them? Had they been part of his remarkable revenge?

Leonard sat in a sort of booth at the rear of the bar, the kind of place where Victorian businessmen might have met to sign papers and exchange bills of sale.

"Tell me how you did it, Leonard." She was trying to sound strong. "Nothing else can happen till I know how you did it."

"Well, what can I say?" He didn't seem angry, more like confident perhaps, but in a laid back kind of way. "Perhaps I am not as stupid as you think. Perhaps I have heard of these sort of things happening before. We all have to protect ourselves against scammers these days. Believe me, no-one is really as safe as they like to think they are. A little piece of software on a computer? A little bit of drug in a drink? Who can guard against such things?

"Is it possible that I could have worked out where you lived from peeking at some small piece of evidence in your handbag? Your drivers' licence maybe? Is it possible that while you were still asleep at my place I could have slipped down to the shop on the corner and got them to cut me a key? Is it possible that when you downloaded an email from me it put a bug on your computer? Is it possible that I added an app. to your phone while you were at the toilet? I am not going to say that I did any of those things, but anything is possible. Maybe there could be even more to come.

"There will be no need for that." Lisa grimaced. "You win. I give up."

"Fine." Leonard smiled. "Show me the money."

"I don't have that much money," she told him, "Not right now. I spent what you gave me and I can't get any more out of the bank till I get more work, and I can't get any work till you stop harassing me, but I promise. I really do promise that I will give it to you. I will give you all of it just as soon as I can."

"Then I want you to sign an agreement." His eyes were steely with determination. "I have to have something, at least for my pride. You will sign that you will agree to pay me back with whatever you have. Anything that you have that I want."

When Lisa emerged from the shadows of the pub she felt an immense wave of relief. Something in there had scared her, though she wasn't sure quite what it was. He had not threatened her with violence, not at all, and yet in the darkest recesses of her unconscious mind, she felt that she had been in great danger. Perhaps she had been expecting him to force himself upon her. Rape, after all, could be the ultimate act of revenge for a man who felt that his male pride had been hurt. But it hadn't happened. He hadn't even hinted at harming her in any way, so why did she feel so rattled? Perhaps it was on account of his friends watching from the shadows. Perhaps it was her own sense of guilt. She just didn't know.

As she crossed the plaza by the supermarket and walked towards the train station she began to feel a tingling in her head as if her scalp was starting to grow tight upon her skull for some reason. It wasn't unpleasant as such, but it was distracting. Perhaps, she thought, it could be stress related, adrenaline caused by fear pushing up her pulse rate and her blood pressure, pumping more blood to her brain. But hopefully, now the tension would subside. She was free of all this nonsense and was never going back. She was finished with all this trickery. She would never do anything so incredibly stupid again.

She reached the train station and got on board, looking round several times to be sure that she wasn't being followed. She really needed to be clear of this place. No-one had followed her, at least there was no-one as far as she could see. Then she felt a hand touch her, in fact it was two hands, more than two perhaps and she spun around but there was no one standing close. She grasped for the handrails and the vertical poles, pulling herself tight against their shining metal as the sensation strengthened of invisible hands touching her, gripping her body.

"Get a grip," she told herself, trying to make a bad joke as she held on to the handrails ever tighter. "This is a panic attack and you need to control it. Think of something else. Look at the other passengers."

But the other passengers were not as they should be. Some of them she hated at first sight. She found herself wanting to slap them, to tear her nails across their faces, to bite them, to sink her teeth right into their cheeks and bite out a big dripping lump of bloody flesh. Some she saw as sexually inviting, as compelling, she found herself wanting their attention, wanting to have them. She could smell their sweat, smell their breath, smell their blood, and even their semen.

Her chest began to fill up with weight, causing her to crouch where she stood, still holding tightly onto the handrails. She knew that something was wrong and yet she could not focus her attention enough to think about what it was. Perhaps he had spiked her drink with LSD. Was this what it did to people? She couldn't be sure but why did it matter?

An older woman stepped towards her. No words were spoken but her gesture and her expression suggested concern and the offer of help. Lisa hiked up her skirt at the front to expose her stocking tops and screamed, then laughed as the older lady recoiled away.

Then her train reached the station and she staggered from the carriage and onto the platform, wide-eyed and open-mouthed with spit dribbling down her chin. She lurched forward, her legs wobbling at the knees, staggering past the ticket gate without swiping her card. The short journey to her apartment was bewildering. She had lost her shoes and she found herself hanging onto bus-stops and lamp-posts for support, oblivious to the traffic or the passers-by. Crossing the footbridge over the railway, she scrambled up the steps on her hands and knees. On the other side of the bridge when she reached out and touched the wrought-iron Victorian railings, the metal seemed to burn her hand and yet no mark appeared. Then she knew she was going to vomit, and it was not like ordinary vomit but huge amounts of black bile which sprayed out into the air in front of her, and tasted rusty, like the taste of blood. She felt her bowels move and managed to tear off her panties just in time, squatting on the pavement for relief then dragging herself towards her own front gate, so desperate with panic that she didn't even realise the door was open as she crawled in onto the polished wooden floor.

Leonard, somehow, was already there, sitting on the sofa, calmly waiting for her, relaxed and confident with a brandy-glass in his hand. He seemed in some way stronger, richer and older than she had thought of him, even just an hour ago when they parted at the pub. He was smiling, but his smile held no warmth, only triumph.

She tried to speak but her tongue seemed to have grown longer in her mouth and she knew that she was only making noises, meaningless noises like a toad croaking or a fox trying to bark. She moved her head from side to side to tell him no. No! Whatever it was she didn't want it. No!

91

From his pocket, he took a single sheet of paper. Then he began to speak.

"You have agreed to repay me what you could Lisa, and I have taken what you had. These unusual sensations which you are feeling are the first stages of demon possession. As time goes by you will find yourself completely controlled by one who serves me. You are never going to get any better. Your body will no longer be yours to control. You might attack children. You might have sex with strangers in the street. You might just kill yourself. It doesn't matter what you do. Your body really has no value to me now that I possess your spirit.

"You sold your immortal soul for nine hundred pounds, Lisa. Nine hundred pounds? You really should have asked for more."

Old men

All through the morning the tired and dishevelled men had limped and staggered up the long dirt road which led to the temple. Every one of them had travelled for hours without food or sleep. Many had burns on their arms and shoulders. Some had cuts to their heads and faces, bewildered eyes gazing out between the crusts of dried blood. Others, more severely wounded, were helped along with their arms around the shoulders of their comrades, but they were a few, a very lucky few. Most of the injured had been left on the battlefield many miles behind and by now they were almost certainly slain.

The troops were in retreat, that much was clear, but to the eye of an experienced soldier, it was worse than that. This was a beaten army. Those men who were still sound of limb were broken in spirit. Many had thrown away their shields and their weapons in order to run away more quickly and now they trudged on wearily with no equipment, looking down at the dusty road before them, simply putting one foot in front of the other, caring only that every painful step would be taking them further away from yesterday's battlefield.

At the temple on the ridge they begged for water from the sisters, and then continued on their journey, following the route which led towards the north, their feet dragging, their shoulders hunched, and their eyes wide and vacant.

"Hold there soldier!" A man on a lathered black horse called down to a survivor. His voice was deep but not melodic. It was the voice of one well used to shouting commands. "You man. Stop there!"

The soldier stopped and turned. His expression of dismay turning to despair as he realised who had hailed him. He looked to either side in search of support, but he had no comrades now among this beaten host and so he just fell to his knees in the dust.

The newcomer dismounted and walked towards him. He was tall, but not abnormally tall. His shoulders and chest were broad, and his slow deliberate walk suggested both strength and confidence. His riding boots were heavier than was normal, with multiple straps and thin steel plates providing the legs with extra protection in battle. His leather riding breeches and jacket were scuffed and creased, they had originally been black, perhaps, but were shades of grey and brown now in those areas which had faded most. He wore a longsword and a dagger at his belt. His hair, thick and curling, hung down to his shoulders, and like his beard, it was turning grey.

"My Lord." The soldier who knelt in the dust shook his head. "My Lord I am sorry. We could do nothing." He had good reason to be fearful because the man who stood towering over him was no stranger.

"Water!" demanded the tall man, in a voice which would brook no delay, and a nun dressed in red robes hurried towards him.

"Not for me, damn you woman. For him!"

He watched the soldier drink then pulled him to his feet, gently but with obvious strength, and perhaps, almost, a semblance of sympathy. He didn't ask for details of the battle, perhaps because he understood that this survivor was not in any state of mind to give a rational explanation. Instead, he straightened the man's equipment and brushed the dust from his hair, like a mother fussing over a small boy. Then he took him by the arm and walked him back, just a few paces down the road in the direction from which he had come. There they stood together, like comrades, and together they stopped the next half dozen men and turned them round to make a line across the road, ready to halt the next cluster of stragglers.

One group, coming up the hill, must have guessed what was happening and they took a sharp turn off to their right, away from the temple and away from the little group that was forming by its walls. They had no desire to fight any more battles, not after what they had experienced. They were leaving the army and going their own way.

Without hesitation the veteran officer remounted and twitched his black stallion into a trot, riding around the fugitives and herding them back towards the temple building, like cattle being herded to a round-up. One soldier was foolish enough to pull out a dagger and he ended up getting a hard kick in the face for his trouble. The others seemed to know who they were dealing with and moved quickly back to where they were wanted.

By the time the sun had reached its zenith, they had rallied a body of several dozen weary men close by the temple walls. The nuns brought more water, and two baskets of fruit. One man planted a spear in the ground, with a small blue and white pennant flickering from its tip. Now they had a flag to rally under. It wasn't an army yet, but it was a start. As the men caught their breath and quenched their thirst the general began to ask questions, determined to learn more of what had befallen their force.

It transpired that they had been attacked in the night, and their camp had been consumed by flames. Even the wooden defences that they had built to protect themselves had become a ring of fire around their position. As the soldiers struggled to contain the blaze they were over-run by a chaotic band of beasts and half-men, howling, stabbing, biting and tearing, and In the midst of the chaos, a huge demonic figure had marched amongst them, slaying anyone who tried to oppose him and casting fires wherever he went. Their tents, their carts, their food supplies had all been burnt and as the pitiful survivors fled from the scene even the grasslands beneath their feet had burst into flames.

"All the more reason we need to be ready! We need to start getting the place in order." The commander stepped through the middle of the line and waved his arm to the men on his left. "You lot stay here and sort out new men as they arrive. The rest of you are with me."

He led his bedraggled crew to the sandstone archway which served as the front gate of the temple. The walls on all sides were stone and stood higher than a man could reach. It was the only building on the road that would be invulnerable to fire, at least he hoped that it would be. Even the gates, with their ornate carvings of religious legends, were created from a type of wood so dense that it could probably smoulder all night before burning right through. This was where he would prepare to do battle. This was probably where he would die, but not yet. First, he would make a stand and fight as he had always fought.

The gates were standing open and his soldiers marched straight in, only to be halted abruptly by the appearance of thirty nuns, these ones dressed entirely in white and armed with light polearms. A polearm is essentially a spear but also features a long axe blade on one side and a strong hook on the other. Against cavalry, it's an ideal weapon. The spear point can be used to hold back a horse which would never be so stupid as to charge onto it. Once the horseman has been stopped he can be hooked from the saddle, or hacked at, overhead, with the axe blade. Normally such weapons would be wielded by tall men with obvious strength, and considerable training, but these lighter versions sat easily in the hands of the women who carried them.

Although they had been allowed into the gates the soldiers now found themselves blocked in on three sides by the armed nuns. They could easily pass back out of the gate if they wished, but otherwise, they were surrounded. Weary soldiers confronting lithe young women, it was a strange situation, but these were strange days.

"What's this? What's happening?" A white-bearded cleric in grey robes marched with purpose through the dust of the temple yard. "You cannot bring men in here! This is a female convent!"

"You're in it," growled the old soldier, "And you're a man."

"I am his Supreme Eminence, Asclepius, Arch-Prelate of Mynpoor, thrice blessed by all the Gods," the cleric announced, "And no-one questions my instructions."

"And I am Ranald Con Connor," the soldier replied, "And no-one stands in my way, not if he expects to live to see tomorrow."

At that very name, the nuns seemed somehow to take on a more defensive stance, although, in fact, their bodies did not move a jot. Ranald Con Connor was a man well known if not well loved. He had once been a mercenary soldier and had risen to command his own troop but had pledged his service to the kingdom and become one of its most successful generals. The Arch-Prelate Asclepius had never met him but he knew the name and he knew some of the stories. More recently Connor had fallen from favour over some scandal at court. The details were far from clear but the outcome was common knowledge.

"If you are Ranald Con Connor then you are retired and banished from court."

"I never said I was retired. It's true that I was banished from court, but I am now recalled and sent here to clean up this mess." He nodded his head back towards the road outside.

"You would be surprised how an army of demons on the loose can refocus the minds of our ruling masters. Now, being as you seem to think you are in charge here, I shall need proper supplies of food and water for my men and we will begin to fortify the building. This is the only solid stone structure between here and the river crossing. This is where I will stop them. Also, you will need to get those nuns away from here. This is where I intend to have my battle and it's going to be no place for women."

"You cannot order me, soldier." Asclepius was as determined as Connor was demanding. "Only the Gods have authority here. However, you and I are here for the same reason. I was aware of these horrific events unfolding in the south and I made my way here fearful for the safety of the temple and of these good women who guard it. I shall help you in as much as I can. But first, you must speak to the Reverend Mother, and get her permission for your men to use the convent. Do that, or I shall bar you from these buildings."

"I see you two have fallen out already. That doesn't bode well." The man who addressed them seemed to have appeared out of nowhere and Connor looked down on him with a face full of fury.

"And you are?"

"I am Zimbarra the Magnificent, and you must know me by my reputation." He wheezed a little, struggling with his breathing. "People love to tell stories about the amazing conjurations they have seen me accomplish."

Zimbarra had dark, well-coiffured hair, so dark, in fact, that Asclepius immediately assumed it had been dyed black, as men may sometimes do to hide their age.

The little man sported a small pointed goatee beard, a drooping moustache, and remarkably pointed eyebrows. Connor was sure they had been deliberately shaved to make them appear more pointed. The overall effect was that the man looked like a devil from a child's storybook. In his choice of clothes, he was as ostentatious as the others were plain. He wore a yellow silk doublet over baggy red trousers tucked into highly polished black riding boots. He sported a lightweight fencing sword in a bejeweled scabbard and an embroidered red velvet cloak, hanging down over his left arm, perhaps to disguise the fact that his spine was slightly crooked and one shoulder stood higher than the other.

"Sadly, I have never heard of you" Connor growled.

"Sadly, I have." Asclepius sighed "You claim to be a wizard do you not?"

"I am a wizard" Zimbarra replied, "And I think you are going to need me to sort out this mess."

"A mess which was created by people just like you." Asclepius retorted. "There's hardly a week goes by without some bunch of rascals go off into the south, searching the ruined cities for magical treasure and who knows what. This would not be the first time they have disturbed something which would have been better left alone. Demons are easy to awaken but difficult to kill. Last year there was even a mummy that strangled someone. We had to burn that. Now we have something much worse and we don't even know what it is."

"Ah, but I know." Zimbarra raised one of his pointed eyebrows. "I know very well what it is and that is why you need me here. In fact, you should consider yourselves rather lucky that I came at all."

"Tell me what you know then, Damn you!" Connor was already tired and didn't want to waste even a single moment on the new arrival. In any case he didn't trust magicians and certainly didn't want one interfering with his battle plans.

"Well, I left my servant holding my horse." wheezed the wizard. "Let me go and make sure they have water for it and then I will tell you what I know."

"Tell me right now or I will cut your head off just where you stand!" Connor stepped towards the overdressed magician, but Asclepius raised his hand slightly as if he wanted a moment to think.

"Very well, very well. If you really are desperate to know I shall share my knowledge" Zimbarra clearly enjoyed knowing that he had their attention. "We are dealing with a Demon Prince. His name I shall not speak, for to do so could draw his attentions upon us and bring us into even great danger. This Demon Prince has the power to command lesser creatures and so the army which has come up out of the desert is composed of a mixture of chaotic rabble, minor demons, goblins and even the savage men who inhabit the wasteland, but what brings them together and offers them victory is the presence of he whose name shall not be spoken."

"And how do you know all this?" Demanded Connor, in a voice like thunder.

"I know this because I am a wizard!" snapped Zimbarra

"And how does a wizard know such things?" asked Asclepius, silently praying for patience.

"Because I used my scrying glass to observe."

"Very well." The high priest seemed resigned. "It might be useful to have someone who understands magic. Demons are indeed magical creatures. But how do we know that we can trust you?"

"Never trust a man who dyes his hair" muttered Connor.

"You can trust me because I have good reason to wish to destroy this demon. He carries a staff of great magical power, which for many hundreds of years was no more than a legend. Now I have seen it and I have seen him use it. I will make common cause with you and will help you to destroy the demon as long as you agree that I may claim the staff as my prize."

"How do we know you are any good?" asked Connor.

Zimbarra turned with a twitch and a gasp of irritation. He looked at a small group of men who had been detailed to dig a defensive trench just in front of the temple wall.

"Dig!" was all he said, and where he pointed the earth immediately began to cascade upwards, out of the ground, like water from a fountain, forming a hole as deep as a grown man and ten paces in length.

"There you are. A few of those will speed up the work for your men. Now, do you understand how good I am?"

Before Connor could reply, Asclepius touched his arm and pointed to the woman emerging from the gate. She wore the same white robes as the nuns on guard but was slightly older, perhaps in her late twenties, though the smoothness of her skin and the general trim of her frame meant she could easily have passed for much younger. Her hair was blonde, suggesting Northern birth, and her lively eyes were a sparkling blue.

"Reverend Mother?" Connor nodded his head uncertainly.

"No. I am not she." Her lips puckered with mild amusement. "I am Lyanna, the commander of the Zealots. The Reverend Mother will grant you an audience. I have been sent to fetch you to her."

"What's a Zealot?"

"The Zealots are the sisters in white." Her tone was patient and good-natured. "The Devots are the sisters in red. Now come with me."

They crossed the courtyard, followed by an escort of six of the armed nuns, each carrying her polearm upright. Connor didn't know where he was going so he followed behind Lyanna rather than walking alongside. Her white woollen robes were almost skin-tight and he couldn't help noticing the conditioning of her body. Her hips and

99

breasts were well developed but her waist was trim and her shoulders broad, suggesting a woman who took regular exercise. This certainly wasn't his idea of a nun.

At the centre of the compound stood a marble statue of the Goddess, portrayed as a young woman holding a bow. On the dais in front of the statue, the Reverend Mother sat in a satinwood chair, not quite so grand as to constitute a throne, but beautifully made nonetheless. Her robes were of plain red wool and she wore no crown, no jewels. A canopy of red cloth above her head protected her from the sun. This time Connor knew who was before him and he bowed low to demonstrate civility. They observed one another in silence for a moment. The Reverend Mother could not have been more different from Lyanna. She was tiny and frail, her white hair and wrinkled skin testifying to her great age, but her eyes were alert and expressive.

"I am Ranald Con Connor ..." he began, but he didn't get far.

"I know who you are Ranald Con Connor." Her voice was crisp and her accent refined. "I know you to be a man with a dubious history and no great lover of religion so now please can you explain to me why you wish to bring men into the temple of the Goddess."

Connor nodded.

"Some weeks ago there were reports that a demon army had appeared in the wastelands and destroyed some villages and outposts close to the Valley of Tombs. A force was despatched to deal with them, led by Lord Ullulay. As far as we know that force was defeated and dispersed. His Lordship has not been heard from since. Another force was gathered from the towns and encampments north of the great river. They were ordered to wait at the crossing and I was recalled from my estate to command them, but the young Lord Vanillien appears to have wished to make a name for himself and passed by here a few days ago without waiting for me. The result of his rashness is only too clear. These few men begging water from your wells are all that remain of what should have been my army.

"These creatures, whatever they are, seem inclined to burn everything they cannot eat or steal. They are using fire as a weapon. I need to stop them before they get to the crossing, otherwise once over the river, they could go off in any direction causing mayhem. The harvest is not yet in and if the fields are burned then the peasant families will starve in the winter. I have decided to stop them here because you have stone buildings and stone walls."

He waited for her argument but none came.

"I have heard of these things of which you speak, and we will aid you in as much as we can, but truly soldier, do you think you can defeat such a demon prince, leading a force which has already beaten two armies?"

Her gaze was direct and Connor had the feeling that he could never lie to this woman as she would be able to see it in his words. In fact, it would not have surprised him if she had said she could see straight into his soul.

"Madam, in truth I do not know if I can triumph. It is always the way of the warrior. In order to prevail, we must risk defeat. But if the fear of defeat should cause us to flinch, then for certain we are already beaten. The only way to gain a victory is to believe in victory, and in truth, I really do believe that victory is possible. These two armies we speak of were defeated even before the battle began, surprised in the night, consumed by fire, and terrified by this demon who leads the pack. From what I have heard there was no real fighting, just a rout. My plan would be to have the men standing ready to fight, sheltering behind stone defences which do not burn. Then let these vermin throw themselves against us and we shall sell our lives dearly."

"Bravely spoken." she nodded. "I would expect no less of a man with your reputation. But what about this mighty demon we have heard of. How will you deal with him?"

"Demons have been killed before." He gazed about him as if to make sure that everyone present was listening. If no-one else can do it I will just have to kill him myself."

The old woman seemed to like his reply, and for a moment he thought that he might have seen her smile, but it was hard to be sure as her face bore the lines and wrinkles of a very long life.

"You have my blessing soldier. Your men may enter the compound and prepare it for defence as required. My nuns will fight alongside you. If the walls should be taken, they will take their station here. By that I mean they will stand exactly here and will fight to the death in order to defend this statue of the Goddess. They will be under the command of the Sword-Mage, Lyanna whom you already know.

Connor turned for a moment to gaze in surprise on the woman who had served as his guide. He had not thought her old enough to be ranked as a Sword-Mage, and he bowed his head slightly to her in acknowledgement. Then he switched his gaze back to the Reverend Mother.

"Lady, I do not think these women should stay. Truly I do not. Their deaths will achieve nothing."

He could immediately sense the irritation of Lyanna beside him but she remained silent. It was left to the older woman to speak.

"Hear me, Lord Ranald Con Connor. This order was established three hundred years ago to protect the temples during the time of troubles. Our sisters train for war and have already dedicated both their lives and their deaths to the Goddess. We shall fight alongside you, or if you choose to flee we shall stand and fight on here alone. This is where we triumph or die and we have no thoughts of surrender or retreat. Do not waste your valuable time arguing over this because within the walls of this convent my word is the law."

When Connor returned to the front gate of the temple he found a small knot of people clustered around Zimbarra who lay on the ground with a rolled up cloak beneath his head for a pillow. One of the nuns was holding his hand and speaking gently to him while another held a clay goblet of water to his lips.

"What happened?" asked Connor, immediately assuming some kind of attack.

"He has merely fatigued himself," murmured Asclepius "When wizards perform magic they call on many forces, but they must use their own vital energies to control them. It can take a toll on them, but usually, they recover. It doesn't affect us priests in the same way because we are merely channeling the powers of our deities. He will survive. Give him an hour."

Zimbarra looked different now. His face was lined and haggard showing his true age, there were grey streaks in his hair. He struggled with shallow breaths and his eyes were wide and rheumy.

Connor turned and surveyed the defences. A steep ditch had been excavated all along the front of the temple, making the stone wall effectively much higher and easier to defend. Despite his natural distaste for the wizard, Connor was impressed. With the small number of men available that work could have taken days to complete. With magic, it had been done in an hour. The wizard might be an annoying little man, but he had got the job done.

"Is there anything you can do to heal him?"

"Most healing is achieved through rest and good food, and sometimes through achieving inner peace. In any case, he is not hurt, he simply needs to gather his energies. He doesn't need any help from me, especially when he has those good sisters looking after him."

Connor was in agreement on that. The sisters were not like any nuns he had seen before, although he hadn't ever seen many on account of never spending much time in temples. To the old soldier it seemed a great pity that such lovely creatures would never have lovers, never get married, never have children. Lyanna only served to reinforce such thoughts when she led him back into the temple to discuss the arrangements for food and provisions. For a moment, as they walked together, he wanted to ask her about herself, and why such an attractive woman had chosen the life of a nun, but he felt it would not be proper and so he let the moment pass.

When they returned to the gateway the wizard was sitting up and looking better.

"So you are a Sword-Mage and you command all the women here?" Connor asked Lyanna.

"I train the Zealots, the younger women dressed in white. I train them in all the ways of the warrior; the sword, the spears, the bow, and in unarmed combat. The Reverend Mother is their true commander. She commands me and she also commands the older women in red, but she is not always present for training, so in reality I am often commanding all of them."

"Training?" Connor smiled. "I would like to observe this training."

If he was trying to make a joke it was lost on Lyanna who promptly ordered up a dozen of the white-robed Zealots. They stood in three lines of four, completely still and holding their polearms in front of them. For long moments they did not move and Connor thought there had been some kind of misunderstanding, then suddenly at a single word of command from Lyanna they began to move as one, leveling their weapons to point to the front, stepping forward in unison, then making a step combined with a thrust, then another step, then another step-thrust, every move perfectly co-ordinated. Then they all turned, facing to the left, making an about turn, facing to the right, then advancing again in that direction, each and every command in perfect coordination with simultaneous timing. Connor had drilled sufficient men in his time to recognise well-trained troops. With such long weapons, even a small mistake could lead to soldiers clashing and obstructing one another, but the Zealots moved with perfection. When at last they had finished the drill they halted in the exact positions from which they had started and Lyanna turned towards Connor and gave a very slight bow.

"An excellent drill," he nodded. "I am highly impressed. As good as any parade-ground soldiers I have ever seen, but can they fight in a real war?"

"My Lord Connor," Lyanna replied, "I have trained these women myself. They will fight as well as any of the men you have in your own army, but with one very important difference, I know that mine will not run away."

There was a moment of total silence. The soldiers standing by sucked in their breath at the jibe and looked towards their sword hilts. Zimbarra raised his eyebrows and Asclepius frowned. The young warrior nuns stood totally still, and yet, somehow they seemed all the more ready, like a trap waiting to be sprung. Connor himself remained expressionless for a moment as if digesting the full implications of her comment. He did not laugh, nor even smile, but at last, he spoke.

"My good lady. If these women have as much spirit as their commander, then truly I believe we could beat a thousand fire demons!" Then he bowed to her deeply, as a courtier would bow to a King, and when he stood up he was smiling.

The soldiers relaxed and Zimbarra wheezed with a sigh of relief. Asclepius cleared his throat and suggested it might be a good idea for all of the troops to pray together. Connor shook his head at that and turned back to Lyanna.

"I must go now and check on my own men, and perhaps when I have got them properly drilled and organised you may let me return the compliment."

She did not answer but gave him a nod, and it seemed that her eyes sparkled just a little more than before.

When Connor had gone Zimbarra turned to face Asclepius directly from the front.

"Don't try to make people pray, priest, like you just did. We don't need it and we don't want it."

"We all need the favour of the Gods." the cleric replied, "Even you, wizard."

"Why would I need your gods?" The wizard's chin stuck out and his goatee beard seemed to poke fun at the holy man. "Go on! Tell me why we need them!"

"You cannot live without the gods." Asclepius sounded like a patient grandfather teaching a child. "They are the ultimate source of all life and all success."

"No!" The little man snapped. "I don't believe they even exist. Look at you! What powers do you have cleric? Nothing! You claim that you have powers to heal the sick and to bring peace to troubled minds, but everything you do would happen anyway, just let people rest and give them decent food and let nature take its course. There is no power in prayer. I have tried it and it doesn't work. It's just a trick of the mind."

Asclepius shook his head and his face grew stern.

"It doesn't work if you don't have faith. But it's certainly better than that which you call magic, dangerous incantations, and arcane knowledge. You are tapping dark arts every time you do that. It will wear you out before your time and when you die you will be in peril of your mortal soul."

"Nonsense," said the wizard, "I am already older than you are and my soul is in no danger at all. Never believe a word a priest says, you would say anything to give yourselves power over the ignorant peasants. You have all those big churches while the poor starve to death in the streets outside, and then you start preaching about the love of the gods."

"And you wizards only use your powers to bring yourselves personal gain." the cleric replied. "You are immoral and unprincipled by your very nature, tinkering with forces you cannot control."

"Whereas you priests claim to control forces which do not really exist." The magician was clearly in no mood for backing down.

"If your gods and your prayers are so powerful, then why did you even need to be here? Surely you could just say a prayer in your big Cathedral and the whole problem would be solved. You constantly threaten ignorant people with the power of the Gods but none that I know has ever seen any evidence of that power."

"Do not tempt the Gods, wizard." Asclepius rumbled. "Be warned that your pride may yet be your undoing."

They fell silent and looked away in opposite directions, each convinced of his own rectitude and the others insincerity.

At some length, Connor returned. Lyanna was with him and she carried an armful of apples from the convent gardens.

"Hey, wizard! Is that a toy sword? Can this good lady use it to cut up the apples?"

Zimbarra turned glowering and whipped the rapier from its scabbard. The blade was in perfect condition and glinted in the sun. For a moment it seemed that he might thrust straight at Connor, however unwise that might be, but then he looked at the fruit in Lyanna's arms and his eyes narrowed.

"Throw me an apple! Come on, throw it! Throw it to me damn you soldier."

Connor took an apple and tossed it towards the little man. He took it clean on the point of the rapier, as easily as a cook putting a knife through a steak.

"Here you go. Now throw again. Throw it right at my head."

He made it look effortless, skewering the apples on the tip of the sword as easy as a child catches a ball. The sword did indeed look small enough to be a toy or a training weapon, but in skillful hands, it would be deadly, and Zimbarra seemed skillful enough.

They sat against the temple wall and Lyanna cut the remaining apples into quarters while Connor took a closer look at the wizard's blade.

"Good quality blade."

"The best." Zimbarra nodded. "It's damascened steel."

"Yes, I can see." Connor held the hilt close to his face with the blade pointing to towards the sky so that he could see the wave patterns in the metal where the smith had forged and folded the red hot steel.

"How old?"

"About two hundred."

"Impressive but could you not try something just a bit bigger." Connor was holding the weapon between his fingers like a noble lady holding a paintbrush. "This would never have the weight to drive through armour."

"I can't use a heavy one because I need to make all my movements from my wrist." Zimbarra took back the sword.

"I have problems with my back. It was already curved when I was born. When I was a child, I had to wear a back-brace and use a stretching frame. Even now it isn't right. If I swung with my shoulders and twisted my waist I could make it worse and just collapse on the spot. Then how much use would I be? With this light rapier, I can just

106

stand straight and let my fingers do all the work. Anyway, even the strongest armour has gaps at the joints and the edges. An accurate thrust can find them and go through them. This will kill you just as well as any broadsword. It just needs to be properly handled."

Connor nodded and turned away towards a soldier on guard.

"You! Yes, you, my good man. Get round to the back of the temple and fetch a flagon from my tent. Make sure it's a full one. I wish to teach this argumentative wizard where the best red wine comes from."

He took four spears and a blanket and somehow managed to put together an awning to shade them all from the afternoon sun. Then they sat quietly, each secretly wondering what the hours ahead would bring.

When the sun went down Zimbarra finished off his wine and pulled his short-cloak around him. "I am tired now and that will weaken my magic. I shall sleep until you need me. My servant has put up a tent at the rear of the temple. Send for me if you think they are close."

When the wizard was gone Connor stood silent for a while and then, having no desire to speak to a minister of religion he went off to check on his guards, leaving the Arch-Prelate Asclepius to keep watch on his own.

The troops were tense that night, but no longer shaken. They had a good stone wall to defend and that always made men feel more steady. They were a mix of survivors from many broken regiments but somehow, without really intending it, they had gathered into groups who had something in common. Some were camped with men they had served with over many years, comrades they could rely upon in the press of battle, but many had found fellowship with strangers who just happened to be from their own region and they seemed to behave accordingly. The fair-haired warriors from the north tried to show no fear, belting out cheerful songs on a marvelous range of subjects. There was a bawdy ballad of a honeymoon night which went comically wrong. There was a heroic saga of ancient warriors killing giants. There was a rowing song with a rhythmic chorus that all could join in. There was even a song about a prince who had a pet pig. Connor pursed his lips into a sort of wry smile. It didn't matter what the song was about as long as it stopped the men thinking too much about what was to come.

Some mercenary archers from the east were deeply involved in their prayers. It served the same purpose, thought Connor, but not something he valued much himself, so he hurried on past them to the other side of the main gate where a group of raw-boned Western men were sharing stories of their home lives and childhood.

".... well the butcher knew that I had been with his wife that night. He couldn't prove it mark you, but he knew it, and the rumours just kept on going round the town that he was going to get me and probably bloody well murder me, and me still just a lad and not half his size. It was pretty clear I had no chance. So one night I was coming up the Sandgate when suddenly he jumps right out from no-where with a big bloody bit of wood in his hand and swings at me. So I takes off back the way I had come and I gets as far as the top of the harbour steps, I could damned well feel his breath almost right on the back o' me neck. Now I just had enough sense to realise I was going a bit too fast and was scared of crashing right down them steps, so I swung me hand out and caught hold of the gatepost to stop myself. But the butcher being dead drunk as it turned out, he had no such thought and he went crashing on past me, across the top of the steps and into that little wall there I tell you, and straight over the side. Down he tumbled, and I was thinking he would land in the water. Just his luck there was a fishing boat tied up below or he would surely have drowned, but that be as it may he was in an awful mess. I pulled him out of the boat and left him on the quay and run and hid. When he came too next day he could hardly walk, his nose was broke and his ribs were cracked but it seems he couldn't remember a thing. From that day on everyone in the whole bloody town thought that I had gave him a right pasting. I was getting bought drinks forever and a day..."

How much was true and how much was a yarn, it was always difficult to say. The westerners respected the art of the storyteller, so a little bit of embellishment was generally expected and easily forgiven if it made the tale more entertaining.

The southerners were a different sort, private and inscrutable, they sat quietly, alone, sharpening knives and fingering their beads. This was their land. Some were not even soldiers. They had lost their homes and perhaps their families. Now they had stopped running and had fallen in with the army. In their silence was determination, to win the coming battle and exact some revenge, or else to die and follow their lost ones to the next life.

When Connor got back to the watchtower Asclepius was still there and they both stood for a while looking out into the silence of the night.

"You don't live here priest" It was really a statement, not a question. "This place is women only is it not?"

The cleric nodded. "You know it, Connor. My Cathedral is in Mynpoor and I minister there, and in the capital of course. I only came here when I heard that the demon lord threatened."

"Why did you come?" Connor spoke with no attempt at respect. "You know you are likely to die and there's nothing you can do here. Why did you come?

"I came because it was my duty to come. I have spent my whole life telling people to stand up for good and oppose what is evil. Now in this moment of crisis, I must be seen to be true to my teachings."

"Good and evil? What does that mean?" Connor spat into the dust. "If a child starves to death on the street outside the royal palace you bastards say it's the will of the Gods, and nothing wrong with it, but if he steals a crust of bread to feed himself you say he is evil and will be judged. I have no time for all that pig-shit."

"Don't you have any beliefs?" The cleric wasn't showing any annoyance.

"Oh, I have lots of beliefs," said the old soldier, "I believe that a dog is more faithful than a woman. I believe you can never have too many weapons. I believe in standing up for myself and always taking revenge on anyone who wrongs me. I even believe that there are Gods, but I don't think they give a damn about what happens to us. We are just like beetles beneath their feet. They can crush us and never notice. You are wasting your life doing service to them, for truly I tell you they really don't care."

"I don't do it for them." The priest was actually smiling gently. "I have never really done it for them. I have done it for me, and for the people. Actually I agree with you about the poor and my own order lives a life of relative poverty. I have no gold. I do not hunt. I wear only plain fabrics. It's true that our temples own lots of land, but a large part of our produce is given to the poor. I want to help people as much as I can in this world, not just the afterlife."

"Ha." Connor scoffed, "Well you had better be ready for the afterlife because that's where you are going to be tomorrow. Seriously, priest, you cannot survive this. You should go. You should go now. If you stay here you will die and what will that prove?"

"It will prove something to me." Asclepius suddenly seemed more intense. His eyebrows dipped towards his nose and his lips pulled in tight. "It will prove that I lived and died true to my faith. I have spent my whole life preaching a set of beliefs, and telling the wonderful stories of men a thousand years ago who did great deeds for their love of religion, but I have always had a tiny doubt in my mind. Would I have done what they did? Could I have done it? Do I really have their faith? Do I have that strength? Do I have the true belief? Or am I a fraud, saying prayers out of habit and living the easy life of a high priest because there is nothing better to do? I have to know whether my life really means anything. So here I am and I will do whatever I can to fight this thing, and if I die tonight then indeed I will die. But I shall die true to my beliefs and assured of my place in the Mansions of the Gods."

Connor held his peace for a moment, perhaps waiting to hear if there was anything else, then, at last, he nodded with just the hint of a smile. "Very well priest, but try to stay behind me when the fighting starts, and perhaps you might just live a little longer before you go off to those mansions.

"The Gods will decide." The cleric's voice was almost a whisper. "If the Gods in their wisdom should see fit to grant me one more day then I shall thank them for their mercy."

"What would you do with the time?" the old soldier seemed to be teasing him now. "If they did give you more days, what would you do?"

"I have always wanted to make a pilgrimage to the East," mused the cleric. "I am told they have temples there which make ours look like the most humble village shrine."

"Ha! Temples! What use are temples?" Connor scoffed. "Give me a decent fortress and I will be happy. There are castles in the northern mountains which would stop this demon rascal, whatever it is. That's where I would choose to make my stand. That's where I would fight him."

"So why are you here?" Asclepius swung round to face him directly. "You were banished by the palace, cast aside after a life of service. You owe them no gratitude, no debt of honour. You asked me why I came, but what about you?"

Connor grinned at how easily he had let his own question be turned against him.

"I've been a soldier all my life. It's what I do. I've lost a few fights but I've never lost a war. I need to win this one to remind them all that I am still the best. If I were to let this pass then I would grow old as a nobody. That's a choice I would not care to take. I must fight this battle, and I must win it, for otherwise, I have nowhere else to go."

"And if you die, soldier," asked the priest, "Do you not worry about what comes next?"

"Damnit no!" The warrior tossed his head. "I can worry about the afterlife when you bury me in the ground. Give me a victory tomorrow and I will celebrate with cold beer, hot food, and a warm woman. That's all the paradise I need."

Asclepius seemed to relax and began to smile. "You are good at your cynical act Connor, but not good enough for me. You have more human goodness about you than you wish to show."

"How so?"

"Well, you certainly had no time for Zimbarra when he arrived here. But when you learned of his weakness, with his back, you felt regret for your earlier testiness, did you not? You even sent your soldier to fetch more wine to share with him. You are not as hard hearted as you try to pretend."

Connor merely shrugged and they stood for a while in silence, looking out into the gloom to the south. Normally there should have been only darkness out in the plains but tonight there was an orange glow, where distant villages and fields had been set on fire by the marauders. After a while, Zimbarra joined them, a woven blanket wrapped around his shoulders against any possible chill in the night air.

"I must off to make my prayers." Asclepius excused himself, not wishing to renew his argument with the little wizard. "Send for me in the temple if they come."

Connor followed moments later and walked back through the temple yard, towards the storehouse in the northeast corner where supplies had been laid out for his men. Lyanna was there speaking to two of the women in red. They were perhaps the oldest nuns he had seen at the temple, apart from the Reverend Mother. He would have guessed they had each seen fifty years, but it struck him that they looked healthy and attractive for their age. The convent gave women safety and good food. These two had done well on it. In fact, at his age, he might easily have thought on them as attractive, but for the presence of Lyanna who outshone them as the sun outshines a candle flame.

"May I make free with this food?" Connor asked, trying not to gaze too intently at the young nun.

"By all means my Lord." Lyanna smiled. "Everything which we have we will share with you."

He took two apples and some grapes and sat himself down on a wooden bench.

"Are you not afraid?" He asked her, hardly knowing what else to talk about.

"Afraid?" She picked up a large golden melon. "No. I am not afraid. We use meditation to control both fear and anger. I am only concerned that I should fully do my duty to the Goddess and to my companions here."

"I am impressed. I have seen many men rigid with fear on the night before a battle."

"They should put their trust in the Goddess." She sat down beside him. "Would you like to share a melon?"

Connor gazed for a moment at the smooth yellow fruit in her hands and then realised he was staring at her breasts. He jerked up his gaze towards her face and was almost overpowered by the gentleness of her eyes.

"What on earth made you want to become a nun?" The question seemed to just jump from his lips, although he had actually been thinking about it all through the day.

"I grew up here." She replied with an air of natural honesty. "I was brought here as a child and I do not know why. I can guess that my parents must have been northerners, from the fair looks they gave me, but I don't know who they were. Perhaps they died in some tragedy, or perhaps they were hung as thieves. It makes no difference. My whole life has been here and I have trained for prayer and battle since I could walk and talk. I don't think of it as a convent full of nuns. I think of it as my home, full of my family."

She handed him a thick slice of yellow melon.

"But you, why are you here?" She took her turn to ask the questions now. "Why would you come here to die? You have great repute as a soldier but here you have only a handful of men and a temple to defend. Why take the risk?"

Connor shrugged. "I wanted one more chance to lead the army before I grew old and died. When they asked me I said yes. I didn't know that some young idiot would get our force destroyed before I even got here."

"So it's vanity really." Her smile was almost sympathetic. "It's all about your reputation. Is that worth dying for in a hopeless fight? Is it more important than your life?"

"My life is worth nothing," the old soldier scowled. "It is worth less than nothing, and if I die in this battle it will be a blessed relief."

"It's wrong to speak like that." Her blue eyes seemed deeper as her expression grew sorrowful. "The Gods have given you a life and you should live it with rejoicing."

"I curse the Gods for giving me life." He sounded bitter but not angry. "Everything that has ever mattered to me has been stripped away from me, and I, with all my efforts and a lifetime of victories, I have earned myself nothing but sorrow."

"I heard his eminence say that you were banished from court." She reached out and took hold of his arm gently, not by the hand but above the wrist. "But I don't know anything about what happened. Tell me, if you can."

Connor paused for a moment as if he would refuse to speak. Then to her surprise, he began.

"It was five years ago. We were at war with the Kashkan tribesmen who dwell in the mountains of the far north. They had raided and I had thrown them back. This had happened many times over the years, but at last, the King decided that enough was enough and it was time to teach them a lesson. We would raid their territory and cause as much destruction as possible. It's what we would call a punitive raid. He put a Royal Prince in charge of the army, Prince Agene, but really I was expected to make the important decisions and teach the Prince about the realities of war. Agene was not a fool, not a bad man, but he was immature. He was twenty-four but he acted like seventeen. As we marched into the enemy territories there was a point where we came to one limb of a mountain range. The enemy retreated up the Western side of it, but if we followed them there was always the chance that they might cross over and come back down the East side to outmaneuver us. Likewise, if we went the other way. Of course, we could split our forces and go both ways, but then they could attack one of our forces with all of theirs, and we would be outnumbered."

"So what did you do?"

"It should have been quite straightforward really. Agene was to stay put with a strong force of infantry to guard the point where the two trails split. I gave him a few light cavalry as well, for scouts. I took the bulk of the cavalry and light infantry up the Western trail. If I was attacked I could fall back easily, leading the enemy into a situation where they would have to fight our whole force. If they attacked down the other side of the valley I could move back quickly to support him. Agene was camped in a really strong position, on a small rocky ridge with reliable troops. All he had to do was hold his position, like a cork in a bottle, while I pushed the enemy back and burnt their villages and crops.

"I take it something went badly?"

"Indeed it did. After we had marched for a few days we caught up with them and fought a series of battles. We did well, but their army wasn't completely beaten. On the other side of the mountain, a small skirmishing force attacked Agene and he went after them, following them up the Eastern side of the range, always close but never quite close enough to fight a proper battle. A good commander would have recognised it for what it was, they drew him out of his position and then they sucked him into the wilderness. When he had gone far enough they turned on him, deep in the forests among the marshy streams, where they were most at home. He suffered a check and began to fall back, but the men I was chasing had crossed the mountains in the night by secret paths and they were waiting for him, behind him, cutting off his retreat. He lost his nerve and rode away, leaving his men to their fate."

"Did they all die?"

"No, some survived but many died. A lot of them were men I had known for years and led into battle many times. But that is war. They died a soldiers' death and I cannot complain at that. If we had used the same trick and won we would have called it a great victory. But it was worse than that. With his force defeated the enemy had a clear route south, sweeping down into my province with almost no-one left to stop them. My own troops were with me, still searching the northern forests. By the time we got word and marched back south, it was too late. My lands had been ravaged, crops destroyed, towns and villages burnt. I had left my wife and child in my castle at Stackstead but for some reason, they had tried to escape south to Larkhall and were caught on the road in an undefended village."

Lyanna didn't ask if they had died. It was obvious from his voice and she didn't wish to increase his pain.

114

"Later, when it was all over, Agene told his own version of events at the court, making out that I had been to blame. I think most people knew he was lying, but he was a royal prince and I was just a commoner, a jumped-up mercenary captain. I could have forgiven him if he had admitted his mistake, but the lying made me angry and I called him out."

"What does that mean?" Lyanna asked.

"I challenged him to a duel."

"You killed him?"

"No, more's the pity. People knew about it and it was stopped. They banished me from the court to get rid of me. I have spent the past five years in exile on my own estates, guarding the northern border against raiders and growing old before my time."

She took his hand, gently, and raised it towards her face, kissed it and then let it go.

"I am sorry for your pain. I cannot say that I know how you feel, for I do not know, and I will not tell you that the Gods have a plan for you, because that would only anger you against them. All I know is that you seem to me to be a good man, and if you survive this fight then you should try to build a new life. If five years have passed there would be no shame in finding new love or even changing your life to do something different. Life is beautiful and is meant to be lived."

He realised that her body was resting warm against his, and for a moment he was struck by her beauty, but then he remembered that she was a nun, after all, and he wriggled away awkwardly, mumbling something about needing to take some wine back for the men waiting at the gate.

"Our best wines are the sweet red ones." she smiled. "That's if you like sweet things."

When he got back to the gate Zimbarra was carefully drawing arcane glyphs of protection on the stonework.

"I went to get some wine." Connor held up the jar as evidence.

"All is well." the wizard nodded. "I am here."

"Then I shall have no fears," glowered Connor. "If the demon lord turns up with all his armies you can turn them into rabbits and we can cook them in a stew."

"A stew eh?" The wizard's eyebrows were up again. "Like the cauldron at Merrideon. That was quite a stew wasn't it?"

115

"Were you there?" The old soldier's attention was captured by the mention of one of his own great battles from days gone by.

"No," answered the wizard, "But I admire the way you handled it."

"What would you know about the way I handled it?" Connor replied "I didn't even attack. The city just surrendered."

"Ahh! You are too self-effacing, Ranald Con Connor." The wizard's eyes were twinkling with mischief.

"I know exactly what you did. After you beat Gudungeon's army at the battle of Geraint's Farm, you sent emissaries out to tell the local people that the war would be passing their way and they should seek sanctuary quickly before the troops arrived. It made you seem like a true gallant gentleman."

Now it was Connor who raised his eyebrows.

"But you knew exactly what you were doing, you sly old fox." The wizard wheezed a little to get his breath. "You even sent warnings out to areas far beyond the city, to villages far off from your route, and everywhere your messengers went they set fire to haystacks and copses so that the horizon was black with the smoke of war. You caused a panic without killing a soul."

Connor shrugged. "If none were killed than you should not complain."

"Oh no! Oh no, no!" Zimbarra protested. "No, no. I don't complain at all. I admire you. Thousands of refugees set off for the safety of the city, long before your troops were anywhere near it. The authorities had no forces to stop them, no plan to control them, and above all, no food to feed them. They had already given what they could to their own army as it marched up towards you. By the time that army fell back there to organise a defence the place was already full of people and on the brink of starvation. That was the cauldron at Merrideon. How long was your siege, about three weeks? That was because you herded all of those hungry people into the town, and stirred them all up in your cauldron. If not for your trick with all those extra mouths to feed that place could have held for three months or more. I understand you perfectly my friend, and I think you did very well. The war was over with just one battle fought. Very efficient, and we might even say it was quite humane."

"How do you know all of this?" asked Connor.

"I know all of this because I am a man of letters." The wizard raised his head proudly. "I have correspondents who write to me with their

116

reports of grand affairs and I repay them by sharing my own knowledge and analysis."

"Then I should hang you for a spy!" Connor laughed. "Or maybe I should pay you to spy for me. But why do you bother?"

"Because I enjoy it," said the wizard. "Because it amuses me and stops me getting bored. I was born with this twisted back and could never do the things that other boys did. I sat on the balcony of my room, gazing out across the fields, reading books and writing letters, fighting battles with toy soldiers and writing stories of imaginary campaigns. When I grew older I studied the histories of the great commanders, and as you became famous I took it upon myself to follow your progress."

"Really?" Connor genuinely seemed surprised.

"Yes. Really! I'm writing my own account of your campaigns. It isn't ready yet but one day it will be a history of some importance. Perhaps if we live through this night you could help me with the answers to a few questions."

"Such as?"

"Well, at Carrola, you had to cross the river with the enemy in force on the far side. You detached your cavalry and sent them up-river raiding and burning towards the next bridge."

"That's right," Connor agreed, "And he sent his as well, to cover me. But my cavalry force was much weaker, my real strength was in my spear-blocks and with his noble cavalry gone my army was far superior. We stormed the bridge the next morning before his horsemen could get back.

The wizard nodded. "The cavalry move was a feint. Yes, I understand that, but what if his cavalry had not followed yours?"

"Well then mine really would have crossed the river at the next bridge." Connor gave a casual shrug. "They could have laid waste to the villages beyond and cut his supply lines. He couldn't ignore that. Sooner or later he would have had to send troops to deal with my cavalry, and at that point I would have taken the bridge."

"I travelled that area myself in my youth," said Zimbarra. "Those beautiful small villages so high up on the hilltops, surrounded by orchards and vineyards. That cheese they make, the big flat ones, and the red wine. It's as close to paradise as I will ever get, not being a religious type."

117

"You and I both." Connor smiled, "But if you like it so much why didn't you stay there?"

"I did for a while, but then I had to leave." The wizard turned his head away, gazing into the darkness. "There was a lovely young lass with thick black hair, and I paid her a few coppers each week to tidy my house and wash my clothes. Of course, it didn't take long before we were in bed together. Then I got to know her best friend and soon the three of us were getting into bed together. It was too good to last. One day there was a knock on my door and her mother was there."

"Angry?" asked Connor.

"No, she had made me a pie and we ended up in bed together. Life got a bit complicated after that and I decided it was time to move on."

"And where are you now?"

"I have a small castle at Rockbridge. It was built by Ballan Drew"

"Ballan the Builder?" Connor was impressed. "Now there was a man who could really build castles. What defences do you have on your main gate?"

"Well, being so high up in the mountains there's no moat," said the wizard, "but the entrance is on the second level with just a small stair running up the side of the building and a gap at the top that's covered by a drawbridge. Impossible to get a battering ram up, or a horse. There are flanking towers, either side, and an entrance tunnel with a portcullis at both ends.

Connor paused for a moment, reconstructing the layout of the building in his mind. "Well, that's a lot better than we have here. Normally with a gateway as weak as this, I would light a bonfire at the gates to stop the enemy getting through, but that's a bit pointless against a fire-demon. When they do come, and I am sure that they will, that may be where I stand in the fight."

"You would put yourself at the place of greatest danger?"

"I'm not afraid to die." Connor looked Zimbarra directly in the eye. "I'm not as fit as I used to be and one day I will go the way of all flesh. But I would like to achieve something before I go. You know, something worthwhile, maybe capture a kingdom or take horrific revenge on an enemy." He smiled at the thought. "I need to do something people can tell stories about so that my life seemed worthwhile."

"Slaying a Demon-Lord?" The wizard's eyebrows twitched up.

"That would do."

Zimbarra offered Connor a handful of grapes. "Well since they haven't turned up yet, perhaps I can do something useful while we wait, like putting a few enchantments on your sword."

"No need really." Connor slipped his longsword silently from its oiled scabbard and it appeared to flicker slightly in the greyness of the early dawn. "It's a wonderful damascened blade, been in my family for generations, and it already has two dweomers cast into it. It gives off a bit of light in the dark, enough for me to see my way but not so much as to attract enemies, and it's also said to cause fear in opponents."

"Very useful." Zimbarra raised his eyebrows. "Do you have any way of knowing if it really does cause fear in your opponents?"

Connor curled his lips a little. "Well, most people look pretty fearful when they see me pointing it at them." He grinned at his own joke, and then they both laughed together.

"Then if ever you buy another sword just ask." Zimbarra could feel the old soldier's attitude warming to him. "I have much experience of working with weapons."

Connor looked thoughtfully at the magician for a moment and seemed to be reassessing him.

"Well, in fact, I do have another weapon. Perhaps you would like to see if you can work anything on that."

"Fetch it." Zimbarra shrugged. "We can see."

"And maybe fetch some more of that wine?" he shouted after Connor as the old warrior disappeared into the shadows.

The edge of the sun was beginning to creep into the sky, transforming the darkness into shades of blue and grey.

"Shall I die today?" asked the wizard, speaking as much to himself as to any other.

"Only the Gods can answer that question." The answer came unexpectedly from the gateway behind him. Asclepius had returned from his prayers.

"I was just thinking aloud." wheezed the magician, turning awkwardly to face him. The priest was only wearing one sandal. He held the other in his hand, dangling by a broken strap.

"When you think about dying it should make you reflect on how you have lived your life." advised the cleric.

"Spoken like a true priest, your holiness." The pointed eyebrows went up. "You never miss a chance to teach us, sinners, that you are right and we are wrong."

Asclepius shook his head.

"No my son. I do not claim to be any better than you are. At a time like this when we face great danger, we must accept that in the eyes of the Gods we are all equal."

Zimbarra stretched and tried to loosen his shoulders with an expression of pain he could not disguise.

"You know I was talking to the general there, and I decided that he and I are really not so different. He's not afraid of dying. All he cares about is his reputation. He wants to be remembered for something. I can understand that. Of course, I am afraid of dying, absolutely, completely sick in the guts afraid of dying. But as long as I can stay alive the next most important thing is my reputation."

"Ah, you admit to pride!" said the cleric, "And all this time I thought that your only weaknesses were your vanity and your appetite for fancy clothes, and good food, and strong wine, and pretty women, and lots of gold and for a grand castle in the mountains."

Zimbarra was almost ready to reply when he realised that Asclepius was actually teasing him, and instead of opening his mouth he merely raised his pointed eyebrows a little further.

"So tell me," the priest continued, "If you get burned away to a cinder tomorrow, what will that do for your reputation?"

The magician slowly stroked his moustache with one finger and his thumb.

"If I get burned to a cinder tomorrow it just won't matter anymore, but if we win then the name of Zimbarra will be celebrated far and wide as a hero and a wizard of great power. Ha ha! Then we will see about the fancy clothes, and good food, and strong wine, and the pretty women, and the gold."

"Then I shall pray to the Gods that you live to be a very old man and that you get to enjoy it all." The cleric seemed quite kindly now.

Zimbarra picked up the sandal and began to fidget with the broken strap.

"Is your faith truly that strong priest? Are you really not afraid of dying?"

"It has been said that death is just another path, one that we all must take"

"Very profound." murmured the wizard. "Who said it?"

Asclepius smiled gently. "Actually, it's from a book. A very wonderful book which I read when I was just a novice. It has shaped my entire life. But please try to understand me. I don't actually want to die, that's not what religion teaches. We are not a death cult. Only the dark forces see death as an end in itself. When these creatures come, as they surely will, I want to win just as much as any of you. If we can ride out of here tomorrow, hearing the birdsong and feeling the warmth of the sun, then I will give praise to my Gods for their mercy. Life is beautiful. With all its challenges and setbacks, life is still beautiful."

"Amen to that" Zimbarra smiled and handed back the sandal. The strap which had been broken was now fixed. "Have a little gift, priest, a magic mending spell from an evil old wizard."

"You are not evil." The Priest's voice was kindly now. "You just like to say that because you think it enhances your reputation. It's that pride again. Thank you for mending my sandal. I hope you will survive the night whatever our differences. He took hold of Zimbarra by the hand and the forearm and muttered a short prayer.

"That will not protect me, priest ..."

"Let the Gods be the judge of that." Asclepius seemed somehow mildly amused. "Some things, you will find, are beyond our understanding."

Connor returned a few minutes later with perhaps the largest sword that Zimbarra had ever seen. Standing upright it was as tall as Connor himself, a full-size two-handed sword. The cross-guard alone was as long as a man's forearm and decorated at each end with a knob that resembled a fist. A single garnet was set in the pommel, winking out like a huge red eye. From the way the old warrior handled it Zimbarra could tell that it was heavy, probably too heavy for the little wizard to even lift it.

"Where in all the nine hells did you find that thing?"

"I brought it with me, strapped to the side of my horse. We have had it on the wall of the armoury since long before I was born. In the old days, when men fought mostly in big pike blocks they used to use them to chop down the spears. One big fellow swinging this would disorder the whole block, and then the rest of the troops could crash in amongst them. It's a bit on the heavy side but it's made from wrought iron you see, not steel, so when the stories started to circulate about demons I thought it might be worth bringing with me. What do you think?"

"I think it's a bloody monster," Zimbarra grimaced, "But I know what I want to do with it. Put it down on the sand over there and leave it to me. Does it have a name?"

"We call it Eternity," Connor chuckled, "because if I hit you with it you'd be finished for all time"

Zimbarra grinned, then rolled back his silken sleeves and drew a circular line in the sand around the sword. He stepped back from the circle and went to work with various chants. At first, Connor was interested but he soon grew bored and went off to take a piss. When he came back the mage was still chanting so he sat down against the wall to rest. Within moments he was asleep. When he awoke the sun was fully up and Zimbarra was talking with Asclepius a short distance away.

"Awake my Lord? Let me show you what I have done." He lifted the great weapon and swung it above his head before dropping it to the ground at Connor's feet.

The general picked up the sword, but where it had once been painfully heavy it now felt much too light. "This is no good, it won't strike with the same force!"

"Ah, but that's where you're wrong, try picking it up by the blade"

Connor looked bewildered. The weapon felt amazingly light when he picked it up by the handle, but as heavy as ever when he lifted it by the blade.

"That's one of my specialties" smiled Zimbarra "The blade is just as heavy and does just as much damage, but the spell makes it feel lighter in the hand of he who uses it. In effect, it's as if you were three times as strong as you are. Now call its name."

Connor called out and Eternity flicked up from the ground and into his hands so quickly that its actual movement could not be seen. One second it was in the dust and the next it was in its master's grasp.

"From now on don't tell other people the name, or they could do that just as well." Zimbarra winked.

"There is one more thing." He began to sound perhaps a little smug. "Actually, you may even think it's the best thing. Well, I would anyway if it were my sword.

"Look at the edge. It's still just as sharp as it was, but now it's what we call a vorpal blade. When it hits a target with sufficient speed it will trigger a spell. When that happens, the spell will... well, it's complicated, but try to imagine a tiny break in the fabric of the universe creating an opening into another dimensional plane. Just as the sword touches your demon, if it hits him with enough force, a kind of gap is appearing in the creature so that the sword can go straight in without any resistance, like a knife cutting through a flame. By the time the matter phases back into place, the structural integrity of the monster is already compromised."

"Marvellous." Connor nodded. "And what the hell does any of that actually mean?"

Zimbarra turned with a swagger and proudly stuck out his chin.

"It means it will cut through the skin of a demon much, much better than any other weapon can do. That's what it means. In fact, it will cut through any solid material just as easily as a knife will cut through water, but only through the surface. Once it has got past the skin, or the armour, it will be past the circumference of the spell, and after that it will only be as effective as any other huge iron sword being wielded by any other warrior.

Connor swung the massive weapon in a circle then brought it to rest as his expression turned cynical. "Were you just pretending all the time?" he asked Zimbarra.

"No! What pretence do you speak of?" the wizard's face darkened.

"The way you're standing." Connor pointed at him. "The way you swung the sword. Your shoulders! Your back! There's nothing wrong with you."

Zimbarra spun towards Asclepius, but the Arch-Prelate had already gone.

As the morning sky grew brighter they could see ever more smoke on the horizon, multiple black smudges stretching away to the left and the right where villages and fields were burning. Asclepius had gone off to do some sort of prayer for the souls of those many poor peasants who must have died in the chaos of the night. As there was nothing in sight on the ground yet, Connor and Zimbarra went back into the convent buildings in search of breakfast.

Connor was horrified to find that there was no meat but Lyanna explained that kindness to animals was one of the principles of their order, along with sobriety, service to others, worshipping the goddess and a few other things. So there was never any meat. It was forbidden. She took a large melon and sliced it in half, and then into segments, and offered him one. They ate it with their fingers, as children like to do, with their eyes peering out over the edge. Her eyes were blue, the bright shining blue of the northern tribes. He noticed she was wearing a different type of robe today, in fact, all of the women were. This garment was split down either side, from the thighs to the ankles, so that although the legs were still covered they would have complete freedom of movement in battle. He decided he should not be paying so much attention to a nun's legs and switched his attention back to those crystal blue eyes. Was she laughing slightly? It was difficult to tell behind a melon. They dined on the fresh fruits, mainly grapes and more slices of yellow melon, although there were apples as well. Then the alarm bell began to ring and all thought of food was put aside.

It took most of the morning for the enemy to fully assemble and the defenders of the temple had plenty of time to prepare. Connor would have liked to have had corner towers for his archers, but it was a temple, not a fortress and he had to make do with what he had. At least it was stone, he reminded himself, as he watched the men filling fire-buckets from the well in case the inner buildings were set alight. He finished oiling his longsword and slid it into the scabbard, then took up his position with the troops on the walls, leaving the larger sword back near the statue until such times as he might need it.

The view from the wall was truly hellish as the marauders made their first charge. The bulk of the troops were goblins, as tall and as broad as a short fat human, but with bestial faces resembling both an ape and a pig. There were humans as well, robbers and outlaws and wild men of the southern desert, but all of these seemed insignificant compared to the small group of demons who led the charges and directed the attacks. If the demons could be killed then the rest would almost certainly turn and flee, thought Connor, in fact without their leaders to control them they might even eat each other. He allowed himself a smile. It was good to be back in command, to know the thrill of battle and to feel that rush lifting his heart.

The temple walls were as high as a man could reach, and now that a ditch had been dug in front they presented a real obstacle to the attackers, but some among them carried slender tree trunks cut from the woods nearby and they were propping them up like ladders against the stonework. At the top they were met by those same soldiers who had run from them in battle just three days earlier, but this time it was different. Now it was daytime and they stood prepared, and they knew what they were facing, and they defended a strong position, and they had a leader whose name was a legend in the army. As each goblin hand grasped the top of the wall it was cut off by a defenders sword. As each enemy head rose above the parapet it was met with a slash to the neck. Young lads made their first kill and old hands sung their battle songs. The convent walls became like a butchers yard as the troops hacked and slashed with their sandals slipping in the blood and their sweat running into their eyes. A few men who had lost their weapons now had polearms borrowed from the nuns, awkward to use at close range, but useful for prodding at a man who was climbing up a ladder. Asclepius the Arch-Prelate stood in the centre of the courtyard, just in front of the great statue, chanting prayers of protection and some incantation which he would claim could dispel fear, although Zimbarra later said he had felt plenty of fear and that was probably true of everyone else.

Then suddenly, up and over the wall, came a terrifying figure which stood a head and shoulders taller than the tallest man. It looked in many ways like an angry bull, with a huge muscular body, a bestial face and bovine horns, its green glowing eyes alive with hate. Behind it the enemy forces came on with renewed determination, some of them managing to get a footing on top of wall now so that they were able to fight on even terms.

Connor was too far away to do anything but watch in horror at the bulky monster towering over his men. It turned towards him as if it could sense his presence, stretching out its powerful arms and bellowing a roar of hatred and defiance.

Then came a flash! It was like a burning arrow, a line of bright yellow flame tearing through the air, from the level of the courtyard to the height of the walls. It took the demon in the chest and burst clear through it, leaving a black smoking hole the size of a skittle ball. The creature crashed down from the walkway and fell stone-dead in the ditch at the foot of the wall. For a moment all eyes turned to Zimbarra, who took a small comical bow then turned away in search of another victim.

But the onslaught was gathering momentum and other attackers had now climbed up to establish a foothold on the parapet, penned in on either side by defending troops. Others, in their increasing numbers, swarmed up the ladders behind them and it seemed that the temple walls must soon be overwhelmed.

Lyanna barked out a command and the older Devots in their red robes began to walk towards the stairways ready to reinforce the fighting men. Another magical bolt shot out from the fingers of the wizard and another of the demons fell down from the walls. Some of the men even managed a cheer.

One group of invaders, who had taken a short section of the wall jumped boldly down from the battlements and into the courtyard, where no-one remained to oppose them but Lyanna and the Zealots, the younger nuns in their white robes. Connor could do nothing to help her for in that moment he had another wave of goblins upon him and he swung at them with his longsword, taking the head clean off the first and then cutting the arm off the second on the backswing. A third one had got to the top of the wall and was standing balanced on the parapet ready to jump down. The tip of Connor's longsword caught him lightly in the belly, lifting him up into the air so that the creature's own weight drove the point home, then the commander flicked him round to the back so that the dying body slipped free from the blade and plunged down onto the tiles of the courtyard.

Behind him, Connor beheld a sight which filled him with awe as the women in white engaged with their attackers. For all of their lives they had drilled with the polearms and their training revealed itself in the disciplined style of their combat. A jab with the spear-point could drive the enemy back, then a sweeping move with the axe could cut his feet from beneath him, or just as easily sever his head at the neck. Where an enemy threatened with a sword a sister would catch his arm with her hook. As he tried to break free she would jab him with the spear-point forcing him backwards and the whole drill would begin again. When the fighting paused for a moment the women dressed their ranks. Every second Zealot pointed her weapon towards the enemy, threatening them and forcing them back. The others laid their polearms back over their shoulders, then swung them up and over in a huge arc, like a fisherman casting with a rod, or a boy chopping wood. Down came the axe blades, cleaving the goblins straight from above, chopping off the arms of some at the shoulder and splitting others down through the head as far as the teeth. With a lifetime in soldiering, Connor had never experienced anyone fighting like this, so graceful it was more like a dance than a battle. The enemy had been brimming with confidence when they had poured down from the wall. Now they were hard pressed and struggling to form a battle line which could hold against the ferocity of the Zealots' co-ordinated attack.

Lyanna ran back a few steps towards the great statue and raised her polearm up into the air, both hands at the top of the staff, just where it joined the axe head. She skipped forward three quick paces and plunged the butt-end to the floor, flicking her legs up into the air and swinging her whole body out over the line of the enemy. She came down behind the enemy ranks, landing on her feet like a trained acrobat. Then she pivoted the weapon in her hands and grasped the bottom end, swinging it like a scythe, taking out the legs of three or four of the enemy troops to leave them hamstrung and lamed upon the ground. Their comrades had but an instant to reflect upon the danger behind them, and in that instant, they hesitated, and their hesitation was fatal. Attacked from both in front and behind, they fell easy prey to the skillful blows of the warrior nuns.

Connor saw another demon blasted by Zimbarra with whatever sort of magic missile he was using and then it seemed that this particular encounter was over, the remainder of the renegades jumping down from the walls and scurrying back towards the cover of nearby trees.

All along the wall, it was the same story, the enemy rabble had been kept at bay long enough for the wizard to shoot down their leaders, now they were falling back towards the woods in a confused rout. The men gave a cheer and fired off the odd arrow without much thought as to whether it might hit anything. Down in the courtyard, Asclepius had the wounded taken aside and laid out in well-organised rows where he passed among them working healing spells with the assistance of three of the oldest Devots.

From the wall Connor watched the enemy reform. In the initial attack, their chaotic enthusiasm had made them seem overwhelming. That was probably how they had broken the two armies sent out to meet them, fomenting sheer panic through the speed and ferocity of their charge. Now, as they struggled to form a line in the field beyond the temple they seemed far less threatening. Their numbers were certainly not overwhelming, almost equal to the numbers he had inside, and now that he had seen the nuns fight he knew he could count on them to lay it on just as well as the men, perhaps even better. He allowed himself a slight smile. That damned wizard had suddenly come good. Whatever it was that he was conjuring up, the demons didn't like it one bit.

The bell began to toll and all eyes turned towards the front as once more the enemy line began to roll forward. Then Connor noticed that something was different. A figure of sorts was emerging from the scrubby bushes where the goblin army had cut their trees to use as ladders in the first attack. It was something big and it made the hairs on his neck tingle.

He had heard them speak of a fire-demon, and that was what he had expected, a demon made up completely of fire, like the straw doll which is cast into the bonfire at a bridal party and bursts into flames to symbolise the passions of love. But that was not what he saw now. This monster was huge, twice as tall as any man, and for the most part, it was black. Not the black of leather, nor the black of steel. This creature was the dirty grey-black of the dust which is found in a chimney or a pile of wood ash. But it was not entirely black. Where a human should have had eyes, or a nose, or a mouth, or indeed any vent or void in its body, this grotesque entity had jagged holes which revealed what lay within, a fiery inferno of swirling flames, and as they watched it raised its head and spat a great gouting column of burning matter to the ground before it, flaring up the height of a man's head and burning all of the grass and shrubs for the same distance on either side.

The monster moved forward at a walking pace, its smaller followers trotting to keep up. It carried no tools to break down the wall, but in one hand it held a gnarled wooden staff the height of a tall man. At fifty paces it flung out its arm in a sweeping gesture towards the temple and it seemed, for a moment, as if somehow the air itself seemed to ripple. Then the outer wall of the temple courtyard exploded and burst into the air, leaving a hole the size of a haystack with nothing but a pile of broken stones and a plume of dust to mark where once the boundary had been.

On came the demon oblivious to any threat. A few of the archers garnered the courage to take a shot but their arrows seemed to snag in the creatures hide for just seconds before they burst into flames and shriveled to ash. Another blast from the staff of power and the entire gateway was burst asunder in a flurry of tumbling stones and splintering wood. Down in the courtyard, Asclepius became aware of what was happening and started more incantations to protect the defenders from fear.

Zimbarra fired off an energy bolt, which caught the monster on one arm. It tore away a hole through which flames began to flare, but the gap simply closed up again. He launched another spell which seemed to float slowly towards the demon-lord, growing as it drifted through the air and then at the last moment turning into multiple huge balls of ice, but the demon walked on through it, no more troubled than a woman walking through rain in a marketplace. Spitting liquid flames from its mouth it passed through the ruins of the gateway and fixed its path towards the great statue, but to reach the dias it would first need to pass over the bodies of the Zealots who had sworn to defend the temple with their lives. Nothing in their training could protect them from this.

Zimbarra had studied that staff in the hands of the creature, that artifact of immense power believed long-lost by the wisest of magicians. He knew that a single blast of that hellish stave could destroy any part of the temple, be it the statue or the shrine, and he knew that the brute had a dozen other ways to kill the young women standing so bravely before it. Desperately hoping to save them the wizard tried once more. From a fold in his sleeve he drew forth a delicate wand, intricately carved from an exotic red-coloured wood. With a word of command a single bolt of blue-white lightning shot forth at his target and blasted a hole through the belly of the monster, which did not fall but turned slowly and with malice towards the small magician.

"Die wizard!" It was no human voice, but a cracking sound like the nose a roaring bonfire makes when piles of small wood and twigs begin to catch and flare up.

Then came a flash, a circle of fast moving steel. It was Lyanna coming in from the side, whirling her polearm high in the air, high enough to catch the creature's arm, near the wrist, strong to cleave it clean through so that the magical staff and the monstrous hand both dropped, disconnected, to the ground.

The demon now swung towards Lyanna giving Zimbarra time to back off a little way, but even as it went for the young woman Connor himself came in from behind her, rushing in close and striking upwards, thrusting his longsword up through the groin of the beast and burying it deep in its belly. The monster's head went up and it screamed furiously at the heavens, then its foot kicked out and its massive hoof caught Connor in the ribs and sent him spinning through the air, to land in a sitting position at the base of the stone platform where the Reverend Mother still sat in her chair in front of the statue of the Goddess, her expression serene in defiance of the attacker.

Towering over the stricken body of Ranald Con Connor, the Demon Lord spat out a huge gout of liquid fire which utterly consumed him in flame. Then it raised its head again and gave a triumphant roar towards the skies.

Lyanna dropped her weapon and ran to the stricken general. His hair was gone, his clothes were burnt to rags, his skin was peeling away to leave his face unrecognisable, the flesh on his arms and chest had turned black, smoking and blistered.

"I'm sorry." was all he gasped, as she cradled his head in her lap. Then the monster fixed them in the fury of its gaze. Its hand had already regrown and now it was visibly changing shape, morphing towards some even more hideous beast, the like of which no mortal man had ever seen and lived to tell.

From a hidden pocket, Zimbarra pulled out a crinkled scroll of ancient parchment. He read one single word from the scroll and gestured at the fire-demon. The result was remarkable. The scroll itself simply crumbled to dust and disappeared, but a shimmering transparent ball of light appeared in the air, completely encircling the creature. On the walls, the soldiers still fought. In the courtyard, the women still stood on guard. On the steps of the statue, the Reverend Mother shuffled slowly forward, but inside that miraculous globe, the monster itself seemed frozen in time.

"Do something quickly." screamed Zimbarra "I don't know how long this will last, and I don't have any more scrolls."

Asclepius called out a command and knelt beside Connor. Taking the hand of the dying man, he began to pray. The Reverend Mother struggled down onto her knees and took his other hand, while a dozen or more of the Devots in their red robes also linked hands, so as to form a prayer circle which began and ended with the fallen soldier, his charred head resting on the bosom of Lyanna.

From the ruins of the gateway, two of the enemy soldiers advanced towards the prayer circle. Zimbarra drew his blade, a delicate foil so light it might have been given to a child for his first fencing lesson, were it not for the exquisite gold wirework on the hilt and the prestigious makers mark on the blade. As the first man lashed at him Zimbarra parried the blow and flicked his own weapon under the attacker's cutlass, converting his position to a lunge which powered his weapon straight through the raider's heart.

The second man sensed his own danger and tried a more practiced approach, leading forward carefully with the tip of his sword, but Zimbarra met the blade with his own, the two touching side to side at the point where they crossed, then he turned his point slowly round the other's, like a fencing master giving a lesson to a new student, easily turning his guard, so that his own sword could pass through the opponent's defence and skewer him.

Behind him the Arch-Prelate continued to pray, his powers amplified by the efforts of those in the circle.

From the battlements, one hopeful soldier shot an arrow at the Fire Demon. It reached the glimmering sphere and then stopped, suspended in the air, for in that sphere time stood still.

The battle on the walls seemed to be dying down, but the praying went on and the gigantic demon still towered over them all. Then, just as suddenly as it had formed, the glimmering sphere disappeared as if it had never been. In that moment of horror, the demon seemed to take a mighty breath and then it spat its fire again, this time at Lyanna as she sat cradling Connor's body in her arms.

Zimbarra threw up his arm and made a chopping motion. A wall of iron sprung up in front of the spot where Connor lay. The monster's burning bile engulfed the wall and flared and flickered but did no harm to the little group who knelt in prayer behind its protection. It was the wizard's last throw. He had gone beyond his limits now and he fell to his knees exhausted, his hands stretched out on the floor to support him. His head sunk down onto the tiles, his hair turned completely white, and the wall of iron faded out of existence.

There are moments, it is said, which we never forget, although in truth we often remember little of the details of any important moment. Human memory tends to cling to one or two outstanding fragments of a situation, a single picture etched on the brain or a single sentence, even a word.

In all the remaining years of her life, whenever Lyanna reflected on this moment, she always remembered that instant when Connor opened his eyes and said one word, "Eternity."

The General sprung to his feet as the massive two-handed iron sword appeared in his hand. His first stroke was from right to left, swinging at an angle. It took the demon on the side of its knee, severing the bottom half of its leg. Then Connor spun fully round in a circle, a trick he had loved when he was much, much younger, building up speed and momentum, scything that mighty two-handed sword straight through the creature's spine and cutting it completely in half. As the broken demon's body hit the ground, the old soldier swung the blade up high and brought it down to in a great sweeping arc, to sever the monster's head from its neck, and there it lay, dead at his feet.

With their commander lost the chaotic warband suddenly lost all cohesion and began to rout. The battle was won. The enemy fled and the soldiers began to celebrate.

***

It was four days later when the three companions took their leave. The dead had been buried and corpses of the enemies had been burnt. The army column had marched out with their wounded trundled along in farm carts. The rubble had been cleared and the rebuilding of the wall was being planned. There was no longer any reason to delay. They presented themselves before the Reverend Mother and thanked her for her hospitality, then Lyanna escorted them out to the road where their horses were waiting. Some of the sisters had brought fruit for them to eat on the way and they stashed it into their saddle-bags before they mounted. Connor looked down on Lyanna and thanked her but could think of little else to say, in fact he found it difficult to think of anything except how beautiful her blue northern eyes were, then he realised that his gaze had wandered to her breasts and he quickly looked away. She touched his leg lightly and wished him well. Then the three men set off on the road leading north.

At the side of his saddle, Zimbarra carried the magical staff, wrapped up in a bale of white cloth and tied with strips of red ribbon. The red and white wrappings created a jaunty effect, but in fact, these were the only materials he had been able to beg from the nuns at short notice.

"What will you do with that?" asked Asclepius.

"Well, first I need to spend time with it, meditate with it, and learn what it really can do. I don't want to go knocking any buildings down unless I really intend to. But when I have the mastery of it then I think I will go questing down in the deserts. There are other artifacts and ancient books just waiting to be found. Would you like to come with me?"

The priest shook his head. "I have other plans. There are things I need to do while I still have the years left to do them. Our triumph over the monster has focussed my mind."

"Is your faith restored then?"

"It never needed to be restored, although it feels as if it may have been confirmed, but more important than that I have learned not to worry about it."

"So what will you do now?"

"Oh, a pilgrimage to the east, perhaps."

"So really you are just going wander off somewhere?"

"Not all who wander are lost." Asclepius laughed a little, as if enjoying a private joke.

"It's from that book again. The one I told you about, which I read when I was young. I shall wander with a purpose. There are temples and shrines I have never seen. There are libraries with ancient books, and people to meet who are masters in their fields. I have so many things to do. So many things."

"Not all who wander are lost," Zimbarra repeated. "I like the sound of that, priest. It's the sort of thing a wizard might say. I shall remember it."

They passed a family of farmers returning to their lands, who clapped and cheered as they went by.

"And what of the mighty Ranald Con Connor? What will you do?" the wizard turned the conversation towards the warrior, who seemed fully recovered from those terrible burns and not a mark on him, except that he now had almost no hair.

"I have no idea what I will do. I just wanted to get out of that place as quickly as I could. I couldn't stop thinking about those women. Better to be gone."

"No harm in thinking about women." Zimbarra sat up very straight stroking his jet black droopy moustache.

"Yes, but it's not just thinking about them. I could hardly get on my horse this morning. My prick was up like a flagpole."

"Not your fault." Asclepius called out from behind them. "It's that spell I did. Remember I told you it was a restoration spell. Rather than just curing your wounds it regenerates your whole body. Very difficult to perform. I haven't ever achieved it before, and I wasn't sure if I could actually manage it but it seems that the Gods were with us. That, and a bit of help from the Reverend Mother. It's the spell. That's what's affecting you."

"What will it do to me?"

"Oh, nothing to worry about" Asclepius was smiling now, more than they had ever seen him smile. "You should expect to be somewhat rejuvenated. You might feel quite young again. As your hair grows back you may find there aren't any grey ones. If you keep active you could lose a little bit of fat, or put on a bit of muscle."

"And this other thing? Feeling like sex all the time?"

"I don't think you should complain about that." The wizard raised his pointed eyebrows.

"But will it last forever?"

"Nothing lasts for ever." Asclepius replied softly, "The spell is so rarely accomplished that we can't really be sure what it will do, but it's not just a passing phase. You really are going to feel like a younger man. Let's suppose that in twenty or thirty years' time you might be back to where you are now. Enjoy it, man! The Gods have been kind."

"Kind indeed" Connor marveled, "But their kindness had me much in a pickle this morning, in the bath-house. It was quite a struggle to remind myself that they were women of holy orders."

"Every order is different." Asclepius mused. "These were founded to guard the temples and that's why they are allowed to use spears and axes, in fact, any weapons. It's true that they don't eat meat or drink alcohol. But they aren't celibate.

"What does that mean?" The wizard's eyebrows shot up. "They can have sex?"

"The ones they call Zealots have never had sex. If they give themselves to a partner, whether male or female then they become a Devot, but then they must love the partner with all their devotion. For them, their love for their partner becomes an act of worship to the Goddess. It's one of their principles."

"So, the red ones?" puzzled the wizard, "Where are their men now?"

"Well, those who have taken male partners can leave the convent if they wish." Asclepius explained." They might return later in life if their husband dies. Those who fought with us yesterday were mainly women who have chosen female partners, and they will probably spend their whole life living together in the convent. It's a nice enough place for women to grow old."

"Sounds like it would be a great place for me to grow old!" said Zimbarra stroking his black hair back behind his ears.

The horses walked on for a moment, their riders in silence till Connor spoke again. "Then what happens to the younger ones, the Zealots, if they don't choose a partner?"

"Well, they can stay there as well, as long as they wish." Asclepius shrugged. "Lyanna, for example, she can just stay there and serve the Goddess like the others, unless she should one day find a worthy partner whom she can devote herself to."

At that moment they realised that their horses had slowed and had now become quite stationary, pausing as the three men gazed at one another thoughtfully.

"Sometimes you must take opportunities when they arise." Zimbarra broke the silence.

"I think I have changed my mind about traveling today." replied Connor, slowly turning his horse back towards the convent. "Now that I have won my last great battle I may have to turn my attention to other things."

"Like melons?" suggested the wizard.

Adventurers

It started off as a joke and we really didn't expect it to end the way it did.

There were six of us, three couples, and we were great friends. We did all sorts of things together. Ivan and I rebuilt old sports-cars, and Sean went with me to sword-fencing class and we did karate club in an old church hall with a dusty wooden floor. The girls went shopping together and tried to find cute little coffee shops. We all got together for nights down the pub and drives in the country. We were a great bunch of friends and we had all sorts of fun, but one special thing we did, more than anything else, and that was Dungeons and Dragons. You have probably heard of it, a fantasy game played with little tin soldiers, fighting dragons and looking for treasure. Maybe you think it's a bit geeky, but for us, back then, it was a bit of a cult, our own little world which normal people could never understand. We would go round each other's houses, have a game and some food and maybe some home-made beer. We were great friends, but Dungeons and Dragons added something extra.

Then we saw an article in the press about the Reverend Green from St Mary's Church, who said that parents shouldn't let their children play these games because they could come under the influence of demons. And demons, he insisted, were not a game, they were real.

Well, of course, we were highly amused. Some dopey old vicar thought that demons were for real. We made a few jokes and had a good laugh, but then we wanted to take it one step further, well I did. To be honest, I never did know when to stop, so I wrote a letter to the editor of the newspaper. It was meant to be funny of course, "tongue in cheek" as they say.

We said that we shared the Reverend Green's concerns about demons and we wanted to help. We explained that we were a party of experienced dungeon adventurers and that if the Reverend Green would like to tell us where he saw these demons we would gladly come and fight them. We signed ourselves with the names and titles that we used to use when we played the game. I was Karl the Paladin, my girlfriend was Naomi Dragonslayer and so on. We all signed it but we used my address because I was the smart Alec who wrote the letter.

The editor of the newspaper never replied and the letter wasn't published, but that didn't matter. We had made our point and had a bit of a laugh at the Reverend Green's expense and we all kept copies of the article and the letter. I've still got mine somewhere. That was the end, or so we thought.

It was later, several months later, when an unexpected letter arrived. This was long before the days of the internet or the mobile phone. A first-class stamp was about as fast as you could get.

Dear Sirs,

Please excuse my intrusion but we find ourselves in a situation of great peril and are needful of your assistance.

For some considerable time, our family home in Lavenham has been most inconveniently infested with one or more malicious entities which we take to be demons. We have requested help and advice from the church as well as the local police but we have received no support or assistance whatsoever. Recently we contacted several national newspapers and asked them whether they would cover the story but again our pleading evoked little interest. One newspaper, however, did forward us your address and stated that they had you on record as potential experts in this field and therefore we entreat you to lend us your assistance forthwith for we are sorely discomforted and have nowhere else to seek protection.

Yours faithfully
Rupert and Dianna

Well, of course, we treated this as one hell of a joke. In fact, it seemed, the newspaper editor had played a joke on us, passing my name on to this crazy couple. But we were interested all the same. The old-fashioned language sounded very suitable for fantasy role play and the letter really was postmarked from Lavenham, a tiny little village out in the wilds of Suffolk. It was the perfect place for something creepy to happen. We even thought about those re-enactment people, who dress up as knights and vikings at the weekend to perform at shows. Maybe it was something to do with them.

There was a phone number so I gave them a call and the guy who answered played it all dead straight. He was a bit posh but very friendly. He was convinced that the cellar of his house was being haunted by a demon and he wanted us to come and sort it out. He even said it had happened before, they had records in the family of demons being exorcised from the premises or whatever, so I asked him to post me some copies and sure enough, they arrived, old historical documents in swirly handwriting from all the way back in the seventeen hundreds talking about this house being haunted and the demon being banished.

The bank holiday weekend was coming up and the weather was nice and so we thought that maybe we should all go for a drive and take a look at the place. So that was it. We decided to go for it. If it turned out to be a hoax we would just have a long weekend in the country. If it turned out to be real, then all bets were off. We filled up the cars with all sorts of things that we thought we could use and booked ourselves in at the local pub, a nice old place in the centre of the village.

Lavenham lived up to all of our expectations and more. The entire town is amazing. It's full of real medieval buildings, made from big solid timbers and whitewashed plaster. People call them Tudor houses, but they are older than Tudor, medieval really. Shops, houses, cafes, everything was like something out of a Robin Hood film. There isn't a building less than five hundred years old in the whole village. The biggest of them all was the Guildhall. Talk about stepping back in time, the place is magnificent. If you've got a spare weekend I can truly recommend it, but not if you are scared of demons!

Rupert and Dianna were a lovely old couple, delighted to see us and still completely convinced that they had a demon in the cellar. We met them in town and followed them back to their place, a half a mile down the road. That was the first real shock when we saw the size of the house. It was huge. It was a proper stately home, and bigger than the town hall. One end looked like it had started off as a castle, with crenulations and lancet windows, and then there were more modern bits built on at the other end. We had been expecting a cellar as big as a spare bedroom but, apparently, this place had cellars running around all over the place and not even a proper map of them all.

Then there was another surprise. There were no electric lights in the cellar. Well, apparently there were electric lights but they just didn't work and none of the local tradesmen were willing to go down there to fix them. So we decided to give it a miss that first evening and we just sat chatting with Rupert and Dianna and drinking their malt whisky and their red wine which I have to admit were both of a most excellent quality.

So it was at ten o'clock the next morning, with slightly fuzzy heads, that we finally set off on our quest to investigate the cellars at Lavenham House. We each took various bits of gear but perhaps the most inspired was my friend Ivan who had done a bit of pot-holing in his time and had brought along a protective helmet with a flashlight on the front, like the sort coal-miners used to wear. We had candles and flashlights as well, but that helmet was a good move. Jacqueline insisted we stop at the local church, so she could fill up a tumbler with holy water from the font. She had also bought a big carton of table salt because one of her books said demons couldn't cross a line of iron or a line of salt. I thought she was overdoing it a bit really but it's all about role-play, so why not.

The first few rooms were nothing special, just dark cellars with bits of old gardening equipment, cardboard boxes, and empty bottles. We left a candle burning in each one so as to light our way back if anything went wrong. Then we came to a big storage area which had a lot more junk in the middle and wine racks around the side and two heavy doors at the far end. We reached the right-hand door and swung it open and Sean volunteered to go in first. He always played a dwarf in our games so I think he wanted to show he was cool with underground adventures. Jacqueline followed him in, just because she was his wife I guess and I started over towards the other door.

"Have you come to find me?" It sounded like someone talking quietly but through a big amplifier, so it was soft and loud at the same time if that makes sense. The voice was behind us and I nearly died of shock. But it was only a child, perhaps ten years old, wearing a long white smock.

"And who might you be now?" asked Ivan in a pompous, half-joking sort of voice.

That might not have been a problem, but as part of the act he had raised up a crucifix, a Catholic one, the type with a little effigy of Jesus nailed onto it, and he pointed it straight towards the kid. That was when it all got a bit hairy-scary. The little guy screamed and it was the most damnably awful scream I had ever experienced in my life. That noise alone was enough to turn my belly to jelly and I staggered backward in shock towards the wall. I heard the heavy door behind me slam and I saw Lynne and Lorrie go tearing off straight out the opposite doorway, back towards where we had all come in.

The spooky kid rose up off the floor. He didn't jump, He didn't fly. He rose up off the floor slowly like he was somehow hovering in the air. His eye sockets were deadly black so his face looked more like a skeleton. Then he flicked out his hands and conjured some kind of circle of yellow flame, which seemed to shoot out in every direction at once. I ducked behind a piece of old furniture and that probably saved me because the dust sheet covering it went up like a flare. I ran down the side of the room and suddenly empty wine-bottles started flying past my head and smashing off the walls. I tripped over a box and then when I tried to get up an old shoe hit me right on the head. Somehow I managed to get out through the cellars, coughing through the smoke as I followed the trail of those candles and I didn't stop running until I was clean out of the house and gasping for breath in the middle of the front lawn. To this very day, the thing that amazes me most is that I didn't just jump in the car and go speeding straight back to London.

Rupert and Dianna were remarkably calm about the whole thing, and not the least bit surprised at the state we were in.

"Was it the child?" Asked Dianna. "Sometimes it's the child and sometimes it's the big one with wings, but we don't really know if that's two different creatures or if it's just one that makes himself look different."

I didn't even bother to answer, kneeling there on the grass on my hands and knees with my heart pumping as if I had just run a marathon.

Then I heard Rupert ask, "Where are your friends?"

Have you ever made a big mistake and then suddenly it dawned on you? Left your cash card in the machine or left your bag on the bus? Have you ever felt a sudden moment of total panic? Well, I had just witnessed a demon, a real supernatural demon, for the first time in my entire life and now it hit me that two of my best friends were still down there in that cellar, possibly fighting for their lives or possibly dead. I was numb with the shock. I couldn't even begin to imagine what to do.

"I think you all had better come with me," said Rupert most politely, walking towards the old wing of the building "Dianna, darling, please could you make us all some tea."

The room he took me into was an armoury and it would have been worth coming all the way from London just to see that on its own. There were helmets and breastplates from the English Civil War. There were muskets and rifles from Waterloo. There was even an early Victorian machine-gun. Rupert led us past all of these, and on to the far end of the room where the selection of weapons could only be described as medieval; big nasty broadswords, falchions, war-hammers, axes, and spears.

"These are the ones you need." He nodded at the collection. "These ones are iron, not steel. They've all been handed down my family over the years. Each time a demon comes through, this is what we have used to slay them"

To be honest, I didn't fancy it at all, but I saw Ivan pick up a spear, and a sack full of iron spikes so I took up a sword and a hammer. Lorrie found a big heavy iron cross that looked like it should be standing in a graveyard, and Lynne took a normal sword but grasped it in two hands to allow for the weight. We stood looking at each other and I remember thinking that it just wasn't going to happen, that we were never, never, never going to go back down that bloody cellar.

Then Ivan just said, "Well you're supposed to be the Paladin so I think you had better lead us."

It was mad. It was just so totally mad. I swung the sword round in a circle and started to run. I ran out of the armoury and straight back across the lawn and back into the house and down the stairs. I think if I had slowed down to a walk I would have stopped altogether but I just kept running, and shouting something, I don't know what, and we charged through the darkness and surged into that big room, but it was empty. The child or the demon, or whatever it was had gone.

We tapped on the heavy door, using the special knock that we always used when we turned up late at each other's houses for parties, it was kind of three taps, then one tap, then another three.

"Is it you?" Sean called.

"Yes, it's me," I called back, and the door opened.

They weren't as frightened as I was expecting, perhaps because they had slammed the door at the first scream and hadn't seen anything else.

"Careful don't disturb the salt." Warned Jacqueline. She had done it just as she said, a line of salt across the whole doorway, like a draft excluder, but for demons.

I gave Sean the war-hammer and he gave me a funny look. He always used a war-hammer when we played Dungeons and Dragons so I figured that would suit him fine. He came out into the big room and we all stood there wondering what to do next, although it was a bit obvious really as there was still the other door, the left-hand door, the one that we hadn't opened yet. But in the end, it didn't really matter because as we stood there thinking, I suddenly caught the smell of sulphur, that smell you get after a firework display, and a tiny swirl of dust or smoke started to form into some sort of pattern and in the passing of a moment the demon morphed into shape right in front of us.

I could best describe it as being like a huge pig walking on two legs. It had a face like a wild boar, big piggy ears and rough bristles of facial hair but with long sharp teeth like a shark and tiny red eyes which were absolutely glowing and alive with evil. Its hands were larger than human hands, with fingers ending in vicious claws and its feet were cloven hooves. The strangest feature of all was the wings because they looked too small to support anything of such size and weight. It was a demon, sure enough, a real demon right in front of our eyes.

Then it all just kicked off. Jacqueline had stayed put in the room with the line of salt across the door and I don't know if that made her just a bit braver than the rest of us but she threw the tumbler of holy water all over that thing and it turned towards her roaring in anger. But it didn't cross the threshold into the room. It didn't cross the line of salt. For a moment it just stood there roaring with smoke coming out of its fur wherever the Holy Water had splashed it. That gave us time to react and everyone started to move.

Ivan made a good lunge with that iron-shod spear and took the monster right through the side, while Sean belted it right on the head with the hammer. The rest of us pitched in with whatever we had. I tried to chop at its neck but I was behind it and the wings were getting in in my way.

The beast spun around and caught Sean with a hell of a slap from one of those big clawed hands but lucky for him he had raised his arms to swing the hammer so he took the full force on his arm, not his head. Ivan's spear was still stuck into the thing and he was holding on so tight that when the monster turned around it dragged him clean off his feet. Then Lynne stepped in, like that woman from Lord of the Rings and chopped her sword down on the back of its leg, but maybe not hard

142

enough to do any real damage. Lorrie swung that metal cross up in the air with both hands and whacked it down on top of its head, like a schoolgirl smacking some kid with a book.

By now the demon had managed to pull out the spear from its side and it spun right round towards me so just by good fortune the cut that I meant for its head went straight through its neck at the front. The head flipped backwards and was kind of hanging upside down as if it was a hood on the back of its neck. That must have really annoyed the beast because it came straight towards me roaring like a train. I staggered back against the wall and I remembered one move from the sword-fencing class. They call it a stop-hit. I grasped my iron long-sword with both hands and pointed it straight at its chest. As the demon threw itself at me it plunged straight on to the blade, but I managed to brace the pommel against the wall behind me and it came on at me with so much force that it drove itself all the way onto that sword. I was pinned up against the wall so that its filthy matted fur was all over me and the rotten slime from the wound in its neck was pumping right out into my head. Lorrie ran in and started battering it with that heavy iron crucifix. Then a metal point exploded from its chest where Ivan had given it another good poke from behind and very nearly speared me into the bargain.

I staggered away and picked up the hammer and I remember thinking how the poor old demon didn't really have much of a chance when there were six of us and we were all bashing it up at the same time.

So that was pretty much the end of it. The sheer weight of numbers seems to have pulled us through. We had killed the demon, or should we say vanquished it, for some people believe that demons don't really die, they just go back to the abyss from which they came. We made a bit of an effort to be sure it really was dead, we cut off the head and hammered a spike through its heart. The main thing was, we had survived, we had won, and we celebrated our sense of relief by knocking nine bells out of that dead demon carcass.

Eventually, we opened the other door, just to be sure, and to our amazement, there was nothing there. There really was nothing, no walls, no floor, no monsters, just pure swirling darkness.

"It's always been like that," Rupert told us later. "The family always talked about it. We call it the void. That's probably where they come from".

143

So we closed the door again and jammed the handle with an iron spike and Jacqueline poured some salt along the floor just in front of the door. Then we made our way back through the cellars and out into the sunlight. We dragged the demon's carcass outside and built a bonfire at the bottom of the garden, where we burnt the stinking thing till there was nothing left but ashes.

Sean's left arm was broken so we had to call up an ambulance and Jacqueline went with him to the hospital in Bury St. Edmunds. Dianna asked the rest of us to stay for lunch, but we gently turned her down and told her we would eat in Lavenham at the hotel. I think we all felt that we had experienced more than enough excitement for one morning, perhaps for a whole lifetime, and it was time to get back to somewhere normal.

Of course, we thought that was the end, but in reality, it was only the beginning. Word gets around and people get reputations. It was only a matter of time until someone else came along who was seeking assistance. There are far more of these situations than the public realise and once it's known that you have actually slain a demon there are always plenty of people lining up and asking for help. But that was the first one, the one that gave us a chance to prove ourselves. It taught us a lot.

Rupert and Dianna are lovely people. I was glad that we were able to help them. "Keep in touch," I told them. "If it ever happens again you know where to find us"

"Yes of course." Rupert smiled. "And you keep in touch too. Any time you fancy a weekend in the country the place is yours. You can go horse-riding, use the library or the armoury. Just make yourselves at home. I shall always think of you as part of the family now"

He gave me his card and I popped it in my pocket. "The Reverend Rupert Green."

The true story of Doris Bither

Doris Bither was a young mother with four children living in Los Angeles, California.

In 1984 she contacted paranormal investigators Barry Taff and Kerry Gaynor, claiming that she was being repeatedly assaulted by invisible entities. Bither alleged that she was attacked and raped by a group of invisible demons which she believed were the spirits of three men. She had, apparently made these claims to others but had been dismissed as a fantasist and a liar.

Taff and Gaynor began their investigation on August 22, 1974. The demon entities were described as being human in outline but translucent and semi-solid, like a human shape made from some kind of fog. It was said that they would frequently harass all of the occupants of the house. The children claimed that the demon spirits were frequently present and always able to appear at will, inside the building. They reported that they often felt themselves being pushed or hit when there was no-one there and suffering painful assaults which felt like being bitten or scratched. Years later when they were grown up, the children continued to support and relate the accounts of the demonic incidents.

Even the investigators felt frightened and sensed hostility whilst in the building. They did not witness the attacks as such but were aware of various phenomena such as whispered voices and strange lighting effects, like balls of light floating through the house. Taff claimed to have photographed these orbs and said the frequency and intensity of the incidents decreased with time.

The most extreme attacks took place in the bedroom when Doris was alone. She claimed that two of the demons would hold her down while the third raped her. Her children, sleeping in the adjacent room would hear her screaming and throwing objects and had witnessed severe bruising on her body, her legs, and her inner thighs. One of her children is said to have reported: "There were times when we would see it happen in front of us" said one. "It was like as if a man was standing in front of my mother and would start to beat her. Imagine a woman being beaten. You could see her being picked up and thrown around. There were sounds, noises which sounded like slaps, but there was no-one there to actually do it."

Bither was known to have had a traumatic childhood with a history of physical abuse and to have regularly misused illegal drugs as she grew older. She had also been in several abusive relationships. Her relationships with her own children were difficult and often a cause of stress. The whole family were living in conditions which can only be described as poverty. The house itself had been condemned as not fit for human habitation, on more than one occasion.

In 1982 a feature film entitled "The Entity" was produced, based on these reports.

Doris Bither died of heart failure in 1995. To this day the case remains an excellent example of the central problem facing all paranormal investigations, exorcisms, and indeed religion in general; to those who already wish to believe this story appears to provide overwhelming proof of demons and the supernatural, but to those who have already decided that they do not believe the entire story appears to be easily fabricated. Ultimately nothing can be proven or disproven and all belief is based on personal inclinations.

Underworld

I have never seen a prisoner so angry. This was no ordinary man, but a hard-boiled violent criminal, with a record as long as your arm, so the possibility of an outburst was no surprise, but this was something different. It wasn't directed at us, nor at the coppers that arrested him. He didn't seem to care about us at all, and yet he cursed and threatened and punched the table. He even banged his head against it until in the end, I had to get him by the shoulders and pull him back to stop him from hurting himself. Then he turned towards me as if he had only just recognised me and he looked me straight in the eye.

"I asked for you special Vic. You need to get them for me."

Steve Berry was a well-built lad, with a swarthy complexion and a thick mop of black curly hair. Down in Cornwall, where I grew up they tend to describe those types as "Spanish looking". In Devon, they just call them country boys. In most parts of the country people might describe him as looking like a gypsy, or a pikey, take your pick, but it always comes down to the same kind of guy. Ruffians, casual labourers, petty criminals. I've seen them drunk, I've seen them fight, and I've seen them getting away with more than they should, but I've never seen one of them quite so angry in a police station. Not till I saw Steve Berry that day.

They had called me in to work on the Sunday morning and I knew it had to be something important, though I never for one moment had any idea of what it would turn out to be. Normally I would have been taking my boy to his Colts' rugby game down the lane, but the job always has to come first. I had got used to being a detective inspector, and with all the government spending cuts there was not much chance of ever getting any higher. Young coppers can be off duty, but with

147

people like me, there's never a clean break between your private life and the job. Whoever made the decision to bring me in had made the right call, but they could never have imagined where it would lead.

Berry was a petty criminal, a serial offender, but in the past it had always been predictable, run of the mill stuff; drunk and disorderly, stolen cars, small time drug dealing, causing an affray and grievous bodily harm. You could take your pick from all that lot and more. That week, however, we had put him in the frame for a rather more serious matter relating to the disappearance of a young woman.

Mary Strawbridge was a local girl and was well known to police. Nowadays they call them sex workers. When I started we used to use the term "common prostitute". It makes no difference. Any policeman in any country knows that you can't stop the world's oldest profession. The best you can hope for is to keep it off the streets so that respectable people don't get offended and teenage kids don't get involved. Mary had grown up in Ipswich, on the north side of town. She was a good-time girl when she was younger and ended up on the game when she found herself with a kid to look after. Now that she had gone missing she suddenly had lots of family worrying about her. They hadn't seemed particularly bothered about her when she was standing outside the Royal Oak in a mini-skirt and high heels, but now she had disappeared and they all wanted answers.

Mary on her own was one thing, but it rung all the wrong bells at our end. Over the past two years, we had felt mounting pressure from on-high to deal with issues of human trafficking. The authorities were always busy watching Dover for illegal migrants, but it seems that the better-organised gangs were getting very clever at using the East Anglian coast. Grimsby, Great Yarmouth, Lowestoft, and Felixstowe are all still working ports, but poorly staffed and poorly supervised, and there are hundreds of miles of deserted beaches facing out towards Europe across the North Sea. None of it is more than two hours' drive from London, where unfortunate young women could be put to work in the twilight world of the sex industry. That was all bad enough, but the murders of five prostitutes in Ipswich a few years back marked the beginning of a new phase. Female missing persons' cases began to increase at a rate we just couldn't keep up with. It doubled in a year, then doubled again the next year and it was still growing. Local women were still disappearing, but no more bodies were turning up so it might be murder or it might be trafficking. From a sleepy backwater, we had suddenly found ourselves on the front line, and on the front page. Everyone from the Sunday papers to the Salvation Army was calling for action, and we had to be seen to be doing something. Our usual informants hadn't been much use. Some of them said they might have heard rumours of a foreign gang controlling the people trade, others were suggesting that there could possibly be a ruthless new operator on the local scene, but nobody really knew anything, and if they did they were afraid to say. We had clear information that Steve Berry was the last person to be seen with Mary Strawbridge. We hoped that might give us some sort of lead into these disappearance cases.

When our lads had a tip-off that Berry was holed up in the back room of the Rose and Crown it was no easy matter to arrest him. He had plenty of muscle and he came out punching but we had few big lads of our own, old style coppers who could handle themselves, and they soon had him handcuffed and into the van. In the morning when he had sobered up he was beside himself with rage. He didn't ask for a lawyer, though he knew his rights well enough. The only sense they got out of him was when he asked for me by name. Me of all people, would you believe? I must have arrested him more times than any other officer in the force, and we had given each other a few hard knocks down the years, but it seems he had a bit of respect for me as a straight copper who would hear him out and get things done. So there I was, down in the cells on my morning off, and him in one hell of a mood.

Smoking is banned in all public buildings now, but we sometimes bend the rules a bit in the nick, if we think it will help to get them talking, so they had given him a couple of ciggies before I got there, just to help him get calmed down. It wasn't working. He was cursing and swearing and swinging his fists in the air. Then I stopped him banging his head on the table and he looked up at me and he said it;

"I asked for you special Vic. You need to get them for me. They killed Colin"

That was the bombshell. "They killed Colin. There weren't no need to do that."

Everyone knew Colin Saunders. He was a hardened villain with a passion for violence. I had nicked him myself more than once. Colin and Steve went way back to schooldays. My sergeant glanced across the room with eyebrows raised. Colin was the vicious one, and Steve was his big mate who always backed him up.

"Who killed him, Steve? You know you need to tell us"

"I am telling you. I want to tell you. The bastards at the farm killed him."

"Which farm are we talking about Steve? Which farm?"

"Tasker's Farm, near Dunwich."

It didn't ring any bells with me but I called in a civilian staffer and sent her to find out, while we dragged as much information as we could out of Steve. He admitted picking up Mary Strawbridge, the previous weekend but denied any kind of foul play. He had been sent to collect Mary from the pub while Saunders picked up two other women then dropped the three of them off at the farm. Berry had followed in his own car and stayed parked on the road outside, listening to the football on the radio. Ipswich versus Norwich was a local derby game, and taken very seriously by the locals, even though the two towns were 40 miles apart. A few minutes had passed, and Steve wasn't really paying attention. Then quite unexpectedly Saunders had come tearing out of the building towards his BMW, but before he got close they had shot him. Berry saw the whole thing, a shotgun blast in the legs to bring him down and a bullet in the head to finish him off.

"Didn't you do anything then Steve?"

"Nothing I could do. I don't carry a shooter. You know that. I just had to stay quiet and hope they didn't see me."

"And did they?"

"No, of course, they fucking didn't. If they had seen me I wouldn't fucking well be here talking to you. Would I? There's a great big shed right next to where I was parked so they couldn't see me at all from the house. I only saw them when they come out in the yard after Colin and they all had their back to me right then so I just sat tight. Then when they had gone in I let my motor free-wheel down the hill till it was safe to start the engine."

"That was a week ago Steve, so why did you not come and tell us straight away then?"

"Because I was going to find a way to fucking kill them myself. That's why. Now I can't do that if I'm locked up in here so I need you to nick the bastards."

So that was it. Steve Berry sang like a canary and gave us as much as he could. He wasn't going to protect the scum who had killed his best friend, and if he couldn't get revenge on them he was quite happy to let us do it for him. Forget all this nonsense you hear about honour among thieves, they'll cut each other's throats anytime it suits them. We questioned him for quite a while before he even asked about a lawyer. It didn't matter by then. He had told us all we wanted to know.

Something serious was going on at that farm. Berry knew that Colin was expecting to be paid in drugs, not cash, and that gave us the unholy trinity we had been searching for, drugs, guns, and disappearing people, the three great trading commodities of the modern criminal underworld. It was two o'clock in the afternoon when we put in our request for the use of weapons, and by six we had got the ok.

We had a joint briefing with the men from the Eastern Region firearms unit at four o'clock the following morning and were ready to move at five, so as to hit the target site before six. It's generally agreed that dawn is the best time for a raid. Usually, the villains are still asleep and even if they are half awake it's difficult for them to put up a fight when they are running about in their underpants and bare feet. Also, there's less chance of any bystanders getting hurt or getting in the way, not that we were concerned about that on this occasion. The farm was fairly isolated, nothing else for a mile or two. Our main concern was for the girls in there. We didn't know if they were still alive, but we had to make that assumption. A surprise raid was our best chance of clearing everyone out with minimum casualties, at least that was what we thought.

The building was no longer part of a working farm. When the last owner died his neighbour had taken over the land but sold off the farmhouse. This kind of amalgamation is very common in modern farming. Berry was dead right about the approach to the place. We were able to park our lead vehicle on the road, behind a big shed, where we would see the gateway and the farmyard, but we couldn't be seen from the house. That would be our command car. The rest of the vans were further back down the road out of sight.

There are no stone quarries in Suffolk, at least none that I know of, and you can see that from the building style of the older farmhouses. This place had red brick up to three feet and then plastered wall above that. The plaster might have been a pretty shade of pink at one time but it was now fairly drab with many years of weathering. The main house was two stories, but at one end there was a three storey wing with a half-timbered gable. Further back there were sheds and stables and a large barn, but no sign of any animals. There were several cars in the farmyard, not just the usual Range Rover that every farmer in the country seems to have. Some of them looked quite pricey and I noticed one was a BMW with Albanian number-plates.

On a normal suburban house we would have knocked down the front door, then rushed up the stairs, but today our luck was in. The men who were sent to cover the back reported an old-style sash window had been left partly open which gave us the chance to get in quietly. I don't know what you think a farmhouse should look like inside, maybe old oak beams and antique furniture. This place wasn't quite like that. There were patterned wallpapers and patterned carpets that might have been fashionable in the seventies, long red curtains made from fake velvet and furniture that was modern, but grubby and worn. The place smelled of dampness, take-away food, and cigarette smoke. There was one other thing that struck me straight away. There were a couple of video cameras on tripods, and several items of sexual paraphernalia, handcuffs, chains, a leather gag and a couple of horse whips. Someone had been making home movies, but not the kind you would want to share with the neighbours.

The first priority was to rush up the stairs and try to catch the villains while they were still in bed. We were all wearing body armour but the specialists from the firearms unit led the way and it seemed to go pretty well, none of the bedroom doors had locks and some of them weren't even shut. We went straight in and got them bang-to-rights before they had really woken up. It's always the best way and we had got it spot-on. Except we hadn't got them all.

At one end of the farmhouse, there was a wing set at right angles to the rest, so the ground plan of the house would have looked like a capital T. Well that bit at the top of the "T" had another floor higher than the rest of the house. We had seen it from the outside but we just hadn't located the stairway yet, moving about in the semi-darkness. It turned out that there were a couple of more suspects up there and they must have heard us. Just as we slapped the handcuffs on the prisoners, some lunatic came running round a corner blazing off shots from a pistol. I was jumping for cover so quick I didn't even see what anyone else was doing, but the sergeant in charge of the firearms unit was a crafty old bugger, and a crack shot, so it turns out. He had held back at the top of the staircase, and as soon as this guy popped up firing the sergeant took one calm shot and that put him down. Then another fellow called out from above. He said he didn't have a gun and he wanted to come down. None of ours were hurt so we cuffed the prisoners and read them their rights and then sent for medics to look after the wounded man. It seemed like a job well done.

Two members of the firearms unit stayed there with the prisoners in the bedrooms while we went back down to search the ground floor. I had a flashlight and so did my sergeant. The kitchen was huge with a wood-burning stove and a stone flagged floor. In the middle of the room was an old solid-oak table, the only decent antique in the place, and on the table there was a large ashtray, a bag of what looked like cannabis and a shotgun.

It was while I was looking at these that they told me they had found the women, or at least they had found some women. In an outhouse behind the kitchen, there were three females with lengths of chain padlocked around their necks. They were badly upset, and only partly dressed with no shoes and smudged makeup, but they were alive, and one of them was indeed Mary Strawbridge. I stuck two of my female officers in there and sent for blankets from the vans, and bolt cutters to set them free.

The girls should have been pleased to see us, no matter what their previous views on coppers might have been. We didn't expect them to jump for joy, but I was taken aback by just how terrified they seemed to be. They were crying and panicking and pleading all at the same time, perfectly normal for trauma victims in shock, but I felt we were missing something. Then one of them, in between the tears and the hyperventilation blurted out something about "the others", and that changed everything. If there were other women here on the farm they might still be in danger, and if there were other gangsters we might all be in danger. They had probably heard the gunfire from the bedroom and could either have run away or been getting ready to take us down.

I took the advice of the firearms commander, and it made sense. We would work our way through the buildings safely and sensibly, minimising the risk to our men. If a villain got away we could always catch him further down the road, but we weren't going to put a copper's life at risk and make some poor woman a police widow.

Two men covered the front of the barn, and two went around the back of it, while the rest of us searched the stables. I don't remember what I was expecting but it certainly wasn't this. In the very first section, there were considerable amounts of drugs, probably just imported from the Suffolk coast. We could see how they had done it. They had bought five-litre plastic containers full of some stuff for the building trade, liquid chemicals to make cement waterproof or something similar. They had poured out the liquid somewhere and pushed an empty plastic bag in through the neck of the container. Then they had filled the bag with powder using a funnel. When the bag was nearly full they had tied it at the top and sealed it, then let it drop down into the container. Then all they had to do was refill the container and put the top back on. If anyone took the top off, all they would see was this white gluey liquid, and if they tested it, no worries, just waterproofing. Here in the stable some of the containers had been cut open and the bags of drugs were being taken out. This was turning into a good days work and we hadn't even had breakfast yet.

The second section of the stable block was empty of drugs. There was a bucket in the corner and a pile of blood-sodden straw on the floor and on top of the straw lay the corpse of Colin Saunders. I have seen murder victims before and I think I could have handled that as I moved on quickly to the third section of the stables, but the sight which met me there was even more sordid. The naked bodies of two adult females were dangling from the roof beam on meat-hooks, for all the world like something in an old-fashioned butcher's shop. One of them had no legs. I ran for the nearest door and struggled out into the farmyard, where I vomited, not just once, but two or three times. Then someone shot me.

***

Soldiers in battle can be badly hurt by a bullet, even when they're wearing body armour. That's because a high-velocity rifle bullet has a lot more power behind it. But this was just a handgun, a pistol, the bullets are much smaller and although it kicked me backwards and knocked me off my feet, I got nothing worse than a slight bruise and a nasty shock.

Before I could get up there were a few more shots and then silence. There must have been someone sitting just inside the barn. They hadn't been able to see us from where they were, not until I came crashing out of the stables, spewing up my guts in the farmyard. That's when they had shot me, but then as they came out into the open the firearms unit had shot back and had taken them down.

I remember someone helping me to sit up. Even though it was still quite grey in the early morning I remember the scene quite clearly. At the bottom end of the yard, two of our men were taking the prisoners towards the van, and by the stable door, the three women were standing wrapped in blankets with the women officers. Then, from somewhere, there was a roar. I suppose it was like a lion, though I have never been to Africa. For all I know it could have been anything. The women in the blankets began to scream, gunfire rang out and the place went crazy. A dark shape like nothing I've ever seen crashed right in among the firearms squad sending them reeling like toys. One flew up in the air and landed right beside me with his leg at an impossible angle. I saw another one lying down in the middle of the yard, his weapon gone. A couple of ours were firing but I didn't know at what. Someone else was shooting from somewhere and I saw one of our men in uniform go down. Then there was that flash of black again. I have often wondered if such a thing can really exist, a flash of black. It wasn't a shadow, it was too powerful for that. It wasn't simply a dark object, it wasn't solid, in fact, it was the exact opposite of solid it was like a pulse of energy, an awareness, a threat, but my lasting impression was just that it was black. Then there was an awful scream. I was on my feet now and struggling to believe my eyes. It was if a statue had come to life. The thing which was standing right in front of me was beyond comprehension. Imagine a bull, a fully grown powerful bull, with hooves and horns all as big as you could ever see on any bull, but walking almost upright on its hind legs, ten feet tall with claws for hands and a mouth with teeth like a wolf. What I saw in that yard was something like that, but my words will never be able to describe the horror I felt when it seized up one of those helpless women and tore off her head with its teeth.

An armed officer stepped forward and opened fire. He was as brave a man as I have ever seen. He stood with his legs spread and his M4 carbine levelled from the shoulder, and he began pumping bullets into that beast. Any one of those bullets would have brought a man down but this creature just turned round to face him and walked towards him almost with a swagger. He kept on shooting till it lashed him with its claws and sent him spinning against a wall, with his body armour ripped and the padding falling out like a burst pillow. It leaned forward, bending over him like a dog sniffing a bone, putting its face right up to his and those hellish jaws opened with another roar. Its teeth were as long as my fingers.

155

I did the only thing I could do. I ran in close behind its shoulder, clutched my Glock 17 pistol in both hands and started shooting straight into its brain from just behind the left ear. It turned on me with a devilish scream and swatted me away with the back of one hand.

I could hear the commander of the firearms unit shouting "Fall back! Fall back!" but I couldn't see anything at all, except that giant beast which was now moving towards me. I could see perfectly well of course, but faced with such a vision of chaos nothing else registered. My entire attention was focussed on that one impossible incarnation of horror. I rolled to one side and struggled to my feet, with the blood pounding painfully in my head. I could hear my own heartbeat and yet I couldn't hear the gunshots or the screams of the women. Perhaps I was already in shock by then, or perhaps I was deafened by the gunfire. Acting simply on instinct I levelled the gun and fired off another five rounds, aiming at its body but not knowing if any of them found a target. The state I was in I could have been shooting clear over his head. Then something grabbed me from behind and pushed me out of the way, holding me up so my feet could only just touch the ground, forcing me forward and dragging me right out of the gates at the bottom of the yard. It was my sergeant, Charlie Avis, and there is no doubt that he had just saved my life. Two men from the firearms team were standing on the road pouring in bullets while the rest of us struggled back towards the vans, and somehow, thank god, we got away.

By ten in the morning, the county police headquarters was like a lunatic asylum. We had grown men crying like children, hardened coppers trembling too much to even drink their tea. We had senior officers calling each other idiots and liars, we had stress counsellors and publicity specialists and union reps from the police federation, and of course, we had hostages and prisoners terrified with fear. The only one thing we didn't have was the press. This was to be a totally private affair. We have all signed the official secrets act and not a word was leaked.

We had captured six men and rescued the three girls we went looking for, but one officer had concussion, one had a broken leg and one had severe lacerations to his chest and his back. Apart from myself, two had been hit by bullets, and one of those was critical in hospital. The worst news was that one of the women we went to rescue had been killed, torn apart by that nightmarish thing.

No-one knew what the hell it was. A monster? A man in power armour? A mad bull? An alien from outer space? We were too much in

156

shock to believe our own eyes. It happens sometimes. The brain tries to rationalise things. I had once done a training course on dealing with victims of trauma as witnesses. They had warned us that people who have suffered an overload of stress often lost track of the truth, "Searching after Meaning" he had called it. The mind tries to cope with what has happened by changing the details of the story so that it will make sense.

When they pulled me aside and started talking to me I really didn't get what they meant. I was telling them everything I could but they didn't seem to understand any of it, they just didn't. I remember I started to get irritated because they weren't really making any sense. I might have been losing track. In fact, from that point onwards I really don't remember anything, until I woke up in a cell.

"Morning Sir!" It was Bungle, a veteran custody sergeant, just a year from retirement and as good a bloke as you could ever meet in the nick. "Here's a mug o' tea and I'm getting you sent up a full English breakfast from the canteen."

It turned out that they had sedated me and put me to sleep in a cell for the night, though I don't remember anything of that. I had a bugger of a headache and a mouth like the inside of a bus driver's glove. It was like having a monster of a hangover without any of the pleasant memories of getting drunk. At the time I wasn't too happy about it, but I suppose looking back they had done the right thing. The full English breakfast soon arrived and that got me feeling a bit better, but the more I started to feel sorted, the more I got to worrying about what the hell had happened yesterday. Something awful was going on, or perhaps I was just going mad.

The rest of my boys had been sworn to secrecy and sent home, but I had been kept in for a reason. All that became clear when they told me I had a briefing lined up in the Chief Constable's office. No normal policeman ever set foot in that place, with its fitted carpets and mahogany table. They made jokes about it in the canteen, why did he need his own private toilet and all that sort of thing. Now I was in there and feeling bewildered. He shook my hand, as if we were old friends, and pressed me to sit down in a real leather armchair while his personal assistant dished out latte coffee in those trendy china cups, the big wide ones. There was another senior officer present, a superintendent from SO19, the elite firearms unit from Scotland Yard in London. I had seen his lads unloading their kit from a couple of vans in our car-park.

Superintendent Phillips was his name, though he asked me to call him John. Once we had our coffee the Chief Constable told his secretary to leave the room. That left just the three of us, and one other man in plain clothes whom I didn't know.

"As far as the rest of the world is concerned" Superintendent Phillips began, "Everything that happened yesterday never happened at all. None of us can ever speak about it, we can never write about it, never give an interview or make a film. Officially it just didn't happen."

The three men exchanged glances while I just said nothing and kept trying to look calm and collected.

"But of course we know that it did happen, and we believe every word of what you have said, Victor. That's why you were, 'put to sleep' last night. We need someone who has had eyes on the inside to help us sort this out, and you were the most senior officer at the scene yesterday. We need you, Victor. I know it's a lot to ask after what you have been through yesterday, but we really need you, and your boss says you are tough enough to see it through."

It was absolutely the last thing in the world I wanted. I had been scared shitless out there and I still didn't know what we were dealing with. All I really wanted was to get home to my wife and the two kids. If they had offered me early retirement with my pension at that very moment I would have taken it like a shot, but all they really offered me was another chance to go back out there and get killed.

Then I thought of the lads who had gone with me yesterday. The men from our own local firearms team who had been tossed about by that thing, and I remembered Avis pushing me out of harm's way, otherwise, it could have been me, and then I heard my own voice saying. "So what's it all about?"

Phillips put down his coffee and posed for a moment with his hands on the arms of the chair.

"Victor. I would like to introduce you to Jason Stark. Jason is a civilian consultant who works with SO5."

Well, that was a surprise for a start. SO5 is a specialist section of the Metropolitan Police. Last time the special operations units were reorganised it was tasked with investigating child sexual abuse, a grim area to work in, but a growing source of concern for both the public and the politicians.

"Sorry Sir," I said. "But there must be a misunderstanding. All of the females in the case were adults as far as I could see. I don't know of any link to children."

"Strictly speaking Inspector, children are not my concern." Jason Stark was in his early forties. Slim, tall and clean-shaven, he could easily have passed for an off duty army officer. His eyes were steely and searching, deeply set either side of a hooked nose. He reminded me of a picture I had seen of the Duke of Wellington, or if he had worn the right sort of hat, he could have been Sherlock Holmes.

"I am a civilian consultant to the Metropolitan Police." He said, in a public school accent. "They call for me when they need me. My specialist area is the occult."

"The occult? For SO5?"

"Yes, the occult for SO5. There are frequently cases relating to minors which also involve the occult. Often it's when we get immigrant families carrying out exorcisms on children they think are possessed. Then something goes wrong and I get called in. That, however, is perhaps the least frightening side of our work. Unfortunately, it can be very much worse. We have had to deal with quasi-religious cults which practised systematic child sexual abuse, murder for body parts and even human sacrifice by satanic groups. So when SO5 think there is an occult dimension they call me in. Today, however, I am here at the request of SO19."

It was a bit of a relief really, to hear him talking about the occult because I quite frankly had no idea what we had experienced at that farm and I desperately needed an explanation which could answer a few impossible questions. He could have told almost anything at that moment and I would have taken it in.

"So, what's the connection?"

"Well we can't be sure until we get there, but we think this may be an interpenetration scenario. We get them from time to time. A non-corporeal life form succeeds in reaching the earthly plane and attempts to establish a foothold. It has to be dealt with before a rift can be opened."

"A non-corporeal life form?" I asked him. "What the hell is that supposed to mean?"

"It means a demon, Inspector Strong." Stark looked at me straight and he was deadly serious. "We are most likely dealing with a demon."

159

Suddenly my sense of reality snapped back and I started thinking like a hard-boiled copper again. "You can't be serious. A demon? Nobody is going to believe that!"

"We don't want them to believe it." He came straight back at me. "That's the last thing we want. If there was ever a moment when the general public realised that it was possible to gate in demons from other planes of existence they would all start giving it a try and we would quickly be over-run. Look how much trouble the idiots have caused by just flying drones over airports or firing lasers at aircraft. We have to keep this sort of thing secret at all costs.

"Has it ever happened before?"

"More times than you would want to believe. Following the Mothman incident in West Virginia in 1966 both MI5 and the CIA set up projects to monitor paranormal intrusions. The first priority is always to eradicate the creature. The second priority is to keep it secret.

"And is it really possible that someone could deliberately call them in?"

"Aleister Crowley did, in 1914. At the start of the First World War, after the Germans had captured Mons, the French army was in total chaos and the British were in full-scale retreat. Crowley was an occultist who had friends in high places in the British establishment and they called upon him to gate in a non-corporeal to disrupt the German advance."

"The Angels of Mons?"

"That's it. Not a legend after all. Just a closely kept secret."

"And what about you?" I asked him, "Have you ever experienced any of this yourself?"

"Do you remember that case a few years back?" Stark put down his coffee cup. "The remote Scottish Island where there were rumours of a satanic cult and child abuse? That was one of mine, except there was really no child abuse involved. Some damned fools had summoned up a demon and then they didn't know how to control it. We invented the child abuse story as an excuse to evacuate the island while we got things sorted out."

"So what about those women at the farm? What are they doing in all of this?" As soon as I had asked the question I had a feeling that I wasn't going to like the answer.

"I suspect they are food, Inspector." Jason Stark looked me right in the eye, without even a hint of emotion. "The demon needs to eat, and the men who are serving him don't want to be eaten, so they pick up a few women who won't be missed, maybe have sex with them if they fancy it, and then pass them on to be fed to the demon. Have you had many disappearances around here recently?"

I looked across at the Chief Constable, who coughed slightly and raised his eyebrows. "One could say that."

"Are you an exorcist then?" I tried to change the subject. I was trying to take it seriously now and I thought it was a reasonable question.

"I have done exorcisms in the past, but that isn't what we need here, not as far as I can tell. Think of demon-possession as a kind of long-range remote control. Most demon possessions involve a human or animal being taken over by the spirit of a demon, but the demon itself is not in this world. That is why you need an exorcism, to drive the demon spirit out of the human body, then it disappears back to wherever the demon really is."

"The situation which you have here is much more serious. I am trying to explain to you that the actual demon itself has managed to get a foothold on earth. It is actually here, physically here. It has made the journey into our world and we have to take it out. If we leave it more trouble will follow, I assure you. We have to kill it, Inspector. We have to kill it straight away and we need you to be part of the team."

It isn't easy to be surprised when you have had a long-term career in the police force, but by this point, I was almost in shock. There were a hundred questions I could have asked without ever believing any of the answers. So I just said what he wanted to hear.

"It doesn't worry me, Sir. What do you want me to do?"

There and then he ran me through the basics of how to deal with demons. He was so matter-of-fact about it, you might have thought we were dealing with a cat that had got stuck up a tree. But no, he was teaching me how to fight a demon. The most simple precautions were defensive measures, magic circles, protective charms, even symbolic tattoos to protect against possession. To actually fight them, and to hurt them, would take iron weapons, not steel because iron was a totally base metal and could not co-exist with their ethereal life forms. I think what he meant was that anything else pretty much passed through them, like a knife cutting through a cloud of mist, but iron hit them and damaged them just like any normal body. The bullets we had been firing the day before would have been made of lead, covered in an outer shell of cupronickel, that's what they mean by a full metal jacket. From what I

161

was hearing now, those bullets could maybe hurt the thing but they couldn't kill it.

To actually kill a demon, totally and completely, he said there were spells, but that took time, and the creature wasn't just going to stand there and let us do it, not unless we had trapped it or disabled it first. Another possibility was to find an amulet or lucky charm of some sort, in which the monster kept its life. If that amulet was destroyed then the life contained within it would jump back to the ethereal plane and the demon's body here on earth just dropped dead, and could be burnt. There were also special weapons, enchanted with spells, though they were very rare and hard to find.

"Do you have any of these weapons?" I asked hopefully.

He nodded and took out a small wooden case, about the size of a paperback book, lined with purple velvet inside. On the velvet lay the smallest dagger I have ever seen. The blade was shorter than the handle. I looked at in disbelief. It was too short to even cut through an apple at one go.

My expression must have betrayed my thoughts because Stark really did take the words out of my mouth.

"You are wondering how anyone could ever get close enough to use this without being killed first. I know. But beggars can't be choosers Inspector. It took me years to track this one down and I don't know of any others outside the Vatican treasury. It's all we have got."

"My men are trained for this." Phillips broke in. "They have weapons which will disable the monster so that Jason is able to finish it off."

***

At least we were going in broad daylight this time. Darkness gave us no advantage over a demon, in fact probably the opposite as we figured that he might well be able to see in the dark. It seemed quite surreal to be standing in a pleasant country lane on a warm spring afternoon, with a team of men wearing full tactical gear and preparing to kill a demon. Their weapons were something to behold. Everyone, including me, had a Heckler and Koch MP5/10, which is a larger calibre version of the normal 7.62 submachine gun used by police forces all over the world. The MP5/10 uses 10mm ammunition, and these guys had their own specialist bullets made from solid cast iron. Two of them also had wide barrelled guns, like the kind we generally use for rubber bullets. They could fire a sort of barbed spear, but their range was limited because they had a bobbin of nylon wire that would unravel as the harpoon flew towards its target. Two more carried sawn off pump-action shotguns loaded with iron ball bearings the size of a pound coin. We all wore protective helmets, not normal police issue but more like those worn by the goal-keepers in ice-hockey games, a network of welded iron bars coming down over our head and neck, quite literally designed to stop us getting our heads bitten off.

This time we set up at a road junction two hundred yards from the farmhouse and advanced to the scene on foot. Two snipers set themselves up where they could establish a crossfire of the site to guard us as we moved forward. When we came into the farmyard it was empty, apart from the parked cars, and we could see that someone, or something, had cleaned up. There were some bloodstains but no bodies, and any equipment which had been dropped in the struggle was now gone, though there were still shell cases where two of our men had stood by the gate blazing off rounds to cover our escape. We checked the house and stables where we had been yesterday but they were clear. It was obvious to us all that the big barn was where the danger was most likely to be found.

The SO19 boys had their own inspector, a ginger-haired Scotsman called Derek MacKinnon. He was a little bit intense maybe, but he knew what he was doing and I could see he inspired confidence in his men. He chose six of them to go with him in the first wave including the two with the shotguns. Jason Stark came with us as well and I give him credit for that. He was wearing a tweed jacket and a tie. You would have thought he was out for a day at the races, not a fight to the death with a flesh-eating demon. I had the option to stay outside but I wanted to see it through so that made nine of us. One of them had put a video camera on a stick around the corner to see what was inside the barn, but it all seemed pretty quiet. Too quiet I thought, after yesterday. MacKinnon gave the word and we stepped forward into the darkness together. I was terrified, to be honest, and I feel certain that the others were scared as well, but it was the only thing we could do.

The two with the harpoons stood by the door and four others stayed outside with Phillips at the entrance. It is very unusual for a superintendent to be out in the field, but I suspected that John Phillips was old school and enjoyed getting out of the office.

163

Inside the barn, it was gloomy but not dark. The first thing that struck me was the smell. There were certainly chemicals in there, something volatile, like amphetamine perhaps, but there were also worse smells, a bit like sour milk, sewage and Sunday roast all mixed together.

Part of the barn was being used for storage. There were boxes and sacks and pallets with more sacks. We passed by all of that and moved further in. There were remnants of the days when it had been a working farm, an old tractor and various trailers to go with it, a field harrow, and the big metal scoop that you put on the front of a mechanical digger. There were rusty old tools and bits of leather harness hanging from hooks and nails on the wooden beams. We were so busy looking around that we didn't really look at the floor, not until Stark almost tripped over something and uttered a muffled curse. He had stood on an arm. It was a human arm. It was a human arm from which the meat had been stripped, or perhaps I should say gnawed, for there were clear striations on the bone, or in layman's terms, tooth-marks. As we moved towards the back end of the barn we found dozens of them, femurs, ribs and tibs, all sorts of human bones, many of which showed signs of having been gnawed and eaten by some ferocious beast.

"Fuck me!" I suddenly thought. "What if there's a whole bunch of these demons? We would have no chance. We would end up just like these poor bastards."

I deliberately took my eyes away from the bones on the floor and tried to look upwards instead, just trying to block out that terrifying thought, but the first thing I saw was a wooden crossbeam running the full width of the back wall, about ten feet up from the ground. On the crossbar sat a row of human heads, some of them skulls, some of them covered in withered flesh, some still fresh and lifelike. The bastard! These were trophies. It was eating these prisoners then keeping their heads as trophies. I felt like throwing up but I made an effort to fight it down, knowing how much trouble it had caused me last time. We moved along towards the corner with the tractor. I was trying not to think of what we might find next.

Once again I had that sensation that there was a flash of blackness. I think I felt it before I saw it. Maybe that saved me. It came at us from behind but I was already starting to turn. I dropped to the side and it missed me. The rest of the team were knocked over like skittles. Crouched right beneath the beast I saw it toss one lad right up in the air with its horns, and smash another against the floor with those massive clawed fists. I rolled between its feet and desperately threw myself sideways, taking shelter under a solid old wooden workbench. It was an awkward place to get into, wriggling painfully over metal toolboxes and broken spades, bits of plumbing pipes and vehicle spare parts. One massive hoof stamped down right next to me and I could smell the stench of its body. I forced myself inwards as far as I could, then I banged my head on something which hurt like hell. By the time I opened my eyes again the beast has just about gone past me and by twisting my head around I was looking at it from behind, the powerful legs, the huge hairy hind-quarters, and the big broad muscular back. For a moment I could only think what an ugly arse-hole it had, much like a schoolboy looking at the monkeys in a zoo. Then the shooting started and that brought me back to reality.

One of the SO19 lads must have got off a couple of rounds because I saw holes as big as a pound coin, bursting out like mini-volcanos from that part of the lower back where any normal creature would have its kidneys. I could even hear a buzz, like a mosquito sort of noise as the rounds whizzed by. The shots had gone right through the thing but they didn't slow it down at all. I suddenly realised I was in double jeopardy now. Any bullets they fired at the monster had a good chance of hitting me so I tried to crawl out from under the bench, in the opposite direction, away from the demon, but whatever it was that I had hit my head on was too big and awkward to climb over. It seemed to be some sort of grappling iron or the anchor for a small boat, and in the end, I did manage to flip it one side and crawl through. Looking back I could see we were in trouble. Several men were down on the floor, whether wounded or dead I really couldn't tell, but one was totally covered in blood. Three more were on their knees and trapped in the corner, watching with horror as the beast swung one man by the legs and viciously smashed his body this way and that, first against the tractor and then against the opposite wall.

I could see they were all going to die, and they knew it. The look on their faces told me that they knew it. They had nothing left to fight with. Behind me I heard MacKinnon shout "Victor, get down," but I wasn't in the mood for getting down. I picked up that old anchor, with a bit of rusty old chain rattling from it, and I took a short run towards the fight. I sprung up on the big rear wheel of the tractor and took a swing at the creature's head, but I didn't quite get it right and without any real intent I fell forwards and landed on top of the monster it as it bent down towards those three guys in front of it. For a single mad moment, I found myself riding piggy-back on a demon, how many middle-aged men could ever say that?

Then I struck. I swung that anchor with all the force I could muster, the sort of stroke you would use with a hammer if you were trying to knock tiles off the bathroom wall, not just letting it swing, but whipping it down with as much muscle as I could get behind it, driving the barbed iron fluke at the end of the arm deep into that repulsive little eye, and into whatever it had for a brain.

The creature turned its head round to the right, the fresh human blood of its victims running from those massive teeth, left hand reaching across its chest and up over its shoulder to try to get at me. I dropped to the floor and rolled away again, just as some of the marksmen retrieved their weapons and started to fire. The demon staggered about a bit, with its hands up to its face. I think it would have tried to pull the anchor out if it could, but it was at the wrong angle, or it might have got snagged on some bone or something.

Jason Stark was shouting but I couldn't hear him over the noise of the guns. I picked one up from the floor and joined in too. The Heckler and Koch can run through its magazine in ten seconds. That was how long it took the team to put a hundred bullets into the thing, but it hardly seemed to be affected at all.

Then there were two loud blasts, amazingly loud. I thought someone was using thunderflash grenades, but then I saw the harpoons smacking into the monster's back, their spring-loaded tips expanding inside its body, the nylon lines stretching back towards somewhere behind me. The men at the other end of those lines were desperately trying to tie them to something but the demon turned towards them screaming in rage and pain. It staggered a bit but it wasn't ready to lie down and die. Instead, it turned sideways, facing me directly. I saw the intensity of the hatred in its one good eye and I knew it was going to kill me.

That was when MacKinnon stepped in, the ginger-haired inspector from SO19. He had one of the large bore shotguns and he placed it point blank against the monster's knee and fired, then pumped the reload and fired again. It was an amazingly brave thing to do, and it gave us an edge when we needed it. Tangled in the wires, shot in the knee and struggling with the rusty old anchor that I had jammed into its eye, the monster staggered to one side and then fell over, bouncing off the old tractor and landing on its back.

I could see what the obvious move had to be and I grasped hold of that old field harrow, tipping it up on one end. A harrow is a metal grid, almost as big as a garage door, with large spikes sticking out of one side. They drag it face down behind a tractor to break up the lumps of earth after the land has been ploughed. Think of an Indian bed of nails, turned upside down, but an awful lot bigger and heavier. It took all my strength to get it off the ground at all. At the rugby club we used to practice our scrummaging by pushing a builder's truck down the asphalt path behind the clubhouse, but this took a lot more effort than that. When I had it up on one end I just lifted it a few inches off the ground and heaved myself forward. I staggered forwards three or four steps and then lost my balance and came crashing down straight on top of the monster. Half a dozen of the harrow spikes embedded themselves in its head and chest. I had gone down with it and so there I was for a moment, lying on top of that old iron frame, looking through the grid and straight into the face of the monster, as it lay there with the anchor still wedged into its face.

I saw a trouser leg from the corner of my eye and I suddenly realised that the shooting had stopped. Jason Stark crouched down beside me as calm as could be, leaned towards the monster and punched it in the neck, or at least that was what I thought, then I saw he had hold of that tiny little dagger. He stabbed it just once and with an awful groan it was dead. It was like switching off a lamp. One minute it was a terrifying giant and the next it was dead meat. The troopers from SO19 helped me up and then dragged the stinking body of the beast off their inspector. With so many of their own lads injured they weren't exactly celebrating, but they hugged each other and clasped hands, their emotional release very clear to see, all apart from Jason Stark who just stood there dusting the dirt off his tweed jacket, no smiles, no cheers, just business as usual.

There was nothing else for me to do. There were a few handshakes as they put me into one of the ambulances and I was driven away. Actually I didn't think I needed to be in an ambulance but with the mission over I think it was just their subtle trick for getting me out of the way. Then the veil of secrecy closed in. These people had all their routines worked out. I have no idea what happened to the men we had arrested. They just vanished into the system somewhere and their story never came out. The two surviving sex workers never came back to town. I think they were put into some sort of scheme like witness protection, except it's designed to stop spies and various other people from speaking out rather than just aiming to protect them. In my opinion, wherever they ended up, those two women are just very lucky to be alive.

My Chief Constable congratulated me, said I was a hero, a credit to the force and all that. I think he was still overwhelmed by it all, just as I was. Sadly he told me he couldn't give me any kind of official commendation as the whole matter was so totally top secret, but he did mention that the authorities were looking to seize lots of money and property off the back of this, so it seems our neighbourhood demon had set up quite a substantial operation. You might have thought that my performance might have got me a shot at that promotion I had been dreaming of for the past five years, but I'm afraid it doesn't work that way. All I got was a couple of weeks off work, so I managed to do a bit of gardening and squeezed in a few games of golf. Not a great reward for saving the world.

SO19 hadn't forgotten me though. Just after Christmas, they sent me a couple of complimentary tickets for the Six Nations so I was able to take my boy down to London to see England play Scotland in the Calcutta Cup. That was perhaps the best day out we had ever had together. A "Lads and Dads Day" I was calling it. He loved every minute. At half time I sent him off with the money to go and get us some burgers. Then suddenly I sensed that someone had sat down beside me. I turned to see a man in a very smart suit, but it took me a minute to recognise him.

"Hello Victor," said Superintendent John Phillips. "How do you fancy a promotion?"

Asylum

"Doctor Hartmann, there's a lady to see you." Dorothy's voice crackled on the office intercom. It was Monday 27th June, 1955 and Dr. Hartman wasn't expecting anyone.

From the one-way window beside his desk he could see his secretary in the reception office, gorgeous as always, her long auburn hair cascading over her tight sweater and the seams on her fully formed stockings running straight down from her knee length skirt to those strappy little stilettos.

He forced that image from his mind and switched his attention to the visitor, an older woman, in her fifties perhaps, holding her hat in her hands as she waited. Well, he would see her, of course, he needed the business. Psychotherapy had seemed like a glamorous career when he applied to university, but ten years later he had realised that it just didn't pay, not in northern industrial towns where people took pride in solving their own problems and mental health carried a great deal of stigma. Hartmann needed clients, or patients, or whatever you wanted to call them. Most of all, he needed the money.

He pressed down the intercom button. "Send her in, Dorothy. I can see her straight away."

Hartmann took up his listening pose, his arms resting on the desk, his pipe close at hand but not lit. Some clients were so nervous they smoked like chimneys. He found that filling the pipe with tobacco made it easier for him to say no when they offered him a cigarette. If he had just simply refused they might find it more difficult to feel that he was empathising.

In any case, Mrs. Preston didn't want to smoke. In fact, she didn't want therapy either. She had come to visit him this morning with a totally different agenda in mind.

"My son Ronnie, Mr. Hartmann, he was in there."

Working class people always called him Mister, even though he was a doctor. They were deferential and formal, but they didn't really see psychiatry as real medicine. He figured that dentists probably had the same problem.

"He was only in for a few days, thank God, and our doctor got him out. He's really wonderful, that Doctor Turnbull, such a lovely man. I really don't know how we used to cope before we got the Health Service, Mr. Hartman, I really don't."

The National Health Service had been running in Britain for ten years and it really had made life better for the ordinary people, but for a privately educated American psychiatrist living in England, it was a complete disaster. Why would anyone pay for a private consultation now that they could get it all for free?

"So let me see if I understand you, Mrs. Preston. Your son has had a history of problems since he came home from the army and now he has had an acute episode and has spent a few days in the psychiatric hospital, and you want me to treat him so that he doesn't have any further relapse?"

"Well, yes and no." Mrs. Preston fidgeted nervously with her hat. "It might be useful for you to see him but that's not really what I came about. It's the others, Mr. Hartmann, the other people who are still in there. I want to know if you can do anything to help them."

The story, as it began to unfold, was a disturbing one. Ronald Preston had been a decorated soldier in the final years of the Second World War. He had seen action in Europe and had witnessed first-hand the liberation of the Bergen-Belsen concentration camp. Since then he had suffered from the kind of symptoms which were generally known as shell-shock. It was just the sort of thing that Hartmann had trained for and someone had passed his name to the family. But Mrs. Preston believed that he could get better, with the love and support of their close-knit family. She was a strong, practical, working-class woman, and she was determined that he would get better. Her real concern was that she was very disturbed by what he had told her about his brief stay in the local psychiatric hospital, the climate of violence and fear.

170

"He suffers with his nerves, Mr Hartmann, but he's not mad. My boy has medals for the war and he saw what went on in those camps. He's not a softy, not easily frightened. If he says it's bad in there, then that must tell you something, Mr. Hartmann. It isn't right."

Hartmann was relieved when she left. Whatever she thought of the local asylum, it wasn't his business and he didn't want to know any more, but in the days that followed he couldn't put it out of his mind. In a sense it was personal.

Born in 1923 to a wealthy Jewish family, Hartmann had been just eighteen years old when the Japanese had launched their surprise attack on the American fleet at Pearl Harbour and the United States had entered the Second World War. Like thousands of other Americans, he had walked out the very next day and demonstrated his patriotism by joining the Army Airforce. Not everyone can be a pilot, and he had been selected for training as a radio technician, and had then seen out most of the war at an airbase in England, servicing the planes which bombed targets in Germany and occupied France. When the war was over he had stayed in England to marry his wartime sweetheart. He had trained as a psychiatrist, and settled down in the peacetime world. But for anyone with links to the Jewish community, the war was never really over. Week by week the black and white cinema newsreel films exposed the horrors of the concentration camps, and people began to talk about "The Holocaust". It was the stuff of nightmares, a terrifying comment on the barbarity to which human beings could descend when the structure of civilisation gave way to the forces of chaos.

As the days went by it played on his mind that Ronnie Preston had been part of the war effort too, that he had helped to liberate those camps and had seen those dreadful sights. That made the young psychiatrist feel a certain kind of affinity, maybe even a debt, and he began to take an interest in Cherry Hill, as the local psychiatric hospital was known.

At first, he just asked around, and then he checked out the official figures, and it wasn't long before a discomforting pattern began to emerge. The number of patient fatalities was surprisingly high. It was generally accepted that mentally ill people were at risk due to suicide, or self-neglect, but that could only account for a small percentage figure, perhaps 2% of extra deaths. At Cherry Hill there too many deaths. It was at least 10% above the national rate, maybe more. Some were suicide, some were natural causes, some were illnesses like TB and

171

pneumonia, but to the eye of any trained health specialist or statistician, the numbers were just too big. It was as the sort of increase one might expect from a flu pandemic, but there was no reason for it at all. In the end, he became convinced that he ought to investigate more deeply, to find out what was really going on inside. It was important, he told himself, to understand things from a patient's point of view.

***

At ten o'clock on Monday morning, a young man arrived at the front desk of the admissions and reception desk at Cherry Hill hospital, accompanied by an older man who had driven him down in the car. The young man's hair was dishevelled and he needed a shave. His shoelaces were untied and his clothes had a few food stains down the front. He handed in an explanatory letter, bearing the signature of his therapist. They asked him questions of course, but his answers were poorly focussed and told them little of any value. By two o'clock that afternoon, he had been admitted as a patient.

The psychiatric hospitals of the twentieth century were sometimes called mental hospitals, sometimes asylums, but the ordinary people might simply refer to the mad-house or even the loony-bin. The interior had a distinctive smell, a smell of human sweat and cigarette smoke partly masked by floor polish and disinfectant, suggesting that in the mind of the hospital administrator, keeping the building clean was more important than keeping the inmates clean. The patients themselves lived an aimless existence, unable to cope on the outside and with nothing to do on the inside. The new arrival spent his afternoon as so many did, sitting silently on a wooden bench in the expansive green area at the heart of the hospital. Here and there an orderly walked by, patrolling the gardens like a policeman on the beat, never speaking to the patients, never making eye contact. When the evening meal was over there was more recreation time, empty time, the same as before, aimless time for aimless people, then a bell which signalled that it was time for bed.

From the moment he entered the sleeping wards he found them oppressive. Each room was the size of a village hall, with forty beds so closely packed together that a man could have felt the breath of his neighbour on his face. For that reason the beds were arranged head to foot. Anyone with even the most basic medical training would know

172

that these were ideal breeding conditions for tuberculosis, but that was not the main reason why he felt uncomfortable. As he lay on his back in the darkness, surrounded by the whispers and snores of the afflicted, his mind began to fill with the nightmare images he remembered so well from the cinema newsreels, the horrors of the Nazi camps.

He knew there was a difference, of course, between a concentration camp and a psychiatric hospital, but there were similarities too, and that worried him. He wondered what gave one group of people the right to diagnose another group as inadequate or undesirable, to sweep them off the streets and confine them against their will.

Suddenly he was shocked from his thoughts by a scream. It was the scream of a man. He knew that he had often heard women cry or scream, as a release for emotions and stress. He had never really known a man to scream for those reasons, but this was a man's voice, screaming. Then there was silence and all that he could hear was the beating of his own heart, and the pulsing of the blood rushing through his neck and his temples as if his head was about to burst.

Again the scream! He tried to estimate the direction, and how far away, but it was pointless, he had no real awareness of the building, nothing to base a judgement on, and he lay in the silence wondering if it would happen again, but it didn't and slowly he felt his heart rate subside and he tried to force himself to go to sleep. After what seemed a very long time he heard someone snoring at the other side of the room, and it occurred to him that everyone, absolutely everyone, asleep in that room had been awake during that screaming and had lain there in total silence, not joining in the noise, not whispering, not snoring, hardly even breathing. That struck him as strange, forty psychiatric patients lying totally silent, it struck him as unnatural, almost impossible, but at last, he fell asleep and thought on the matter no more.

In the morning every patient had to join the queue outside the nurses' station. The patients called it "the cage." It was an area like a shop or a post office counter, protected by bars, where the inmates would receive their medication from a nurse before going on to breakfast. He was ready for that, he had practiced hiding the pills under his tongue so he could spit them out when he got outside. He found himself wondering about the integrity of the whole system, using tranquilisers to keep the patients under control, not attempting to cure them in any way, but just keeping them under control.

173

After medication came breakfast, and to be fair it was quite a good breakfast, a bowl of porridge followed by a kipper washed down with a large mug of tea. "Thank god for the National Health Service." he thought, as he made his way out into the hospital grounds, the large central space with lawns and trees and garden seats, where the patients in their hundreds would sit aimlessly till lunch.

It was a pleasant day, warm and dry with only a very mild breeze, and he spent the morning exploring the site, as far as he was able without going out of bounds. He didn't want to arouse any suspicion so made a point of walking slowly, like a man with nowhere to go, sitting down now and then, to spend a while gazing vacantly at nothing in particular. By eleven o'clock he had scouted all of the areas that were open to male patients.

With his explorations complete he felt a sense of anti-climax. There was nothing out of order about the site. Of course, it was far from pleasant, but no worse than any other mental institution of the time. The patients might be sad and lonely but they were not in any way threatening. On one wooden bench, two old men sat, each talking to a different invisible friend, with exaggerated hand gestures, as if they needed to prove to others that someone really was there. Another lay beside the bench, curled up, like a rough sleeper, but with his jacket deliberately pulled right up over his head and face as if to keep out the hostile world. On another bench, three men sat silent. One of them with his mouth hanging open and no false teeth. Behind them, in the shade of a tree, one man stood like a statue, his arms out in front of him, not moving, a strange sight to behold, a schizophrenic patient in a catatonic state.

One old man in a wheelchair seemed to be just a little more focussed than the rest, so the newcomer tried to engage him in a conversation, starting with the weather which was always the most easy thing, this being England. They talked about the sunshine, and about the absence of rain, and how good a summer we had last year. The old man talked about gardening and the young man talked about growing tomatoes.

"My name is Ernest by the way." Said the old man.

"You can call me Eric." said the younger man, then he lowered his voice to a whisper, "It's not my real name, but just call me that for now."

Then they sat for a while without speaking.

174

"I couldn't get to sleep last night." Eric threw in what Americans call a 'curve ball'.

The old man nodded. "First night?"

"Yeah. Not used to so many people in one room. Lots of snoring in my block."

The old man nodded but said nothing.

"Just when I did get to sleep, something woke me up." He tried to sound more stupid than he really was. "Like screaming or something."

"All sorts of people in here." The old man nodded.

"Are they dangerous any of them? Anything I need to look out for?"

The old man looked sideways at him for a moment, then shook his head. "No. Not really. The dangerous ones are over the other side." He raised his eyes and looked towards the chapel. It was only then that Eric percieved that there was another section to the hospital, which could not be seen from the central area.

The main administrative buildings ran from West to East across the site, effectively cutting it in half, with male patients to the north and females to the south. Each of those main areas had its own green space, with benches and trees, surrounded by the solid dormitory blocks where the patients slept, and at the eastern end of each stood the utility buildings, the dining hall and the recreation room. The central building of the whole establishment was the chapel, the point where the male section, the female section, and the administrative building all met, like the junction point on a capital T, and behind the chapel was the fourth section, which housed the criminally insane.

The chapel door had been locked when Eric walked about the site, and when he tried it again it was still locked, so he went to the library instead and read the Daily Sketch, then borrowed a book on the History of the Great War, to keep his mind occupied till bedtime.

Once again he found it difficult to sleep. The beds were uncomfortable and the background noises played on his mind, but at last, he slumbered a little. After breakfast, there was a morning-prayer service in the chapel and he could make out the brick-red outline of the buildings beyond, but the east window of the church was stained glass, so he could only see an outline, nothing of interest. The rest of the day went by without incident and he managed to keep up his act of pretending to swallow the medication then spitting it out later.

The rest of the day went much as before, sitting on a bench, watching the inmates, each in his own crazy little world.

175

Early in the afternoon Ernest pulled the wheelchair up beside him.

"You don't really belong here do you?" the old man murmured quietly.

"What do you mean?" Eric's eyes widened fearfully.

"I don't think there's anything wrong with you. Are you a reporter for a newspaper? Is that it?"

"No! Eric shook his head. "What makes you say that?"

"Well, there's nothing wrong with you. What's supposed to be wrong with you?"

"There's nothing wrong with me. You're right," Eric leaned towards him in order to keep his voice down to a whisper, "but don't say anything."

The old man looked at him quizzically, waiting for an explanation, but Eric just rose from the bench and gave him a gentle pat on the shoulder then strolled away, deliberately making an effort to look like a man with nowhere to go.

In the darkness, after midnight, Eric slipped out of the ward and along the corridor to the toilets, then down a concrete stairway to ground level. He had expected more supervision, but after all, it was a hospital, not a prison, and most of the inmates were incapable of packing a suitcase, much less making an escape. At the foot of the stairs he found a service door opening out into a yard, close to the administrative building and a long corridor. He chose the corridor, not the yard. At the end of the corridor was a storeroom, filled with bedsheets and pillows, pyjamas and white coats, and another service door, leading out into the main concourse.

Eric left the building and walked across the central green, silent and empty now in the darkness, his heart pumping with excitement and a sense of boyish mischief. Ahead of him, the chapel stood majestically in the moonlight, brick-built but in the gothic-revival style, with perpendicular windows and small octagonal towers. The door was closed and locked as he had expected but he circled around towards the back and found a small fenced off area, presumably off-limits to the inmates. That seemed promising and he soon managed to shin over the fence, finding a small back door and an outdoor bunker full of cleaning materials. The small door was also locked, but then as the moonlight shifted slightly in the trees he realised that the window above the bunker had long since been broken and was no longer glazed. Moving carefully sideways he found he was able to squeeze between the lancets of the window and jump down lightly into the nave of the chapel.

In the darkness it took a little while to truly assess the state of the place, but as his eyes adjusted he was able to move around without bumping into the furniture. Every Christian church is built to pretty much the same pattern, with an altar at the eastern end and there is usually a back-door there where the priest and the choir come in. Sure enough, just beyond the south transept, he found a small door in the wall, leading to the vestry.

From the vestry a door led out into an open space, much like the area where the inmates sat in the daytime, but somehow much less wholesome, and immediately as he left the building he could hear that this part of the establishment was not at rest as it should be, for he could hear shouting, muffled shouting, not loud enough to carry beyond the chapel, but definitely shouting, perhaps from within a building, filtering through from behind the glass of the multiple square panes of the ranks of rectangular windows which fronted up the buildings of the special sections.

He didn't try the door at the front entrance as he wanted to avoid any encounters with staff, and in any case, he assumed that in a secure unit it would be locked, so he skirted along the side of the building in the darkness, hearing the shouting more clearly now. It grew louder as he drew in closer towards the walls, in order to hide himself within the darkness of the shadows. Towards one end of the building a line of dustbins were enclosed behind a low brick wall, tall enough, Eric hoped, to give him the height he needed to look in through the windows but before he could approach his nostrils were assailed by an atrocious smell, both sweet and sickly at the same time. As he reached the bins he heard movements in the darkness close by and he thought he saw rats scurrying off to avoid him. He raised the lid of the first dustbin and it was full of something but he couldn't really say what, rotting food waste, maybe. He opened the second and there was more of the same sort of stuff, but this time he thought he could make out a finger, a human finger. He pulled at it and lifted it up. It was a hand, a severed human hand and he reeled back in shock. The next bin contained a human body crouched up in the foetal position. Struggling to compose himself he opened the fourth bin and found another corpse, but this time badly decomposed, hollow eye-sockets gazing up from a putrid decomposing face. The stench was overwhelming and he turned away to vomit.

Looking up from the darkness he could see something hanging in the window of the secure ward, like a coat perhaps, maybe a trench coat or a leather flying jacket, but for some reason he felt uneasy and he climbed up onto the low brick wall which enclosed the area around the bins, raising himself up only so high that his eyes were level with the lower panes of the window and he could look in. At once he realised that what was hanging in the window was neither a jacket, nor a coat, nor any item of clothing at all, but an animal, or at least what was left of an animal, perhaps a large dog, or maybe a goat but it was difficult to be certain as the unfortunate beast had been skinned, and all that now hung by the window was a bloody torso.

Raising his head slightly further and peering through the window his senses were almost overwhelmed by the awful scene of chaos which was unfolding within. The walls of the room, once plain magnolia, seemed to have been daubed and smeared with some substance possibly blood or perhaps excrement, maybe a mix of both, some of it forming signs and symbols, some just random patterns.

Some of the patients seemed to be running amok, crashing over beds and running into one another, throwing chairs and turning over cupboards. Others, clustered at one end of the room were restrained in straight jackets, unable to defend themselves in any way and clearly terrified in finding themselves at the mercy of the most deranged inmates.

A desk which had once perhaps been used in the nurses' station now stood against the further wall with half a dozen human heads upon it. Nearby stood a wheelchair, and in it a decapitated body sat, locked in place with chains, apart from the head which was now possibly part of the collection on the table.

One bed had been stripped of its mattress leaving just the metal frame and wire base. On this makeshift rack lay the body of one unfortunate patient, unmoving, probably dead, his body slashed all over with deep ugly cuts. The flesh of his midriff peeled back to expose his inner organs, folds of intestine had been torn out and could be seen hanging down towards the floor. Another corpse was sat against the wall, with empty sockets staring from an eyeless face and a mass of blood and tendons where the sexual organs had been ripped away.

In the centre of the ward stood a gynaecological bench, to which some naked wretch had been tied down, his feet pulled up into the stirrups so that his nakedness was fully exposed to the malicious intentions of a small band who now tortured and tormented him with a vicious collection of sticks and knives and something which looked like a policeman's truncheon. Eric looked on horror. Nothing in his life or his career had prepared him for such sights of chaos and depravity. He struggled to understand the situation, how these psychopaths had taken control of the ward, and why the authorities seemed unaware.

At one end of the ward was the nurse's station, the cage as the residents called it, and from here emerged more figures, four or five of them dragging another victim who struggled against them for all that he was worth. They held him down on one of the beds and began to tear at his clothes as he kicked and screamed, knowing he was doomed. They crowded around him and bent towards him, bowing their heads towards his body. Then, as Eric looked on helpless from the window he could see that they were biting their victim, perhaps even eating his living flesh.

Momentarily, one of the torturers raised his head from the grisly task and he looked like nothing Eric had ever seen. His face had transformed into that of a beast, brutal and ugly with huge incisor teeth and small evil eyes. His chin and chest were soaked with blood from his frenzied feeding and his hands had somehow become like claws. Eric strained to see through the smoke and bad light, trying to get a clear look at the others, and finding that they also had somehow become altered into bestial creatures.

He never remembered just when he started to run, but run he did, and as fast as he could. He found his way back to the chapel and from there to the broken window and out onto the roof of the storage bunker, and down into a dark area of shadow where he lay curled up for a while, panting and sobbing and desperately trying to make sense of what he had seen, and then he realised something else. The beasts he had seen had been wearing white coats, not the white gowns which are given to senile patients, but the white coats worn by doctors and orderlies. Looking down on the murder and chaos in the ward he had been afraid that the inmates were out of control, but in reality, the inmates were the victims, and the beasts who preyed upon them were members of staff.

What were they, these beasts which tortured and ate living humans? They reminded him of the Morlocks from that book, "The Time Machine", by HG Wells, but in his heart he was afraid of something worse. There was something unholy about these beasts, something demonic. It was the perfect situation, of course, demented lunatics with a history of violence could be locked up in a big institution and no-one would ever care if they lived or died. They could be tortured, raped or murdered. All they needed was a death certificate signed by a hospital doctor and no-one would ever bother to ask why they died.

Beside himself with fear he crept into the bunker and hid himself behind the cleaning materials until the hospital began to stir and the morning routines began. He returned to the ward and went straight to the washrooms, only emerging when he heard his name being called by the orderlies.

"I was at the toilet!" He shouted. "At the toilet."

It seemed to satisfy them and they went off elsewhere then returned to escort the whole group to the dining hall, where Eric gazed blankly at the porridge and didn't eat the kipper, but only managed to drink a small amount of the tea.

An hour later, sitting alone in the grounds he became aware of something approaching and he turned fearfully to find the man in the wheelchair coming up beside him. Their eyes met and at once Eric realised that the other man knew. They looked at one another in a long silence. Eric couldn't speak. He didn't know how to begin, so it was left to the older man to break the ice.

"You went sneaking out last night," said Ernest. "Some people saw you go. You shouldn't be doing that. If they catch you they'll kill you. They'll send you to the other side."

Eric felt a wave of panic and turned his head to vomit, but nothing came up except yellow bile and tea.

"I need to get out."

"Yes, maybe you do, but it isn't easy."

"I can do it." Eric sounded resolute. "I know the system and how it works."

"Best you don't talk to me again," whispered Ernest. "I don't want them to think that I'm with you."

Any patient could make a request to be seen by a doctor, but usually, it required an appointment and the clerk in the office told Eric it would be tomorrow before a consultant psychiatrist could see him. He demanded to see the doctor immediately. He told them that it was urgent, but they wouldn't listen. In the end, he told them that he was a psychiatrist himself and he really needed to see the most senior member of staff on site, but they clearly didn't believe him. He argued. He began to panic. He lost control and they called for the orderlies. He found himself being dragged into an isolation cell and injected with a sedative. It wasn't supposed to have gone like this.

In the middle of the night, Eric suddenly came awake. He could hear something just beyond the door of his cell, something breathing heavily, something bestial. His heart began to beat faster till it was almost jumping out of his chest, then it spoke to him, or rather it hissed at him from beyond the door.

"We know who you are. We are waiting for you."

Then it was gone, but Eric remained awake, unable to sleep, dreading what the morning would bring. In the end it brought porridge and kippers, just the same breakfast as the rest of the hospital, and Eric was starving so he ate it, even though he was terrified at the thought of what they might have put in it. He kept calm this time and tried to appear to be unthreatening in the hope they might let him out, but they locked the door again and he had to stay put.

Sometime later, in the afternoon perhaps, the door was opened unexpectedly and there stood a doctor with a kindly expression and two orderlies. It was all very civilised. They walked down the short corridor to the consulting room. Eric took a seat and the orderlies left. The doctor smiled and took out a leather-bound notebook.

Eric knew how this worked. He knew what would happen. If he began to talk about demons torturing and eating patients in the secure unit they would just put him down as being psychotic. He needed to find a way to convince them that he was sane. The best way was, to just tell the truth. He introduced himself and gave the doctor details of his background and his work. He explained his concerns about the hospital. He outlined how he had deliberately got himself committed in order to see the hospital from the inside. It was going well. The doctor was listening. In fact he was fascinated.

Then suddenly Eric felt a wave of panic as another possibility crossed his mind. He had no way of knowing whether this particular doctor was part of the act. This could all be a betrayal. One of them had been outside of his cell during the night so whoever they were they had access to the whole of the hospital.

It took just a moment to make the decision and he made his move. The doctor was an old man, easily pushed aside. The window was already open on a sunny day, it was easy enough to push it a little further. The drop to ground level was risky but he made it, and soon he was back on the central campus. He crossed over to the garden, with the benches and the trees and there was Ernest in the wheelchair.

"Do you want to get out of here? I have a plan, but we have to go now."

He pushed the wheelchair at normal walking speed, in through the service door on the ground floor of the ward, and stopped at the laundry room. He put on a white coat and wrapped a blanket around the old man, then followed the corridor back to the small service door leading into the yard behind the admin block. Once they were through that door they were out of the secure area. The aim was to look like an orderly wheeling a patient somewhere and it worked. They crossed the yard and entered the admin building, where their way led along a dingy corridor with emulsion peeling from the walls. The old man seemed to be struggling with his breathing. "Probably the stress of it all." thought Eric, and he stopped to check that his fellow traveller was able to cope.

"Don't stop!" Ernest willed him on. "No, please don't stop. Not now, they might know, they might find us."

They moved on, approaching a corner as they passed by a room with an open door with an ancient looking dentist's chair. Eric shuddered and looked away, focussing on the task in hand, pushing the handles, rounding that turning and at last coming to a halt by the fire door. He pushed open the fire doors and they rolled down a small ramp and into a car park.

Eric was free. He wouldn't stop now. He couldn't stop. He just kept moving, out through the gate and down the lane turning right onto the main road that led towards town, almost running, but looking over his shoulder as best he could, seeing no signs of pursuit, not yet, at any rate. Gradually he began to slow down. It was only half a mile to the edge of town, to the high street, the local shops. He would be safe there. People knew him in those shops.

A bus went by, the passengers gazing out of the window at this strange sight, the man in the white coat pushing an old man in the wheelchair. They would probably guess they had come from the psychiatric hospital, there was nothing else up that road for about five miles. Eric didn't care anymore. They were out and he was still alive.

182

The world was still a beautiful place. He took off the white coat and threw it over a hedge.

The very first shop was a tobacconist and newsagent, still open for the evening papers and two policemen were standing on the corner outside. Eric speeded up a little, desperate for that final moment of safety.

"Good evening gentlemen, and where have you two come from?" asked the older officer, "As if I couldn't guess."

"I am a doctor, officer, and this man is in my care." Eric straightened his collar. "We need to make you aware of a serious problem at the psychiatric hospital."

"A serious problem, sir? And what might that be?" The younger policeman joined in. "An escape was what we heard."

Eric stayed calm. He had half expected something like this. It was important to keep calm and not show any signs of psychotic or irrational behaviour.

"Whatever you have heard, I can assure you my story will check out. I am a qualified therapist, I have an office on Anderson Terrace and my secretary will confirm my story. If that doesn't satisfy you then I'm happy to come with you to the police station so that we can sort things out."

The police sergeant smiled but eased away slightly. "Not sure about the station, lads. I think you'll most likely be going back to the hospital, just as soon as they get down here with the ambulance. Now don't move, don't do anything silly."

But it was too late. Eric looked up the road at the passengers walking back from the bus stop. He looked back in the other direction, seeing the ambulance coming from the direction of the hospital. The situation was out of control and he needed help. He sprung to the right and took off down Melbourne Street, leaving Ernest in his wheelchair with the policemen. He cut through the alleyway into Market Square and went through the bottom level of the market hall and out the other side and into Anderson Street, to the office, with the bright brass plate beside the door, "Doctor H. G. Hartmann"

He didn't ring the bell, he just threw open the door and ran in. Mrs Preston was there with her son, Ronnie, sitting down waiting to be seen but behind them, he could see Dorothy, looking beautiful with her long red hair and her tight sweater, her long skirt and her delicate stiletto shoes.

"Something terrible has happened at the hospital" He called to her. "I need help."

"Don't worry." Dorothy sounded calm. "Don't worry. It's going to be OK, I promise." She pressed the button on the office intercom. "Doctor Hartmann, it's that schizophrenic patient that we referred to the hospital. He's here in reception and he says he needs help. He seems very confused and I don't think he has been taking his medication."

Primitive religion

People always thought of me as strange, that much is true, and it was probably my own fault. Our people are very outgoing. They sing and they dance and they laugh, and most of all they tell you what they think, no secrets, no holding back. But I spoke little in the company of others and was not good at the things others did well. I would not talk to people. I don't know why but I just felt that I could not do so. I was a disappointment to the family and my parents must have felt that it would be difficult for me to ever get a good partner for marriage.

When I was caught stealing I had no answers, no reason to give, and no-one to take my side. They beat me and still I had no answers to give, but I talked to myself in my own language, like I had done from childhood, my own little words that no-one else could understand. Was that really so bad?

One morning I was awakened suddenly and the room was filled with people, some whom I knew and some whom I didn't know. They were talking the words of religion. The big man put his face so close to mine and was shouting at me and I had no answers so I spat at him. It was a bad thing to do. I know that it was a mistake.

Then they all went out then and left me and I could hear them talking outside. They sounded loud and angry.

When they came back they had candles and a jug of water. They stood around the bed and started to pray. I didn't know what to do, or what to say, it all seemed to make no sense to me. Then they put their hands upon me and started asking me my name. When I told them my name they didn't listen, they just asked again and prayed again.

"What are you doing?" I asked my mother "What are you doing?"

"We have to exorcise you, child." She replied. "You are possessed."

And so it began. They prayed over me and the prayed with me and they made me repeat prayers after them. They blessed water and poured it into my mouth and when I swallowed it they gave me more, and when I coughed on it they said that the demon was rejecting it.

I don't know how long these prayers went on but I didn't really feel any different. Some of the time I responded to some of the things they said because I felt that it would be over quicker if I did what they wanted, but nothing really happened. Then they left me.

The following day I was kept alone, all day, and given just one bowl of rice and some water to drink. There was a bucket in the room for me to use when I needed it but everything else was taken away from me. I cried and shouted and banged on the wall but they wouldn't let me out.

That evening they came again for more prayers, but only for a very short time and then they went.

After three days alone I broke the water cup and began to cut my arms. I knew they would have to do something to stop me. I wanted them to be afraid of what I would do. I took the bucket and wiped handfuls of dirt on the walls of the room. If they were going to treat me like this, then I was going to fight back.

That night they tied me to the bed with pieces of rope and strips of cloth, and they began to pray again. I tried to break free but the knots held me bound. I screamed and they slapped me, and I screamed a lot more. They heated up knives on the candles and touched them on my skin. When I struggled to avoid the pain they held my arms and legs. Some of the men, when they held me, looked down on me in a way which seemed to say that they would own me now, I was in their power.

The next time that they tried to make me drink the water I just couldn't drink it. I was breathing so hard that I choked on it and spat it everywhere. The big man said that this showed it was working and that the demons were fighting to remain. That's when they started to punch me, on the ribs, in the belly, on the arms. It went on and on, punching, slapping, burning, water and always more praying. The next time they asked me my name I shouted something crazy like "Magegog" or something. It didn't mean anything I just wanted them to stop hitting me, and it worked, they stopped and went into a huddle and maybe because it was so late at night they left me alone after that. Then they went away but I knew that they would be back.

In the night I lay there awake. I was in pain from the beatings and from lying in the one place for so long. I felt so sorry for myself and so alone. I have never been a person who wanted anything from others but at this time I just wanted to think that there might be one person who would be there for me, one person who would take my side and believe in me, but no-one came.

Early in the morning though, the big man came and I heard him talking to my mother outside. He came in and spoke to me. He sat on the side of the bed and said some prayers. He told me he wanted to help me and it would be good if I just trusted him because he knew about these things and he could drive out the demon which possessed me. But I felt his hand against my leg, and I was only wearing a gown, no underclothes, and I started to scream and he slapped my face, several times, and then he left the room and I heard him saying to my mother that the demon was growing stronger and things would need to be done.

Later, when they were gone my sister came to feed me. I cried and begged so much for her to help me but she said she couldn't do anything, and all this was for my own good, and that it was best I do whatever they say otherwise they were going to take me away to another place to do things properly. This time I didn't argue or say anything but I knew if they took me away from here I was going to most probably die.

I asked to use the bucket and I told her I was scared of wetting in the bed and so she loosened my bonds and helped me up. When I was done I told her I needed to put some proper clothes on if they were moving me somewhere else and she took the bucket and went off to get me something.

When she went to empty that bucket I listened so carefully to her footsteps. I waited till she was as far away as possible, and then I just walked softly to into the hallway, opened the door and stepped outside, and then I just ran.

I ran as fast as I could possibly run, considering my bare feet and the state I was in. I really don't know how I ran at all, how I managed to run after being tied up for so long, after being starved and beaten the way I was, to this very day it still amazes me that I had the strength and the willpower to do it, but I suppose when you think you are going to die there's no reason to hold back and so I just did it. I ran.

I ran straight out through the door, wearing nothing but that filthy gown. I ran down the stairwell past the other apartments and out into the courtyard where I sometimes used to watch the boys playing basketball. I ran past that boarded up old shop with the sign outside saying "Independent Ministry of Jesus Church" expecting at any moment that they would all come spilling out of there and run after me, but they didn't. They must all have been too busy shouting "Halleluiah! Praise the Lord!" though the only thing I could hear was my sister shouting at me to come back. I ran past the newsagent and nearly ran into the subway leading to the trains, but I didn't know if I would get past the barriers. I thought about running into the shop and asking for help but I thought somebody in there might know me and might take me back to my wonderful respectable parents who everyone in this part of town thought so highly of.

Then the bus stopped. It stopped at the bus stop, right next to me and I jumped on. I had no card, no money, nothing at all but I just said to the driver "I need to get to the police station." He was a Sikh, I knew by the turban of course, and he looked at me standing there in that bloodstained gown, naked from the thighs down, and he just said "OK". I could see my sister running behind and she was so close, but the bus pulled away and we were gone, clear away up Kennington Road and she was left behind. The bus driver was getting on his radio and we went straight past the next stop, just leaving people standing there. By the time we reached the top of the road, there was a police car there waiting, with the blue light flashing, and they sat me in the car and a woman officer put a blanket around me.

They kept it all out of the papers for months, till the trial was over. By then I was set up somewhere by social services, trying to live some sort of a normal life. I say trying because the fear of being caught has never left me. Probably it never will. If I tell you that I that hate my parents and I hate all religion you have to understand I have my reasons. I don't believe in demons or spirits or exorcisms, but one thing I do believe, I hate their primitive religion more than any real demon ever could.

A messy divorce

It was a messy divorce, just about as messy as they can ever get. Things hadn't been easy for quite some time beforehand with tensions and rows over little things and until at last Robert and Marian had agreed to part peacefully so as not to upset the children. Brian and Sonya were too young to understand all of this so Robert agreed to go quietly. He arranged to stay in the spare room at a friend's house on the other side of the small town where they had both lived the whole of their lives. It was all supposed to be peaceful, civil and friendly.

Then at the end of the first week Robert called round unexpectedly just to see how things were going, but when the children let him in they told him that Marian had just nipped down to the corner shop. Robert felt irritated that she would just go out and leave the children in the house on their own, even for a few minutes. In his mind they really weren't old enough for that yet, so he just sat down and waited for her to get back.

That was when he realised that Marian had left herself logged into her email on the family laptop. It was a Hotmail account that he knew nothing about but now that he had the chance he decided to take a peek and suddenly he saw it all. There were hundreds of email messages, all of them coming from just one man. Hugh Bainbridge was a friend of theirs in another town, not a close friend, but a friend nonetheless. The messages went back about a year. It could have been going on even longer than that. Robert had no way of knowing what might have been deleted. In the last six months they had become particularly graphic with various pictures of both Marian and Hugh in what used to be called 'compromising situations' but was now fashionably known as 'sexting'.

Worst of all for Robert, there were pictures of the two together, pictures of his wife with Hugh in restaurants, in bars, even selfies of them having sex in in hotel rooms. It was obvious that this had been going on long before he had agreed to the trial separation. As he stood looking down on the screen he realised that the answers to all of his questions could be found right there in those messages, a long history of duplicity and deception which had caught him completely off his guard. He had thought he was giving up his home and his children to demonstrate that he still loved his wife. Now he knew that she had taken him for a ride.

Robert quickly changed the password on the mail account to ensure he could access it later, then flipped the laptop shut and tucked it under his arm. Those pictures and messages were his now, evidence he might need for the divorce case to come. As he left through the front hallway he took a felt marker pen from his work jacket and scrawled a parting shot across the wallpaper;

"Curse you for ever Marian you bitch I promise I will see you in hell."

That was the point at which the divorce case became a lot less peaceful, civil and friendly. It was later that week when Marian went out one morning and discovered that her car had been damaged, two tyres punctured and the paintwork gouged right along one side. She phoned Robert at once and they shouted and screamed on the phone. It was natural that she would blame him and it was only to be expected that he would deny it but their nerves were raw now and one thing led to another, with nothing held back in terms of strong language, threats and personal abuse.

A few days after she noticed that plants were dying in the garden and there were huge white patches on the lawn. It seemed fairly obvious that someone had come in the night with weed-killer, and it seemed obvious that this was Robert seeking revenge. More than that, she realised, he actually had a strong motive for making the garden look a mess. That would push down the valuation of the house when the case eventually went to the divorce courts.

"Maybe it was the hairy man, mummy." Brian was her four year old son, a happy little boy with blonde hair and blue eyes, who loved to go to bed in his Spiderman pyjamas.

"What hairy man?" asked Marian bemused.

190

"There's a little man, like the seven dwarves." replied Sonya, the six year old daughter. "We've seen him at night standing outside in the street."

"Are dwarves bad, mummy?" asked Brian.

Marian was of the opinion that dwarves were the least of her worries and that vengeful husbands were a much greater threat. In the week which followed she took on a solicitor to handle her forthcoming divorce and gave him details of her husband's unreasonable behaviour, photographs of the damage to the car and the garden, and of the writing he had scrawled on her wall.

She also took on a dog from the local rescue centre.

"I want one that barks!" she told the manageress, "I don't care if it gets annoying, I will love it all the more for that."

They gave her a beautiful white dog, a Samoyed, and she called it 'Winter' because it made her think of the snow. The children loved it but it was strong and they were too small to control it, so Marian always took the leash when they walked it through the park. It barked at other dogs and it barked when the neighbours came out into their gardens and it barked at the postman and at anyone walking past the house at any time of the day or the night. That suited Marian fine. For a woman on her own going through a divorce, a dog that barked was exactly what she wanted and it was exactly what she got.

The following week an eleven year old boy from further down the road was caught damaging somebody else's cars. Word got around and other people began to talk about various acts of vandalism, to their vehicles and their gardens, bicycles damaged and paint sprayed on their properties. After agonising for an hour or two Marian plucked up the courage to phone Robert and tell him. She was very embarrassed and apologetic. He was quite decent about the whole thing. He thanked her for letting him know and she agreed that he could come and say hello to the kids one afternoon. It was less hostile than before but there was no escaping the damage which had been done, with memories of hurt and distrust now on both sides.

A week or two went by and one day outside the school gates the mothers were discussing the vandalism case when Sonya broke into their conversation.

"He's still there Mummy, the hairy man. We still see him over the road at night."

191

That night, when Marian had put them both to bed she waited in the darkness watching the trees and gardens on the other side of the street, but there was nothing, no vandalism, no dwarf, no child, nothing at all. She had a glass of wine and watched the late night review of the next day's newspapers, and then she went to bed and drifted off into sleep.

In the darkness of night Marian came awake, with a terrible premonition of fear, so much so that she was afraid to move but lay perfectly still in her bed desperately trying to understand what was wrong. Then, from the corner of her eye, she became aware of something dark, forming and growing larger at the edge of the window frame, as if a liquid such as black oil was somehow leaking through from the outside, except that this oil was defying the rules of gravity by spreading upwards and outwards instead of running downwards.

As Marian lay there, stricken with fear and frozen in place, the dark shape came towards her, sliding and gliding across the surface of the wall, oozing its way towards her until it began to form a mass upon the wall above her pillow. She tried to escape but her arms and legs simply would not move, she tried to scream but her mouth could not open. Then to her horror the black mass above her began to form into a shape, first a featureless blob, then something seeming to have limbs, crude misshapen limbs like tendrils reaching out from the wall, and then finally coalescing into a shape which might almost be thought of as semi-human, like an ape, perhaps, or a large dog, or a dwarf. Suddenly the being fell away from the wall and plunged down onto Marian's face, causing her to scream in her panic, waking up in bed to find that it had all been simply a nightmare.

It was after three o'clock in the morning, still dark outside, too early to rise and impossible to go back to sleep. Marian brought the dog and the children into her room and all four slept together, the mother and children in the bed and the white dog stretched out on top of the blankets beside their feet.

When Marian went down at seven to make breakfast, the house seemed unusually airy, the atmosphere fresh, chilly and slightly damp. Every window in the ground floor of the house was standing wide open and had probably been like that all through the night.

Marian phoned Robert and accused him of coming round in the night and opening the windows just to frighten her. He denied it of course, but she reported it to her solicitor and asked him to keep the police informed and then just to make sure that they took her seriously she said that the children had reported seeing him loitering outside on the other side of the road. When she had finished the call she phoned the nearest locksmith and asked him to come round and change all the locks, and put security fittings onto the windows. They agreed one day the following week and then she just she tried to get on as if nothing had happened.

She awoke in the night to the sound of a dog barking, loud barking, frantic barking which just wouldn't stop. As her mind struggled to throw off the confusion of sleep she realised it was coming from somewhere downstairs and the dog which was barking was Winter, the Samoyed, but when she reached the ground floor, trembling uncontrollably with fear, there was nothing to see, nothing in the house and nothing outside. She phoned the police anyway and reported a prowler. At that time of the morning there would not normally have been much happening in a small town, and the local incident car was able to reach her in just minutes. There were two officers, a male and a female, and they searched the house and the surrounding gardens without discovering anything suspicious.

"Did you actually see anyone?" asked the uniformed sergeant, with his pen and notebook in his hand.

"Not this time." Marian shook her head. "Our dog started barking and scared him off, but I know it was my husband, he's been harassing us for weeks now."

The sergeant nodded. "Good watch-dogs Samoyeds. They know when to bark. You've made a good choice."

In the morning Marian looked at herself in the mirror.

"Oh my goodness, girl. Look at yourself."

She felt she had aged years in the past week and she decided to start having a nap in the afternoon, while the children were at school, to try and catch up for what the sleep was missing at night. She phoned Hugh Bainbridge, the boyfriend, and asked him if he would come over for the weekend to give her some security and support. Hugh agreed without hesitation. He only lived twenty miles away and he told her would come straight from work on Friday evening. That made her feel better and she sent a text to Robert.

'Hugh is coming for weekend - you stay away.'

On Thursday, once again they all went to sleep in the main bedroom, Marian, Sonya, Brian and the dog, but soon after midnight the barking woke her up. This time she had kept the bedroom door closed and the Samoyed could not get downstairs. In any case, his barking seemed to be focussed on the bedroom window.

Marian pulled open the curtains and looked down onto the front lawn where a creature stood the likes of which she had never seen before. It was a human, or at least something very close to a human, but short and squat in its build, its naked body more hairy than a normal human but not so hairy as a beast. In one hand it held a heavy metal hammer and in the other a long and vicious looking knife. What terrified Marian most was that it was already looking up, directly at her, as if it had anticipated exactly where and when she would open the curtains. Its jaws hung open crowded with teeth and its eyes were small but filled with hate.

Marian phoned the police while the all the time the dog barked and barked at this apparition and the children hid beneath the blankets. She was told that a car would be with her as soon as possible. She finally knew in her heart that none of this had been her husband's doing and she called him, waking him up to answer the phone.

"Please, Robert what should I do.?" she begged.

"Go downstairs and get yourself a knife." He told her. "Keep the dog with you. As soon as you see the thing and it sees you, hold up the knife and the phone to show it that you are ready to defend yourself and that help is on the way."

I don't know how long the police are going to be." She whimpered at him down the phone. "Will you come over now for me, please?"

"I'm on my way." He said, and switched off the phone.

As Marian walked down the stairs she could hear nothing but the dog, no sounds of anyone breaking in but no sounds of police sirens either. She ran to the kitchen and armed herself with a carving knife. When she opened the doorway to the lounge, the dog went into an absolute frenzy, barking and snarling but not advancing into the room.

In the centre of the living room stood the little man, his body-hair rough and dirty like the bristles on a wild pig. She beheld his fangs, and his claws, and the weapons in his hands, and his small vicious eyes, and she knew that he had come to kill her.

"Why?" That was all she asked.

"You husband cursed you." answered the creature. "It's still there in writing on your wall. You left it there as evidence. I am to be the fulfilment of that curse. By your sins and your hatred you have brought me from my world into this world and now I shall take what is mine by right."

"Please no, forgive me." Marian begged for her life.

"You are an adulteress and a liar, you deserve no forgiveness." replied the creature.

"There must be something, please." She was desperate to gain some time, knowing that her husband and the police, were already on their way.

It was a story that ran for days in the papers. The police arrived to find the whole family slaughtered. A young mother cut down by multiple frenzied stab wounds and horrifically mutilated as she lay dying. Two helpless children with their skulls crushed where they lay in their beds. Even the family dog killed as it fought in their defence, its white coat matted with blood.

The estranged husband was arrested at the scene. He claimed that they were killed before he arrived, but the evidence was stacked against him. At his home he had her computer. He had seen the graphic pictures of Marian and her lover together, enough to arouse jealousy in any man. She had given multiple reports of his threatening behaviour to the police and to her solicitor. She had told them she had seen him standing outside in the darkness. That very evening she had sent him a text saying regarding her lover; 'Hugh is coming for weekend - you stay away.'

That must have been the final straw. There were no signs of an actual break-in, but Robert still had his house keys. She had ordered new locks to be fitted but sadly it would now be too late. Robert had blood from the children on his hands and there was no sign of anyone else having been at the scene. Robert had the motive and the opportunity to kill her, and on the wall, in his own hand writing, he had scrawled the words.

"Curse you for ever Marian you bitch I promise I will see you in hell."

A cautionary tale

In 1975, a twenty-three year old German woman named Anneliese Elisabeth Michel underwent a service of exorcism that would eventually lead to her death, a year later, from stress, malnutrition, multiple injuries and dehydration. The Roman Catholic priests responsible for the exorcism, and Anneliese's own parents were found guilty of negligent homicide.

At 16, Anneliese was diagnosed with temporal lobe epilepsy. In 1970, she suffered a seizure and was prescribed medical treatment. Soon afterwards, she began to report that she was seeing 'devil faces', and hearing voices telling her she was damned and would 'rot in hell'. Normally such symptoms could be associated with schizophrenia, but even the most junior neuroscientist would be aware that brain damage such as a brain tumour can have similar effects.

As time passed Anneliese began to behave in ways which were ever more bizarre. It was said that she drank her own urine, ate insects, and became generally difficult and aggressive, as well as self-harming. One local priest confidently declared that she "didn't look like an epileptic" and decided she must be possessed by a demon. Together with another priest he obtained permission from the local Bishop, to carry out an exorcism, based on nothing but the opinion of these two ministers of religion.

As a result of the intervention of the church, Annaliese was subjected to an exorcism in 1975 and her parents stopped her receiving medical treatment. Her condition did not improve, of course, and further exorcisms followed. After a period of 10 months, punctuated by repeated attempts at exorcism, Anneliese eventually died. A medical post-mortem found that she was dreadfully underweight, and would have been unable to move because both of her legs had been broken during a total of 67 exorcism sessions. Tape recordings of the exorcisms appeared to feature demons arguing with one another. Both priests said the demons identified themselves as Lucifer, Adolf Hitler, Caesar Nero, and Judas Iscariot amongst others. To most rational people this is hard to believe and does not provide any justification for killing a young woman.

Throughout this book, we have entertained ourselves with stories of demons living amongst humanity, but at this point, dear reader, we should pause and ask ourselves a simple, but pivotal, question. "Does anyone really believe that demons exist?"

In the case of Annaliese, there was already a medical diagnosis that she was suffering from brain damage to the temporal lobe, the area which controls language, listening and speaking, including inner-speech which influences logical thinking. It should have been completely obvious that her bizarre behaviour was a manifestation of disabilities caused by her condition, a simple case of mental illness, however a priest of religion decided that she was possessed by a demon, a priest of that same Catholic Church which for centuries has justified the burning of senile old women on the grounds that they were witches.

I hope that you have enjoyed reading this book but please remember that demons, just like gods and angels, are only creatures of fiction and that exorcisms are a pointless piece of theatre which can often lead to severe suffering and even to death. Learn to treat others with tolerance, with kindness, gentleness and love, and you will find that your own life is more rewarding.

Author's Note

I hope that you enjoyed reading these stories as much as I enjoyed writing them. They were written for your entertainment, but they also serve to illustrate an argument which I have often debated with friends, that there are only a small number of stories in the world, which we constantly tell, and retell in different ways, a basic list of plots which appear again and again in our stories and plays and films.

There is the basic love story; the guy gets the girl or the guy loses the girl. There is the cowboy story, wherein the good guy beats up the bad guy. That even happens in space, where most science fiction involves the good human beating up the bad alien. There is the messiah story where someone saves the world, or at least saves his friends. There is the long journey, which might start with the Anabasis, the March of the Ten Thousand written by Xenophon in 400 BC, but is still entertaining us with the Lord of the Rings written in the 20th Century. There is the crime story, where we have to work out "Who done it?" There is also the horror story where we ask "What is it?" There is the survival story, a stranger in a strange land, like Robinson Crusoe.

My own particular favourite is the Beowulf Saga, which was being told in England as early as the seventh century but may refer to a real hero who lived two hundred years earlier. In that story a band of warriors, led by a hero, set out on a mission to help a village which is under attack by a monster. That wonderful tale has been told and retold in many formats and versions, the best known being the classic Japanese film "The Seven Samurai." which in turn inspired the famous western "The Magnificent Seven". It is also the basis of many Science Fiction stories including Predator and the second in the Aliens series.

With all this in mind, I deliberately set out to write these demon tales as new variations based on simple stories with which we are all familiar.

"Getting his own back." is a retelling of the classic tale of Faust, originating perhaps around 1540, wherein a man sells his soul to the devil in exchange for short term gain. In this particular case I took great pride in ensuring that the final result really was poetic justice.

"Digging for Gold" reflects a situation we have all experienced at some time in our lives, where we strike a bargain and then wonder whether it was good value. Hopefully in most cases it will not have been quite as drastic as it was for Lisa. Incidentally, if you should ever have reason to walk down Throgmorton Street, you may find that Arbitrager pub really does exist, and the wine bar beneath it where Lisa enjoyed her expensive cocktail is called "Demon Wise and Partners," but you can't nip in for a quick drink, the tables are reserved hundreds of years in advance.

"Business Unfinished" is based on a genuine murder case which was widely reported in the British press.

I had wanted to write "Through the Circle" ever since I painted a watercolour of the towering red rock back in 1981. The story itself is based on "Goldilocks and the Three Bears" or "Jack and the Beanstalk", which of course really share the same basic storyline. I have actually read that "Jack and the Beanstalk" could be as much as 3000 years old, one early version being called "The boy who stole the ogre's treasure."

"Third Time Lucky" is derived from the tale of Rumpelstiltskin. In the original version, a girl is required to spin straw into gold. Our modern girl is required to make money in other ways, but in both cases, the little man comes to the rescue, then demands the baby in payment.

"Their Satanic Majesties" is another story adapted from a folk tale. In this instance, it is based on Hansel and Gretel, two children who wander into a witch's lair but manage to turn the tables on their captor.

Asylum is not based on a folk-tale but on a very famous psychology experiment conducted by David Rosenhan in 1973. If you would like to know more try searching for the phrase "On being sane in insane places."

"Old Men" is a classic plot line, often referred to as "Three men in a boat," where the entertainment is based on the development of a friendship between people who had previously been strangers. However, on an even more simplistic level, you might recognise the story of the "Three Little Pigs" with fire demon playing the part of the big bad wolf.

"Primitive Religion" is adapted from the story of the Gingerbread Man. "Run, run, as fast as you can. You can't catch me. I'm the Gingerbread Man!"

The true story of Doris Bither is truthfully reported just as it stands on the official records.

"The Exorcist", again, is reported directly from real life, as are the events referred to in the final, valedictory piece.

"Underworld" is a simple retelling of the Beowulf story, and the same could perhaps be said about "Adventurers," except that it was based on an absolutely real event which I was involved in around 1981.

"A messy divorce" was written specially as an addition to the second edition. It follows the most basic plot for any horror story, where the audience are kept wondering 'What is it?' (Whereas detective stories ask 'Who done it?')

Therefore, dear reader, I hope I have made my point, that there are no new stories, just new versions, in new settings, with new characters, and with that I must say goodbye and thankyou for being my audience, this time.

About the Author

Bruce Johnson was born in Sunderland in 1955. He graduated from the University of Exeter in 1977. In 1990 he became a Fellow of the Royal Asiatic Society, with a particular interest in the Hittite civilisation.

Bibliography

King of Kings (2019)

Demon Tales (2019)

Demonspawn (2019)

Contacts

Instagram: Bruce_Johnson_Writes

Facebook Page: Bruce W Johnson: Adventures in Fiction

Facebook Group: Bruce W Johnson: Adventures in Fiction

Website: https://brucewjohnson.weebly.com/

Printed in Poland
by Amazon Fulfillment
Poland Sp. z o.o., Wrocław